Love's Kindling kept me engaged from page amid the Revolutionary War during an ugly time when the British burned villages and killed the innocent, the love story between Zadok and Aurinda struggles along with the fight for America's freedom. Elaine Cooper has mastered placing her readers into the setting. Her research of this area of Connecticut and the towns that were ravaged are captured by her pen in the scenes of Love's Kindling.

— AUTHOR CINDY HUFF

I just loved the redemptive storyline. So many beautiful parts to this story. The theme of forgiveness and overcoming bitterness is such a needed one right now.

Wonderful history, and so well researched. Well done!

— KATHLEEN L. MAHER, ACFW GENESIS AWARD
WINNER 2012

Elaine Cooper has given us another well-researched Revolutionary War story, this time set in 1779 Connecticut. It is filled with engaging characters, war action, broken relationships, and budding romance.

Zadok Wooding and Aurinda Whitney are not only plagued by the war around them, but they also battle emotional and physical challenges which threaten their growing attraction. The issues many of the characters face are not relegated to the eighteenth century, they're timeless. There are faith lessons readers will remember long after the story ends.

— JANET GRUNST, AWARD-WINNING AUTHOR OF *SETTING TWO HEARTS FREE*

A well-written tale of love overcoming obstacles. Despite the terrors of war, an overall sense of hopefulness carries the story through darkness into light. Each of the main characters, as well as the secondary ones, grow with experiences many of us could never imagine, and yet their situations and reactions are relevant even to modern times.

— TAMMY DOHERTY, AUTHOR OF *CELTIC CROSS*

Dedicated to the memory of my dad, Gordon Mueller.
Heroes during wartime are found in many callings.

Dear Jo,
Time to rest
and read. :)
Love, Elaine

DAWN OF AMERICA–BOOK ONE

LOVE'S KINDLING

INCLUDES THE NOVELLA WAR'S RESPITE,
(PREQUEL TO THE SERIES)

AWARD-WINNING AUTHOR
ELAINE MARIE COOPER

Scrivenings
PRESS
Quench your thirst for story.
www.ScriveningsPress.com

Published by Scrivenings Press LLC
15 Lucky Lane
Morrilton, Arkansas 72110
https://ScriveningsPress.com

Printed in the United States of America

Paperback ISBN 978-1-64917-098-9

eBook ISBN 978-1-64917-099-6

Library of Congress Control Number: 2021936285

Cover by Linda Fulkerson, bookmarketinggraphics.com

ACKNOWLEDGMENTS

I am so grateful to a gentleman named Charles Hervey Townsend, Esq. who, in 1879, took considerable time to document his recollections of stories he heard as a boy. In his own words, "it was with the greatest delight that he [the author] listened to the traditional account of the invasion and evacuation of New Haven [Connecticut] by British troops, July 1779, as related by old citizens. And as he grew older, he began to note down their stories, and subsequently to verify them."

Townsend amassed hundreds of pages that documented not just the 1779 attack on New Haven, but also the subsequent attacks on Fairfield and Norwalk as well. Many details of the battles and destruction that ensued would have been lost to history if soldiers of old had not shared their stories with him. His documentation became the backdrop for the fictional story of *Love's Kindling*.

I also want to thank, my husband, Steve, who patiently edited my first draft of *Love's Kindling*.

Thank you also to Alycia Morales (editor), and Shannon Vannatter and Linda Fulkerson, editors and publishers at Scrivenings Press.

Thank you to all my readers in the U.S. and beyond, who have supported my books through the years and encouraged my pen to keep writing. You are a gift to me.

And thanks, as always, to my Lord and Savior, Jesus Christ, from whom all blessings flow.

WAR'S RESPITE

PREQUEL—DAWN OF AMERICA SERIES

1

New Haven, Colony of Connecticut, 1763

Jonas Wooding wiped the sweat and ash off his forehead, grateful for the November breeze. The fire over the forge seemed more tolerable in this arrival of fall weather. He longed for a reprieve from the summer's heat, since it had lingered far longer than his body could tolerate. Mostly, relief permeated his spirit because the war with the French was over. France had finally surrendered.

For seven long years, the king's army had battled. Darkness seemed to still hover over New Haven as those years cast shadows of loss on loved ones left behind. Some wives still wondered if their consort was a casualty. Reports of children crying themselves to sleep, missing their daddas, filtered through communities. Or worse yet, children forgetting who their fathers were altogether.

From the recent news that traveled back to town, Jonas cringed, thinking of so many who would never return. He banged the horseshoe with such a firm force, he flattened the iron too far. Swallowing back a curse, he plunged the sizzling piece into the slack tub and tossed it aside, throwing his hammer down on the anvil. He'd take a break before the ache in his head threatened to worsen.

Jonas had never joined the militia. Instead, he'd stayed home to raise his family and shoe the horses of the community. He often regretted not joining the fight, but he had two sons and a daughter to raise, not to mention the child on the way. Who would teach his sons to be men, perhaps needing to fight someday? Peter was only eight and Zadok, six. Who would educate them to make horseshoes for the mounts, equipping them to support families of their own?

As he stared off toward Long Island Sound, the front door of their home closed. Without turning around, he smiled. Esther approached. Her soft steps, made more awkward in these latter days of her confinement, were as familiar to him as her tender kisses on his cheek. In less than a moment, he felt her cherished lips.

"Husband, you must take a rest. Drink this new cider to refresh you. You've been hammering all afternoon."

"Thank you." He guzzled a long drink then wiped his mouth on his shirtsleeve.

Giggling, she picked up the edge of her apron and wiped the same spot she'd kissed. Soot smeared the white fabric. She suddenly grabbed at her large belly and inhaled.

His heart galloped at her gasp. "Is it time?"

"Nay. Just a good kick from this wee one. Though not so 'wee' anymore."

He sighed in relief and took her hand. "You must rest awhile. You work too hard." He searched the farmyard. "Where are the boys? They must help you."

"They've been playing with friends. Do not fret, Jonas. They have done their chores and need time to play." Esther frowned and stared into the distance. "Is that Abijah Whitney? And who might that be with him?"

Jonas spun around and stared at the veterans in their tattered regimentals as they walked their horses down the street, past the smithy toward the Allan house. Primrose Allan had lived there with her sister, Eliza, until she gave birth to a baby girl, five years before.

The child survived, even thrived, but Eliza Whitney had died during the birthing. Primrose had mothered her golden-haired niece, a treasured friend of his son, Zadok. Would Abijah allow the lass to stay with her aunt?

Esther gripped his arm. "Jonas ..."

"'Tis not our concern, Esther." He placed his soot-covered hand around her. "I know what you're thinking, but the child is his."

"But Jonas ..."

"Be silent, wife. All we can do is pray the man will see reason and do what is best for the child. Besides, he may stay here in New Haven." He attempted a smile—a weak endeavor. War could embitter a man's heart. He'd seen it with his older brother, and he'd never forget the sullen, hardened man who'd come home, only to drink himself into an early grave.

What might the war have done to Abijah Whitney? When he rode by, his stern face did not bode well for the future of Primrose Allan and the child.

Jonas bent down and kissed his wife. "Please, go sit by the hearth."

"Very well." Her voice quivered, but she turned and went indoors. He inhaled deeply and resumed his work at the forge, pumping the bellows with determination to refresh the flame.

TENSION STARTED in Abijah Whitney's shoulders then stretched clear down to his hands, which gripped the leather reins. Shifting in his saddle, he nearly moaned when his back seized.

After such a long journey astride his mount, pain had become his constant companion. But physical discomfort was mild compared to the anguish of returning to the town he'd left Eliza in.

Six years ago, with his wife barely pregnant with their first child, he'd clung to her and resisted letting go. Had some sense that would be their last embrace filtered through to his heart? Perhaps deep within he'd known, and now he regretted ever leaving her to face her childbirth with him hundreds of miles away. Although her younger sister, Primrose, had watched out for her, she was not a midwife. Nor had she ever birthed a child. What a fool he'd been.

The letter scrawled in Primrose's hand after Eliza died bearing his daughter had fallen into the muddy waters of the militia camp. He left it in the muck and mire, never to retrieve the parchment that bore the message which made him doubt the existence of God. Why would a good God allow his precious woman to die in agony? His heart would not be consoled, so he took out his anger and vengeance on the enemy soldiers.

"Abijah. I say, did you hear me?" The voice of his friend, Isaac, permeated the dark thoughts haunting him.

"Nay, Isaac. I beg your forgiveness. Of what did you speak?"

"I asked you what your plans are. For the child."

"Plans? Why, she is my daughter. She will come with me."

Isaac sighed. "The child is how old?"

"She must be five. Or six. I cannot remember." He removed his tricorne hat and swiped his filthy uniform sleeve across his forehead. "Why?"

"Why? Do you think it might perhaps be difficult for the lass if you take her away? Are you planning on marrying the sister, so she can still take care of her?"

Abijah scoffed. "Marry Primrose? Have you lost your senses? She and I ne'er got along. She and Eliza were nothing alike.

Nothing at all." Saying his wife's name out loud elicited tears, but he sniffed sharply to hide them.

Isaac grew silent, then inhaled a deep breath. "Do you consider me your loyal friend?"

The question took him by surprise. "Well, I saved your skinny hide from those Indians and French frogs more than once. Does na' that qualify me as a faithful friend to you? Might I assume that means you're loyal in return?"

Isaac pulled up on the reins and stopped.

Pausing, Abijah scratched his forehead.

"Then hear me out, friend. You must think this through. About the child. What is her name?"

Abijah stared into the distance toward the church spire. "I do na' know."

"You ... you're willing to take a young child from the only mother she's ever known and raise her up ... and you never even learned her name?" Isaac stared at him with mouth open. The man, rarely speechless, seemed to have suddenly lost his tongue.

An inner furor seeped into Abijah's veins. His face burned, and his enraged heart wanted to lash out at all the injustices he'd witnessed in the last six years. "How dare you question me claiming my own flesh and blood? She's all I have left of what was mine. You think I'd be willing to leave my child with a sharp-tongued woman who has no right to her?" The words spit from Abijah's mouth.

"Abijah, please understand my meaning ..."

"I understand it quite well, friend. You've no one to come home to, so you want to deprive me of the one solace left in my life. Well, you can take yer ideas and spit them on the ground. The child is mine, and with me shall she go." He jerked the reins and cantered faster toward the house.

He remembered the way, the map to her door inscribed in his heart. This was where he'd bid Eliza a final farewell. His anger melded into anguish when he drew closer. For there in front of the wooden framed house appeared the younger image of his beloved wife. The golden ringlets he'd caressed every day for the year they'd been married were carried down onto the small head of the child. The girl's laughter filled the air with music.

The lass played with a young boy about her age who kept trying to put a fistful of dandelions into her hair. She ran away from his dirt-covered hands, taunting his efforts with the spunk and sass Abijah remembered from her mother. He stopped his horse and stared at the scene.

The door to the house opened and Eliza's sister, Primrose, came out. She twisted a piece of cloth in her hands.

"So, ye've returned, have ye?" Her caustic tone could sear clear through a less-determined man.

"Aye."

The child turned to look at him with a quizzical expression.

"Aunt Primrose?" The question of his identity burned unspoken on the child's face.

"I'm your dadda, lass."

She tilted her head. "My dadda, was killed in the war."

"Nay, lass, I am here."

She ran to Primrose, threw her arms around the aunt's waist, and buried her face in her apron. Eliza's sister clung to the child with a fierce grip.

"Forgive my friend." Isaac cleared his throat. "He is quite beside himself at seeing his daughter for the first time. I am Doctor Isaac Northrup, camp surgeon for the militia."

"Won't ye both come in for tea?" Primrose's voice trembled. "Come, Aurinda." She guided the child into the house.

"Go gently, Abijah. This could be quite difficult and painful for all of you." Isaac kept his voice low.

Abijah did not answer as he dismounted and tied the horse's

reins to the porch rail. He stared at his daughter's friend, who hadn't spoken a word since his arrival.

"And who be you, lad?"

"I'm Zadok. Aurinda is my friend. Will you move into this house now?"

"Nay, lad. I have land in Fairfield."

Tears welled in the boy. "But … Aurinda lives here. You will not take her away, will you?"

Abijah wanted to lecture the boy about respecting his elders. Instead, he said, "Go home, lad."

The child ran off.

When they crossed the portal into the house, he could sense Isaac's eyes boring into his back.

This would not be an easy task. But it would go as he planned. He had not put his life on the line for king and country all these years to abandon the one hope that had sustained him through the darkness—claiming the daughter he'd never seen. Even if it were by force.

2

"Pappa! Pappa!"

The voice of young Zadok tore at Jonas's heart. No ordinary lament, these sobs of a child in deep distress gripped him. Jonas ceased pumping the bellows, dropped his hammer, and raced toward his younger son, certain the lad was injured in some way. But when he stumbled across the road to meet Zadok, the child flung himself against his father's legs with no blood in sight.

"Pappa, he's taking her away!" The boy wept great tears.

Jonas lifted him into his arms. "Who is taking who away?" He'd nearly forgotten about the return of Aurinda's father when the realization struck him like a physical blow. The veteran had truly taken his child, and no one could do anything about it.

What could Jonas say to comfort his son? He gripped him tightly as Zadok convulsed in his arms, tearing away at the fibers of emotions he usually withheld. Turning toward the house, Jonas carried his son indoors, where Esther met him.

"I was just going out to see what the trouble was. Zadok, what has happened?"

"Aurinda. He's taken her away. All the way to Fairfield."

Zadok resumed the outpour of tears on Jonas's shoulder, soaking his grief clear through his father's shirt and waistcoat.

"Oh, Zadok." Esther's voice held back a sob.

Zadok and Aurinda were such close friends, playing together nearly every day for the last couple of years. Esther's grief seemed as deep as the lad's.

She waddled toward her favorite chair and beckoned Zadok to come sit on her lap. Jonas set him on the wooden floor, and Zadok ran to his Mamma. With little room left on her lap with the coming child, Esther did her best to accommodate her whimpering son. She cuddled him and stroked his head while whispering soothing sounds.

Jonas turned toward the door and walked with heavy steps back outside. This event would cause a great stir in their town. 'Twas not every day a widowed man claimed such a wee one from the only home she'd ever known, not to mention the only mother she'd ever known. Veteran or no, most men would see the practical side of allowing the aunt to take care of the lass.

Why Abijah Whitney made this choice mystified him. Could the veteran not have moved to New Haven or at least arranged to visit the aunt from time to time? What sort of man would do this?

After he inhaled deeply, Jonas started to pump the bellows when he heard screams in the distance. "What now?" He lay his work aside once again and walked toward the disturbance.

The closer he came to the Allan home, the louder the screams tore at his heart. 'Twas bad enough to see his son's grief. But when he saw Primrose Allan beg her brother-in-law to leave the child and then saw the lass laid across Abijah Whitney's saddle, a chill needled up his spine.

He grabbed at the horse's reins before Abijah cantered away and glared at the stern-faced man who gripped the girl. "Is there no other way you can settle this?" Jonas spoke with measured anger. "The child is beside herself with fear. Is this how you want it to be?"

"'Tis none of your affair, Wooding. Release my reins at once." He hissed his words like a snake.

Jonas let go of the leather straps.

But the child grabbed his fingers and would not let go. "Please, Mr. Wooding. Help me."

The terror on her face, akin to the sorrow he'd seen on his son's, brought deep anguish to him. "Aurinda ..."

Before he could speak further, Whitney pried the girl's hands from his and kicked the mount to a run. Jonas would never forget the pitiful sounds coming from the girl while her curls bobbed with the gelding's stride. Her voice soon faded, but the memory of that moment would likely never cease.

The only wails he heard now belonged to Primrose Allan. He forced himself to turn toward the grief-stricken woman.

"My wee babe!" she repeatedly cried.

The man who rode into town with Mr. Whitney attempted to comfort Primrose. Jonas, his feet heavy as lead, clomped toward the two.

"Miss Allan, I am so sorry."

The sobs ensued while the veteran twisted his tricorne hat in his fingers and stared at the ground. Noticing Jonas's presence, the stranger tipped his head. "Isaac Northrup, at your service." The audible strain in the man's voice testified to his concern.

"Jonas Wooding. You are mates with Abijah Whitney, I presume?"

"Aye. Though I wish today he'd been more friend than foe." Isaac tugged at the collar of his uniform and exhaled a breath with force.

"Indeed." He stared in the direction Abijah had gone. "'Twas ... a poor decision he made."

Isaac nodded and stared at his hat. "Aye."

Silence followed except for the wails of Primrose Allan. A

neighbor appeared and put her arms around Primrose then guided her into the house.

"I don't know what to do. I know Abijah's within his rights to take the girl. But the cruelty of it all." Isaac shook his head. "There is no reasoning with the man. The war has hardened him to the point I barely recognize the schoolmate I once knew."

Jonas put his hand on the man's shoulder. "Come down the road to our house. Have some cider, and you can rest. It looks like you've traveled a fair bit and could use some victuals."

"Aye, that I could." Isaac's legs turned stiffly toward his mount, and he untied the reins that secured the mare to a tree. "I'll come back later and bid farewell to Miss Allan. I believe she is none too pleased with my presence at the moment." The weight of a thousand worries seemed to rest on his shoulders while the two men walked side-by-side, Isaac leading the horse.

"So tell me, Northrup, what did you do in the militia?"

"I am a physician by training, so I worked as camp surgeon. I had two assistants, but one of them was killed while helping a mate." Isaac's face waned pale.

Jonas asked no further questions about the war. "There's my house and smithy. My wife has a fresh hogshead of cider you may find refreshing. Step inside."

He held his hand out toward the door in welcome, and Isaac removed his hat before entering. Jonas looked for Zadok, but he and Esther were no longer on the chair. Soon, Esther bustled back toward the main room, steadying herself on the wall every few steps.

"Zadok is asleep, poor lad." She looked up at Isaac.

"Esther, this is Isaac Northrup, recently returned from the war. He is a physician. He is also friends with Abijah Whitney." Jonas cleared his throat.

She tilted her chin upward. "I see." She waddled toward the hogshead and took a pewter tankard down from a shelf, then filled it halfway full. "Here, Mr. Northrup. Some refreshment." Her voice sounded less than friendly.

"It's Dr. Northrup, Esther. Although he is a friend of Mr. Whitney, he is concerned for Aurinda. And for Miss Allan."

Isaac wiped his mouth on his sleeve. "Aye, that I am, Mrs. Wooding. 'Twas no reasoning with my friend. He refused to listen to my concerns. All I can do is watch out for the little lass to be sure all goes well for the child. But my hands are tied by the law. He has every right to take her, despite the obvious pain to so many."

"Aye." A tear rolled down Esther's cheek. She wiped it off and sniffed. "Would ye stay for supper with us, Dr. Northrup? You must be starved after your long journey."

The man smiled for the first time. "Aye. 'Twould be most pleasant, and I'm grateful."

"Mamma, I feel sick." All three adults turned toward the lass whose cheeks were bright red and who rubbed her eyes.

"Alice!" Esther hurried toward Alice, who stood in her shift and shivered. "Let me take you back to bed. I thought you'd been napping quite a long time. My poor babe."

"Let me carry her for you, Esther." Jonas picked up the three-year-old, who seemed feather-light after carrying her big brother, Zadok. The heat that emanated from her small frame vied with the sweltering warmth in the forge. "You burn with fever, lass. To bed with you."

Would this day get any worse? He prayed not, but this latest distress filled him with uncommon foreboding. He'd ne'er seen their youngest child this ill. And with his wife about to deliver their fourth child, Jonas grew overwhelmed with worry.

"May I help?" Dr. Northrup stood in the doorway. "I have some medicinals that might relieve the fever."

"Aye, of course." Jonas combed his hand through his hair, which had come undone from his queue. "I thank you."

Isaac exited the house then came back carrying a leather haversack. "Show me where your daughter lies."

The two men's boots clomped down the hallway. A raucous cough erupted from the lass as both men entered her room.

Esther sat on the edge of the bed, stroked her hands through her daughter's damp hair, then pulled the quilt up to the girl's chin.

"Best to cool her off a bit, ma'am. I know we like to comfort our young ones with quilts, but her fever seems quite high."

"Esther, let Dr. Northrup examine her." He helped his wife stand from the bed.

The two of them watched as the doctor felt her forehead and placed his ear against her chest. Jonas's heart raced when the doctor's eyes narrowed.

The physician patted the girl's shoulder then stood. He inhaled a deep breath before he spoke. "I regret to tell you this, but I believe she suffers from the grippe." Isaac wiped his hand across his face and thinned his lips when he turned toward the parents. "I shall do all I can to help her recover. 'Tis important, Mrs. Wooding, you keep your distance from your daughter, since you will soon be in your confinement."

Redness emerged on Esther's cheeks, and she glared. *There's that look.* The fierce stubbornness of the protective mother— unknown to the doctor and on the verge of an eruption. Jonas often likened it to a mother bear robbed of her cubs.

"I will not remove myself from my daughter's bedside, Dr. Northrup, no matter the danger. My lass needs me." Her anger suddenly morphed into tears, and she returned bedside to comfort Alice.

Isaac's face paled. "I must caution you, Jonas, this grippe is a fierce one." His voice was barely above a whisper. "Many in other communities have succumbed to this illness already. You and the rest of your family must take care."

"Aye." Jonas's throat dried, and he tried to speak but coughed a bit instead. He swallowed quickly, then responded with a weak voice. "I understand. But ye'll not convince my Esther to stay away from the lass. She is our precious wee one." The tears that had remained restrained now gushed.

The doctor took his arm and led him down the hall. Jonas's thoughts ricocheted from the small hands of Aurinda that clung to him as she begged for help to the convulsive sobs of his younger son to the scarlet cheeks of his desperately ill daughter. So much sadness in one day—he could not fathom the thought of any more.

What would he do if he lost his family to this dreaded grippe? Would he have the strength to bear it? He prayed to God the doctor's presence would be the providence he longed for. He clung to the man's arm as he hoped the doctor's medicinals could save them all.

3

Isaac pulled the many-bladed fleam from his haversack. He chose the smallest blade and poured rum over it to cleanse away remnants of the last blood-letting. His normally steady hand shook when he lifted the small arm of the child.

Mrs. Wooding wept in her husband's arms while Isaac prepared to make a small incision on Alice's arm. *Steady, man. 'Tis just an arm, simply much smaller than you're used to.*

"Must you do this? Alice is so very small."

"I am sorry, Jonas. The high fever necessitates balancing out the humours in her body. Bloodletting is the recommended practice. It's been done for centuries." Isaac could feel the droplets of sweat forming on his forehead.

The child, barely alert due to the intense fever, lay still. She jerked slightly when he inserted the sharp fleam. He held the basin below her arm, which hung at the side of her small bed. Her lack of response to the incision concerned him. His throat dry, he allowed the blood to escape for several seconds before he applied a clean bandage to the drowsy lass. Isaac looked at the parents. "Do you have cold water fresh from the well?"

"Aye, I'll fetch some forthwith." Jonas seemed relieved to leave the room.

His wife ran to Alice's bedside and knelt on the floor beside her, an image of grief that had Isaac fighting back tears.

Moments later, Jonas returned with the bucket of fresh well water and a linen cloth. Mrs. Wooding grabbed the material, swished it in the frigid water, and carefully stroked the girl's forehead.

Isaac motioned for Jonas to follow him to the other room. "I fear the grippe has filled her lungs with infection." He kept his voice to a whisper. "We must hope for the best and pray all will be well." He clenched his jaw and grasped his hands behind his back. Although a trained physician, the doctor's arsenal of weapons against disease was painfully lacking. Often prayer became the last—or only—resort.

Jonas shuddered. "Aye." He spun back toward the child's bedroom and stood by the bedside.

The boy he'd seen at the Allan home emerged from another bedchamber, rubbing his eyes. He stared at the doctor and rubbed them again. "Who are you?"

"I am Dr. Northrup. You saw me at Miss Allan's home."

"You came with that bad man who took Aurinda." Tears formed again in his already swollen eyes.

"Aye, I did. Although I wish he had not." Isaac stared at his feet.

"Why are you here?" The boy blinked several times.

"I am a doctor, and your sister is quite ill." He cleared his throat to get rid of the huskiness in his voice.

"My sister?" He ran into the bedroom until his father yelled, "Halt!"

The father emerged, carrying the struggling boy.

"Why is she sick?" The boy yelled. "What's wrong?"

"Listen to me, Zadok." Jonas set the boy down and gripped his arms while he held the child's gaze. "You mustn't go near

Alice. She has the grippe and you could get it from her, the doctor says."

"But I want to see her." By now, Zadok wept uncontrollably.

"I know, son." Jonas's voice remained strong but laced with fear. "But 'twould break my heart if you were to get sick too. Please, do as you're told."

"Come, lad." Isaac put his arm across his shoulder. "Come sit by the hearth and talk with me. It's been quite some time since I've played a game. What would you suggest?"

Zadok shrugged his shoulders but didn't speak.

A knock at the door drew their attention. Isaac answered it, since the parents were with the ill child. When he opened the wooden portal, amazement rippled through him. Primrose Allan's hand remained raised to knock again, and her expression seemed to mirror his surprise.

"So ye've not left New Haven yet."

Her slightly swollen eyes and reddened cheeks did not hide the fine features of her face, nor lessen the overall impression of beauty. Her dark curls, for the most part, hidden beneath a mobcap, persisted in escaping the linen headpiece. Although her stare seared with rage, he discerned the grief her anger attempted to smother.

"Nay, Miss Allan. Mr. Wooding invited me for cider before I follow Whitney back to Fairfield. Whilst here not more than a few moments, his daughter took ill, and I've attended her." He shifted his feet.

"Alice?" Her face paled, and she licked her lips. "Nay! Not their wee one!" She turned toward the boy. "Zadok, I came to see how ye fare since … since Aurinda is gone …" Her lips trembled.

"Please, Miss Allan, there is much sadness here as well." Isaac gently gripped her arm. "Try to focus on bringing comfort to this family. Perhaps you can help Mrs. Wooding so she does not exert herself in her condition."

"Aye, Dr. Northrup." She bit her lip in an attempt to stop it from trembling. "Where is Esther?"

"Come with me." He led her down the hall but noticed Miss Allan give a gentle squeeze to Zadok's shoulder when she passed him.

Throwing her shoulders back in a brave maneuver, Miss Allan slipped quietly into the child's room. Isaac heard the two women weeping. He wiped his nose and went back to the hearth to visit with Zadok, but the lad was gone. He sighed and sat for a moment while he rubbed his head.

A moment later, a hand touched his shoulder. "Thank you for seeing our daughter. What do I owe you?"

"Not a shilling." Isaac shook his head. "My presence in this town has brought enough grief. 'Tis the least I can do to try to make amends."

Jonas's eyes pierced through the dimming light of dusk. "Yer not responsible for your mate. We all make choices, and Whitney made this one on his own."

A ruckus outside drew both men to their feet. They hurried outdoors to find Zadok and another boy in a scuffle. Blood flowed from the other boy's nose.

"What's this about? Peter? Zadok?" Redness crept up Jonas's face.

The boy swiped the blood away with his sleeve. "He started it!"

"He said I'm in love with a lass, and I'll never see her again." Zadok burst into tears.

As he lifted both boys off the ground, Jonas pulled with force on Peter's collar. "Did I not tell you to be kind to yer brother? 'Tis not *you* that misses your friend. And now yer sister is ill and yer mother is fretting about." He sighed and released the boy. The energy seemed to escape the blacksmith like the steam from a slack tub. Shoulders slumped, Jonas walked back to the house.

Isaac stared at the boys, then pointed at Peter. "Go wash up, lad." He took Zadok's arm. "Come sit on the tree stump with me."

Head downward, Zadok trudged behind Isaac.

Isaac lowered himself to sit on the stump, then groaned. "Spent too much time in the saddle the last few days." Looking up at the child, he softened his voice. "Lad, I know you miss yer friend. But I'll make you a promise."

"What?" The child stood with his arms folded.

"I promise you I shall look after your friend, Aurinda, and make sure no harm comes to her."

The child squinted. "How?"

"Well, I will be the doctor in Fairfield, and I'll be sure to check up on her and be sure she fares well. I promise." He placed his hand on Zadok's arm and gave a gentle squeeze.

"But can you bring her back to me so we can play?"

Isaac looked at the ground. "I wish I could, lad. But the law will not allow me to do that. Even though I wish I could."

"Dr. Northrup. Her fever worsens!" Primrose Allan called for his help from the open doorway.

He stood with weary legs and hurried toward the house, Zadok at his heels. He didn't stop at the hearth but headed straight to Alice's bedside, followed by Primrose and Zadok. Jonas picked up his son and removed him from the sick room as he scolded him for his disobedience once again.

"Do you have any hyssop or sage tea, Mrs. Wooding?" Isaac felt the girl's forehead with the back of his hand.

She stood from the chair, which had been placed by the bedside.

"Sit, my friend. I shall make the tea." Primrose Allan scurried away.

Isaac watched her for a moment, then turned back to the patient. "We must get this fever down. Please remove most of her clothes and put cool linen behind her neck and down her arms."

Her parents followed his instructions, seemingly energized by the task. Alice moaned when the cold cloth touched her reddened skin.

"My poor babe." Mrs. Wooding's lips trembled, but she continued to minister to her fever-ridden daughter.

"Mrs. Wooding, you must take a rest, truly. Please allow your husband and Miss Allan to attend your daughter."

"He's right, Esther. We can watch Alice. I'll call you if we need you." Jonas kissed her cheek.

She gripped his hand before she stood with his assistance. With one more look at her child, Mrs. Wooding waddled toward the doorway where Zadok had been standing, looking at his sister.

"Go with your mother, lad." Jonas pointed toward Zadok, and the child obeyed.

Primrose returned with the tea and brought a spoon to administer the healing brew. "I could na' find the sage, so I made hyssop with a bit of cone sugar."

"That will do." Isaac shifted his feet. He helped Jonas prop up the child with pillows. "Make sure 'tis not too hot and give her just a few drops from the spoon at a time."

"I know, doctor." She met his gaze. "I've tended my own wee lass when she was abed with fever."

"Of course you have." He winced and tugged at his collar. "I did not mean to imply you were not capable."

Indeed, Miss Allan seemed the picture of motherly care as she fought back her own tears to tend to another in need. His admiration for her increased, along with his attraction for her. He remembered the kiss Jonas had placed on his wife's cheek, even in the midst of their sorrow. What must it be like to have a wife to bring comfort to her husband? To be there in sickness and health? To be his helpmate and lover?

He shook the thoughts out of his head. He must have been away at war too long. Such a woman the likes of Miss Allan would ne'er want a man who helped steal her own niece out of her arms. Even if the choice was not his. She'd believe he shouldn't be on such friendly terms with a man like Abijah.

The child coughed, returning Isaac's thoughts to the present, a long and raucous sound. Miss Allan carefully laid the child back down on the lowered pillow, while Isaac laid his head on her chest to listen to her lungs. She sounded no better. The thick gurgle alarmed him when he rolled the girl on her side. Without the need to instruct her, Miss Allan patted the child's back firmly to help loosen the congestion.

She truly was a skilled and competent woman—and lovely to look at.

If only she did not despise him.

4

Well past midnight, Isaac startled awake. The house was quiet, save the occasional crackle of the hearth next to him. He pushed himself up from the chair while every muscle ached when he did so. If he hurt this much while still a young man, what would it feel like to be old?

Tiptoeing with an awkward gait down the hall, he found the child with pale cheeks, still resting on her bed. He feared the worst yet saw she still breathed, even though 'twas shallow breaths at best. Miss Allan, barely awake, opened her eyes wide when she saw him.

"How does she fare?" His voice rasped from sleepiness, and he coughed.

"She is quieter, but the fever persists." Miss Allan leaned over toward the child for a closer look. "I do na' know what to do for the wee lass."

"Nor do I at this point." He paused. "I suppose we should pray." It sounded more like a question when he said it.

She glared. "You mean like I prayed for her father to never come claim her?" Her voice stabbed like daggers.

"I think you speak of Aurinda now." He cast a smile her way, hoping she'd see the sympathy in his attempt.

Miss Allan blushed and looked at her hands clasped together in a firm grip in her lap. "Aye. Forgive me, I pray."

"I am the one who needs forgiveness." He inhaled. "I should have found a way to reason with Abijah. I should have …"

She reached out and touched his arm. "There is no reasoning with that man." She removed her hand as though afraid she'd done something amiss. "I never understood what Eliza saw in him."

In the dim candlelight, Miss Allan looked even more beautiful. Why did Abijah dislike her so?

"I think Abijah resented our friendship. Although we were sisters, he seemed jealous we were close." Miss Allan shook her head slowly and stared at the wall, plagued by the ghosts in her past. "After … after Eliza died, Aurinda became me only comfort. She was so much like Eliza, 'twas like I had me sister back." Her lips trembled. "And now she is gone."

She abruptly metamorphosed from sadness to anger, then glared at Isaac. "Yet I prayed to God her father would ne'er return. But he did."

"Surviving the war was not easy for any of us." He cleared his throat. "There were times I thought none of us would return, Miss Allan." He stared at the floor.

"Please, call me Primrose." Her voice softened, "Life is too short for such formalities."

For the first time, he sensed she saw beneath his surface demeanor to understand the war-torn veteran who'd suffered scars of his own. He gave a pensive grin. "Then you must call me Isaac. There are days I wish I were anything but 'Dr. Northrup.' Like today, when all my medical knowledge seems for naught." He paced a few steps then spun around and paced a few more.

"Think how many lives ye've saved."

His shoulders slumped when he stared at the floor. "All I can see are the ones who died."

SLEEP ELUDED Jonas as he lay in bed. Since his mind would not rest, he rose to relieve Miss Allan so she could lie down. He glanced at Esther, who was finally able to get a few moments of rest, despite her fitful slumber. He very carefully lifted the covers so he wouldn't disturb her.

Planting his feet on the frigid floor, he shivered and grabbed his leather breeches, pulling them on quickly, yet carefully, so he wouldn't lose his balance. He didn't bother pulling his hair back in a queue but let it hang free. His waistcoat added more warmth, and his stockings and shoes completed the barrier to the cold, night air. He dreaded the return of winter weather that would bring back the intense cold. Would it also carry more sickness? More death?

He forced such thoughts from his mind and stumbled blindly down the dark hallway. He'd not slept at all. As Jonas entered the room, he focused on his daughter in the bed. "How is she?"

"Mr. Wooding, ye've not slept a wink. Why do ya na' lay down longer?" Miss Allan's expression filled with concern.

"Primrose is right, Jonas. You need your strength. We're here to watch out for her."

Hearing the doctor refer to Miss Allan by her Christian name confused Jonas. What had transpired between those two? He decided not to ponder such thoughts since there were more important things to think about.

He leaned over Alice and felt his daughter's forehead with the back of his hand, like he'd seen Isaac do. "She is still too warm."

"Aye."

He glanced at the somber expression on Isaac's face, and a chill ran up his spine. Did he believe she'd not recover?

The death of one of his children had always been Jonas's worst fear. While he'd seen other families lose one child or more to illness or injury, this deep-seated dread left him weak with terror. How could he cope if Alice died? So small and frail, yet filling their home with joy and exuberance, Alice's presence permeated a room with the brightness of a hundred candles. If her light were snuffed out, how would he survive?

How could he ever face this unnatural progression of losing the next generation when he would still live? Would God put him through this terrible trial?

Dear God, may it not be so.

"May I get you some of that wonderful cider, Jonas?" Isaac touched his arm to get his attention.

"What? Aye. Please."

"Sit here, Mr. Wooding." Miss Allan stood and gestured toward the chair.

The mannerly thing to do would be to insist she keep the chair, but he collapsed onto the wood, too feeble to stay upright.

He reached over and picked up his daughter's hand with a tender touch, like one cradles a flower petal. Her skin, soft as lilacs and pale as snow, seemed luminous in its cast. He caressed her fingers with careful strokes, fearful they might break apart if he pressed too hard.

The contrast between his daughter's tiny, soft hand alongside his thick fingers and coarse skin seemed akin to a gentle wave along the sound, swishing against the harsh grains of sand on the beach. Where did the waves go after they touched the crushed rock? Did they disappear into the ages, like a young life swept away too soon? Would his daughter be carried away on the ocean of eternity?

A shudder that began deep within his soul testified to the truth. Alice had slipped away to heaven, and neither the doctor nor he could stop it. The inner tremble erupted into an outpour of sobs, which wracked his body with the pain of it—an agony from which he may never recover.

ISAAC LAY his ear against the girl's heart, now so still and silent. As he stood, his unsteady legs nearly caused him to lose his balance. He'd seen many a man killed on the field of battle. But seeing this small child's spirit whisked away to heaven would plague him for the rest of his life.

"I know my sweet babe is gone." Mrs. Wooding waddled down the hall, her heart-rending sobs echoing off the wooden walls. "I felt her spirit leave this house. I cannot live without her."

Isaac guided her to a chair and helped her sit. The unborn infant must have kicked, since Mrs. Wooding grabbed at her huge belly.

"Ye're not feelin' yer pains yet, are ye, Esther?" Primrose reached for the pregnant woman's arm and looked at her closely.

"Nay. 'Tis my unborn babe, weeping for her sister gone to heaven too soon."

Her sister? She could not know 'twas a female child, yet the words blurted from her lips in her grief.

"Please." Mrs. Wooding reached toward the child's still body under the covers. "Bring me my sweet Alice to hold one last time."

Isaac started to object, fearful the dreaded illness would spread to the mother, but Primrose touched his arm and shook her head.

"I'll bring ye yer sweet babe, Esther." Primrose carefully wrapped the young girl in a blanket and carried her over to Mrs. Wooding. The child seemed asleep, but it was the final sleep they all had dreaded would happen. Mrs. Wooding smiled through her tears while she draped the deceased child around the girth of her belly then rocked her for several minutes. She sang a lullaby to the daughter whose ears would never hear the beautiful melody again.

As Isaac hurried out of the room to escape this bereavement, he nearly knocked over Zadok, who stood in the doorway.

The boy's lips trembled. "Is she gone to heaven, Dr. Northrup?"

"Aye, Zadok. She has." He could barely swallow for the tears. He wrapped his arms around the grief-stricken boy and carried him toward the still-burning hearth, where he sat and held him for so long they both fell asleep.

When Isaac awoke at dawn, the embers in the hearth barely glowed. Zadok slept peacefully on his shoulder. Isaac remembered what had happened during the night but prayed it would reveal itself to be a bad dream. Even so, his mind understood the truth. The same wish crept into his thoughts every morning after a battle when he prayed the men who were killed were, in fact, still alive. But the nightmare had come true once again.

5

Jonas left the burial ground with his arms around Esther. He glanced behind and saw a sight he would never have imagined—his two sons held each other's hands. The family, at least those who were left, trudged solemnly back toward the house, accompanied by Miss Allan and Isaac. The two friends had shared the worst moments of the Wooding family, and it seemed only fitting they should stay for the rest of the day.

"Might I fix ye some victuals before I return to my home?" Even as she spoke, Miss Allan was already washing some vegetables.

"That would be very kind of you." Jonas stared at Isaac, who appeared nearly overcome with grief.

Jonas wondered what the death of another, especially one so young, had done to the man's soul. Would the veteran surgeon ever recover from the wounds that war had wrought in his heart?

The boys were quieter than he'd ever seen them. Although they often had found their young sister a nuisance when they wanted to play, they now seemed inconsolable. Alice's sweet spirit had woven its way into their hearts. Would either of them ever return to the happy children he remembered?

And what about Primrose? Would she ever get over the loss of her niece, so brutally torn from her arms? Her suffering, akin to the death of one's child, would likely plague her forever.

How would any of them ever be the same? Life had stolen the joy from them all.

Inside the house, the temperature was nearly cold as outdoors. The missing chinks in the walls allowed every puff of the November wind to seep through. Jonas shivered and hugged himself. He left his woolen coat on and stirred the glowing coals in the hearth.

"Let me add a log to your hearth, Jonas." Isaac seemed grateful to have something to do besides dwell on the sadness.

Zadok and Peter hurried inside, hugging themselves to keep warm.

Primrose pointed at them. "Close the door, boys."

"Yes, Miss Allan."

No need for reminders of good manners today, Jonas supposed.

Esther stared at the fire, seemingly mesmerized by the flames.

"Why do you not rest, my dearest?" Jonas placed his arms around her shoulders.

She didn't answer him but did not resist when he guided her toward their bedchamber. When they passed by the empty room that had belonged to Alice, Esther paused and wept.

"Come, my dear." Jonas barely resisted tears himself. He held her frame, which trembled with every step while she all but stumbled down the hall.

◟◞

ISAAC STOKED the fire with the iron rod and stared at the flames. He didn't want to think about these last days of trial and grief. It was almost more than he could bear.

"Drink this." Primrose handed him a tankard of cider.

He stood and accepted the offering. Thirstier than he realized at first sip, he soon guzzled the rest of the drink. When the last drops were gone, he felt strangely refreshed. One need had been met, giving him strength to at least survive.

Life should be more than just survival, however, and he hoped his need for peace and companionship would someday be fulfilled. Somehow, they seemed intertwined.

As he turned toward Primrose, the urge to be close to her nearly overtook him. "Primrose, I ..."

Before he could speak further, she closed the distance between them.

He took her hands and clung to them. "I can't tell you how it pains me what Abijah has done. I never ..."

Her tears melted away the barricades in his heart.

He held her close then drew away to look her in the eyes. "I promise you I shall watch out for Aurinda, to make sure she is well."

Primrose nodded. Overwhelmed by the desire to kiss her, he gave in to the hunger. She responded in kind as the emotions of the last few days seemed to find release in their mutual embrace. He paused to catch his breath only to stop abruptly when he saw young Zadok staring at the couple.

"Oh, dear." Primrose's cheeks grew scarlet. She tucked stray curls into her mobcap and smoothed down her apron.

Isaac cleared his throat and tugged at his collar. "Hello, Zadok."

"Is that fun?" Zadok's innocence shone through the question. "Mamma and Pappa do that sometimes. They say 'tis where wee babes come from."

Isaac's cheeks burned. They must've been as red as

Primrose's. "Well, certainly that can be the *start*. But nay, 'tis not exactly how wee babes begin."

"Oh. But 'tis fun, is it not?"

Isaac grinned. "Aye, 'tis most fun."

A knock at the door gave blessed relief to the embarrassment. "I'll get that." Isaac hurried to answer.

When he opened the door, a man and woman carried a large kettle and loaves of bread. He recognized the minister from the burial service.

"Mrs. Stone, Parson Stone, please come in." Primrose waved them inside and quickly closed the door to keep the warm air in.

"We do not wish to bother the Woodings at this time of grief, yet we thought perhaps they'd not been able to prepare victuals for Thanksgiving. We brought our extra."

Isaac and Primrose stared at each other, then looked back at the Parson and his wife.

"Thanksgiving?" Primrose appeared dumbfounded.

Just like Isaac felt.

"Aye, we did'na wish to cause dear Esther and Jonas any concern for the celebration. Though 'tis a sad day of thanks for them this year." Mrs. Stone's eyes brimmed with tears.

"Thank you. I'm certain the Woodings will be most grateful."

Another knock at the door brought more neighbors with more Thanksgiving fare. A cooked pheasant, fish, garden vegetables from the harvest, apple pies, dried pumpkin, and of course, more breads.

Isaac, Primrose, and Zadok, along with Peter, who'd joined the group, stood with widened eyes.

"Let me bring Esther and Jonas here to bid their thanks." Primrose started to go to the bedchamber.

But Mrs. Stone said, "Nay, dear Primrose, let them rest. They will partake of these victuals when they can. No need for thanks."

The neighbors filed out with tearful smiles then waved farewell to the small group.

Isaac stared with mouth agape. He'd never seen such love and loyalty from a community. He finally found his voice. "This is most astonishing."

"Nay." Primrose held her hands over her face in a prayer-like gesture. "'Tis not so astonishing if ye know the good people of New Haven."

Jonas appeared in the room, his mouth agape.

"The neighbors. They brought victuals for Thanksgiving. I've ne'er seen anything like it." Isaac shook his head slowly in disbelief.

"'Tis an unlikely day to give thanks, is it not?" Jonas' brows furrowed and he rubbed at his swollen eyes.

Zadok went to his father and looked upward. "But Pappa, our friends are so kind to do this, are they not?"

"Aye, Zadok, they are most kind." Jonas forced a smile.

"Pappa, can we not partake? I am quite hungry."

"Aye, Zadok." He patted his son's head. "We all must eat. Especially your mother must partake. I shall bring her a trencher in our bedchamber." He took a clean plate and filled it with several portions of the fare. After he'd chosen what he murmured were "Esther's favorite foods," he turned to bring her the plate. He stopped abruptly and looked back at the others. "Please, Isaac, could you lead a prayer of Thanksgiving at the table?"

Heat flushed Isaac's neck and spread across his face. He'd never said a prayer out loud, certainly not at a family meal, and not at such an important event as Thanksgiving. He stuttered. "I … I don't know."

"I can do it." For such a small boy, Zadok had a large and determined manner.

"Aye, Zadok. I'm certain you can. Very well." Jonas proceeded down the hall with the food plate for Esther.

Primrose stood straighter. "Let's everyone wash our face and hands before we eat." The boys hurried to the basin, licking their lips and stopping along the way to sniff at one or more trays of food.

"Does that mean me as well?" Isaac grinned.

"Of course, it does, Dr. Northrup." She threw him a flirtatious grin.

"Are they going to kiss again?" Zadok's whisper to his brother echoed throughout the room.

Isaac squelched a laugh. "Well, certainly not in front of you curious chaps."

The resulting laughter brought blessed relief as they filled their plates. The mourners seemed to alternate between tears and giggles. Isaac had seen this fluctuation in moods in camp after battles, but he assumed it to be the result of too much rum.

Then he remembered one of the soldiers saying in a drunken voice, 'A merry heart doeth good like a medicine.' He saw it now in the contrast of grief and laughter that filled the Wooding home. It had naught to do with intoxicating spirits but was a medicinal for the heart. Whatever its source, Isaac was grateful for it.

Although he thought he had no appetite, Isaac's growling stomach informed him otherwise as he spooned generous portions onto his trencher.

The foursome sat along the tableboard and bowed their heads. Isaac, relieved that Zadok volunteered to pray, smiled at the boy who saved him from the embarrassment of a life bereft of religious teachings. He held his breath while the lad's small voice rose above the communal grief and the gifts from a kind group of friends.

"Dearest Heavenly Father, we thank Thee for this food. Thank Thee 'tis Thanksgiving, even though we forgot. Please forgive us our trespasses as we forgive those who trespass against us. And … and please watch out for Alice. We really miss her. Amen."

Muffled "Amens" followed the boy's prayer. While they served up the meats and fowl, root vegetables, and breads, Isaac imagined none of them would need salt on their Thanksgiving meal. Everything would be seasoned with their tears instead.

6

Not anxious to leave Primrose, Isaac planned to leave for Fairfield the next morning. Nevertheless, he resolved to keep his promise to her—to make sure Aurinda was well.

His plans changed quickly, however, when Zadok appeared in the main room, cheeks flushed and eyes rheumy. "I don't feel well, Mamma."

Mrs. Wooding cried out and would have collapsed had Jonas not kept her from falling.

Isaac swooped the ill child into his arms and carried him down the hall, placing him on the bed his brother pointed to. Isaac swallowed his fear and felt the boy's forehead with dread. "Now listen, Zadok. You are a strong lad, and I'll do everything I can to treat you and get you well. Understand?"

Zadok nodded with a weak motion.

Jonas hurried into the room with his hands clasped. He groaned when he looked at his younger son "'Tis the grippe, I assume."

"Aye, Jonas. But I've just told Zadok he is quite strong, and he should be fine. We must encourage him to drink, however, and keep him cool."

Jonas nodded while his lips trembled.

"You must be strong." Isaac grabbed his arms and met his eyes. "For Zadok. And for your wife."

"Aye." Jonas stood taller and threw his shoulders back. "What can I do?"

"First, get more cold water from the well. Then ..."

They were interrupted by a moan of pain from the main room.

"Esther!" Jonas's face turned ashen, and the pulse in his neck visibly throbbed. He ran back down the hall.

Zadok grabbed Isaac's arm. "Is Mamma all right?"

"Aye, lad. 'Tis likely her birthing pains." He stroked his fingers through the boy's hair. "Nothing to fear." He forced a smile.

If only he believed that in his heart. Peter carried in the well water.

Jonas placed his hands on the brother's shoulders. "Peter, listen to me. You must try to stay away from your brother whilst he's ill. Understand?"

"But will he die too?" The question hung in the air like spent gunpowder on a breezeless day.

"Not if I can help it. But there is something you can do. Pray for him."

Though Isaac did not believe it would help, it would give Peter hope. And they all desperately needed hope.

JONAS FOUND Esther as she bent over and gripped her belly with both hands.

"My dear wife." He needed to be strong for her at such a time, but his stamina faltered from the last few days. He wanted to believe all would be well, but his faith had been challenged with the loss of Alice.

God, help me be strong for Esther. And Zadok.

Sniffing back tears, Jonas helped his wife down the hall. When they passed by Zadok's bedchamber, Esther looked inside.

"I love you, Zadok." Her lips trembled.

"What can I do, Pappa?" Peter stood in the hall, his face pale.

Shaking his head to clear his thoughts, Jonas said. "Go. Get the midwife."

Peter spun around and ran down the hall. The front door slammed shut.

In obvious discomfort, Esther stopped abruptly. "I have lost my water."

The desperation in her voice cut into Jonas' heart when they both stared at the puddle on the floor.

"'Tis all right, Esther. I shall take care of it." Jonas helped her onto the bed.

She moaned and held her enlarged belly. "I fear something is wrong."

"Nay, sweet Esther. 'Tis just ... all you've endured making you fear."

"Nay, something 'tis not right."

He swallowed with difficulty. "Mrs. Hotchkiss shall be here forthwith." He paced back and forth while pausing every few minutes to look out the window for the midwife.

When Peter returned alone, his heart raced.

"One moment, my dear." He kissed his wife's cheek, squeezed her hand in an attempt to reassure her, and strolled out the door. His walk morphed into a run when he made his way outdoors and stumbled into Peter. "Where is the midwife?"

"She cannot come." Peter's face reddened, and he breathed heavily. "She is at another birthing." The boy's lips quivered.

"No matter, son." Jonas reached out and hugged his son close. "'Tis not your fault." He pulled away. "Now, go find Primrose. Tell her we need her straightaway."

43

Peter ran frantically up the road toward the Allan home. Jonas whipped around and returned to the house. When he shut the door, he could hear Esther moan loudly down the hall. He ran toward their bedchamber as Isaac emerged from the sick room.

"What is wrong, Jonas?"

"The midwife. She cannot come."

Isaac's face paled, and he licked his lips. "What will you do?"

"I've sent for Primrose."

"Will she know what to do?"

"I pray she does."

Terror threatened to overtake Isaac. What if Primrose did not know what to do? She'd been with Eliza when she gave birth. Eliza had died.

Copious sweat soaked his shirt, and his nostrils flared. His thoughts were so jumbled he could not think straight. He concentrated on taking deep, slow breaths. Would prayer help, or was it his momentary insanity that prodded him to do so? He gave in to the prompt.

God, I've no reason to believe You would listen to such a sinner as me. But, if You are real, I beg You to protect this family from more grief.

A loud scream from the bedchamber sent him rushing toward the mother. Swallowing became a challenge, but he forced himself to push past the dry lump in his throat. "Mrs. Wooding, Primrose is on her way."

"Dr. Northrup, I know something is amiss. I have such pain here." Her fingers shook as she pointed below her ribs.

A cold shiver progressed up his spine. He'd seen this once before in the war camp. One of the camp followers about to give birth complained of the same discomfort. The midwife who attended the woman called the problem an 'unnatural position' of the infant and called in Isaac to help her maneuver the large child into the proper birthing placement.

They both tried with every ounce of their strength, yet both mother and child succumbed to their unsuccessful attempts. That incident still haunted him.

Why, when this family had already borne such grief, were they in serious danger of more heartache?

Primrose whisked into the room. She shoved past Isaac and began to tend Mrs. Wooding. "Esther, I fear Mrs. Hotchkiss is on another birthing. Meantime, I'll help ye as best I can."

"I fear something is wrong." Esther grabbed Primrose's hands.

"There now, I'll help ye through yer pains."

Isaac cleared his throat. "Primrose, might I have a word with you? Please?"

Her expression questioned him, yet she followed him out to the hearth. "Isaac, I need to be with her now."

"Please listen. Should it seem things are not going well, please call me in so I can examine her."

"You? But ..."

"I know 'tis not the physician's place. Yet, I am concerned you might need assistance. Please, will you call me should you have any concerns?"

"Aye, I shall." Primrose spun around and hurried back into the woman's bedchamber.

Isaac closed his eyes and inhaled a deep breath before he came back to Zadok's bedside.

Fraught with anxiety, Isaac spent the next hour in attempts to cool down the fevered child while he tried to ignore the cries of the laboring mother down the hall. With each pitiful scream, Isaac's spirits seized with worry. This was not Mrs. Wooding's first child. She should be closer to delivering the babe. Unless things were as he feared.

Again, he resorted in desperation to prayer. If there existed a God who cared about anyone, surely He would be concerned about this family, would He not?

"Isaac." Primrose stood in the doorway. Her face flushed with redness and moisture. "Isaac, can you come?"

He left the child's bedside and scurried toward the bedchamber, expecting the worst. Mrs. Wooding, alert but obviously exhausted, clenched the quilts and whimpered. Jonas followed Isaac on his heels.

"Jonas, do I have your permission to examine your wife?"

The man appeared on the verge of collapse. His head drooped, and his weak voice could barely be heard. "Very well." He stumbled toward his wife's bedside and clutched her hands. "Esther, please let Isaac examine you. Mrs. Hotchkiss still has not come and—Primrose needs his help."

"I understand, Jonas."

In all his twenty and seven years on this earth, Isaac had never seen a braver woman. If only his medical skills could be worthy of her valor.

When Esther's next pain began, Zadok called for his pappa. Jonas left Esther's bedside and stumbled down the hall.

Isaac forced himself to take steady breaths. "Mrs. Wooding, I know 'tis not the usual way, but I beg you to allow me to place my hands on your belly so I might determine your child's position. Primrose fears things are not going like they should."

Esther's eyes bulged as she nodded without speaking. Primrose went to the other side of the bed and clutched Esther's hand. Isaac cleared his throat and oh so carefully placed his hands along the outside of Esther's shift. He pressed just hard enough to feel for the baby's position inside the womb. After he completed his examination, his breathing sped up.

"Thank you, Mrs. Wooding." Isaac stepped away from the bedside. "Primrose, might we speak in the hallway?"

Her eyebrows furrowed while she followed him once again.

"The child is not in the right position." He held both of her arms, making every attempt to smother his emotions. "I've seen this before. 'Twill require strong arms to help remove the obstruction to the babe."

Primrose's face blanched. "But, I do na' know what to do."

"I do." Isaac clenched his jaw and forced his shaky legs to stand firm. "I've seen the maneuver done before. 'Twill require us both placing our hands on either side of the child and pushing hard in one direction. Hopefully, the babe will cooperate and turn with its head downward. Come and help me. Please."

She searched his face. "Aye. I pray God helps us both." Primrose turned and ran toward the bedchamber.

Isaac followed until Jonas grabbed his arm.

"Tell me. What is wrong?" Jonas scanned Isaac's face.

He took a deep breath. "Jonas, go tend Zadok. He needs you. With your permission, Primrose and I shall assist your wife."

"You two?" Jonas inhaled sharply. "Do you know how to help her?"

Isaac could easily fail this man. Again. But what choice did they have? This child would not wait for the capable hands of the experienced midwife. Circumstances necessitated he and Primrose do the deed, lest the mother or baby die. Or worse yet, both could die.

"Aye, Jonas. We can help her."

The expression on Jonas' face did not inspire trust in Isaac's abilities. Stumbling down the hallway, Jonas escaped to Zadok's sickbed.

When Isaac stepped into the bedchamber, the terror on Primrose's face matched his own.

God help us both.

~

JONAS KNELT by his son's bedside. Zadok lay in a fitful, fever-driven sleep, so Jonas took the linen from the basin of cold water and stroked it over his son's arms, forehead, and neck. He frequently swished the linen anew as he brought the freshly cooled cloth to the boy's skin each time.

Exhaustion from grief and concern overwhelmed Jonas, and he placed his head on the side of Zadok's bed, praying while he dropped off to sleep.

A scream of pain caused him to jerk awake. Pushing off the feather mattress, he stood, then stumbled toward the bedchamber. Esther wept uncontrollably. Both Isaac and Primrose had beads of sweat falling from their foreheads.

"I ... I think it worked." Isaac stammered and grabbed onto Jonas's arm.

"What worked?" He clung to the doctor's arms with force.

"The child was in an unnatural position, and we had to turn him around. 'Twas painful, aye, but necessary to save them both."

Jonas pushed past Isaac and Primrose to grab Esther's hands. "My dearest, I am so distressed for you." Tears emerged.

"'Tis better now, Jonas." Esther made a valiant effort to smile. "The strange pain here is gone." She pointed under her ribs. Her expression sobered when she grabbed her belly, which visibly tightened beneath her shift. "'Tis time. Jonas!"

She gripped his hand so tightly it caused him pain. But he did not mind if it meant it would bring her comfort.

"'Tis time to leave, Mr. Wooding." Primrose touched his arm. "We'll stay with her. All should be well now."

"Aye, Jonas, we'll call you." Isaac wiped the dampness from his face and exhaled.

His heart still galloping at a frantic pace, Jonas inhaled with a jagged breath and returned to Zadok's bedside.

7

Jonas left his wife's side with reluctance but returned to Zadok, now wide awake and whimpering.

"Pappa, is Mamma all right?"

"Aye, son, she is well. More concerned about you getting better, so you must drink some of this tea Peter made."

Zadok coughed then furrowed his brows. "Peter made this?" He took a sip. "'Tis quite sweet."

"Yer brother must have added a bit too much cone sugar." He tousled the boy's hair.

The pains of birth Jonas had listened to three times before alarmed him once again.

"Are you sure Mamma is well?" Zadok's lips trembled.

"You were too young to remember when Alice was born." Jonas forced himself to smile. He paused and took a deep breath. "This is what all the mammas endure when they bring their wee ones into the world." His voice sounded strained. "Then, when they look at their new babes, the memory of those pains eases. Their love for their little one helps them forget the pain."

Zadok's brow wrinkled. "Did she cry when she had me?"

"Aye, son. But she loved you so, she said you were worth it."
He felt his son's cheeks. "You seem a bit cooler now. Mayhap
you should rest."

"Pappa, can we pray instead. For Mamma?"

"That we must do." Jonas nodded.

Jonas bowed his head, fearful to ask God for safekeeping for
his family. The last time he prayed, Alice died. Did God listen
then? Would He listen now?

For Zadok's sake, he begged their heavenly Father to protect
Esther and the baby. Each time more cries emerged from the
bedchamber, he prayed louder yet. Despite his own lack of faith
and the fear of more loss, Zadok needed to be encouraged. He
also prayed silently—after Zadok fell asleep—that God would
spare his sons from this grippe. The thought of losing all his
children in one short span of time threatened to shatter what
little faith Jonas clung to.

In the midst of his greatest despair, his head shot upward.
What was that? A small mewling sound emerged from the
bedchamber. It stirred Jonas's heartbeat to a frantic pace, and he
nearly tripped as he headed down the hall to his wife. He paused
in disbelief.

Isaac and Primrose appeared on the verge of prostration.
Primrose sat on the chair, breathing heavily, with moisture
soaked through her clothes. Isaac wiped off his face and
forehead with a piece of linen. He collapsed into a sitting
position on the floor.

Their exhaustion contrasted sharply with the look of peace
on Esther, who smiled at a small bundle cradled in her arms.
The infant nodded its head and looked for a meal, while Esther
complied by offering the hungry child her breast. Her grateful
smile reflected Jonas's relief.

"Esther." He hurried toward her, kissed her cheek, and
stroked the baby's damp hair.

"'Tis a daughter, husband."

Jonas teared up, praying God would forgive him for his doubts. "'It is of the Lord's mercies that we are not consumed, because His compassions fail not. They are new every morning: great is Thy faithfulness.' From the book of Lamentations." He took Esther's hand and kissed her fingers.

"For the Lord is good," Esther quoted her favorite Psalm through her tears. "His mercy is everlasting; and His truth endureth to all generations."

"Mercy." Jonas's love for his wife and children, all gifts from a loving God, brought overwhelming gratitude to his heart. "We shall call our daughter Mercy."

THE EARLY DECEMBER chill seemed warmer in the sunlight that brightened Isaac's spirits. Fatigued from the events of the last several days, he took comfort that, although one life had been lost in the Wooding family, four had been graciously spared, including Peter, who had come down with the grippe right after Zadok. Isaac could not account for the results. His skills had little to do with it.

The same experience reminded him of the battles in war. He recalled Colonel Washington, who sustained bullet holes throughout his uniform and had two horses shot from underneath him. Yet the colonel received not a wound.

Other soldiers who might have survived were casualties of a single musket ball, while comrades to the man's right or left survived without a scratch.

Why did Zadok and then Peter both recover from the attack of the grippe while their little sister succumbed? And why did the experienced midwife in the war camp, assisted by his strong hands, fail to save that mother and child while he and Primrose succeeded with Mrs. Wooding?

Isaac shook his head and took in the soothing sounds of the

waves that swished along the beach of the Long Island Sound. There was much about life he did not understand. Perhaps he never would.

Footfalls nearby captured his attention. Primrose. His heart skipped a beat while the woman approached him. Her hair hung down and twisted into a braid, while the rich, dark color glimmered in the sunlight. Her mere presence elicited a palpable stirring, an attraction for a woman, which he'd hidden deep inside the burial ground of war's hatred. Primrose had resurrected a tenderness and longing he assumed died long ago.

She drew closer and encircled her arm through his while she took in the glistening waters of the ocean's inlet. He no longer focused on the sound but found the beauty of her features encompassed his attention.

"So ye must leave today, then." Tears moistened her face.

"Aye. But I'll return and tell you how Aurinda fares."

Her eyes narrowed. "Will ye?"

"Of course. Do you not trust me?"

"I wish to trust ye. Yet I fear Mr. Whitney will come between us. Just as he's come between Aurinda and me."

Isaac drew her toward him. "I am not Abijah Whitney. I pray you can understand we are old friends, yet I do not share his sensibilities. The war changed Abijah."

Her expression seared through to his soul. "Yet it didna' change thee?"

Had it changed him? Of course—it had in many ways. But it did not make him a bitter man. It made him cherish life more than ever.

"All we endure in life changes us in some way. Sometimes for the good and sometimes not." Isaac stroked her cheek. "I have not forgotten who I am. A physician who does all I can to save lives. Because I understand life is short. And we must treasure those we love and the moments we have together."

A shiver crept up his spine. Would this be their last moment together?

Before he could stop himself, he enfolded her in a desperate embrace, afraid if he let go, he'd never hold her again. Primrose responded in kind, and when they kissed, it brimmed with both fear and passion. He didn't remember how long the kiss lasted, but it didn't seem long enough.

"Please, come back to me. And tell Aurinda how much I love her." Primrose covered her mouth as sobs emanated from behind her fingers.

"I shall. I promise."

She spun around and ran back toward town. He stared until she disappeared out of sight. It mattered not what Abijah thought. He wanted Primrose, and would return for her.

Isaac trudged slowly through the deep sand and returned to the home of Jonas. He found him shodding Isaac's gelding.

"Ah, just in time." Jonas wiped his forehead with his sleeve and released the horse's leg. "Your mount despaired for new shoes."

"'Tis no surprise to me. I cannot remember the last time he was shod."

Jonas grinned. "Not too many smiths on the fields of battle, eh?"

"Nay."

"You said farewell to Primrose?"

"Aye. None too happily."

"Well, you can return anytime. Quite certain she'd follow you to Fairfield if you asked her." Jonas raised his eyebrows.

"I may just do that. First, I must see about Aurinda, as I promised. If I bring Primrose to Fairfield and Abijah stands in her way of seeing the child, I don't know what might happen." Isaac shook his head slowly.

"Aye. 'Tis a whole new battle to contend with."

Wondering what journey lay ahead, Isaac stared toward the

road to Fairfield. "The curious thing is, we have a respite from war, yet I find myself facing battles of a different sort. Pain and suffering, illness and tragedy—'tis always present, whether in times of war or peace. 'Tis the lot of mankind, I suppose." He squinted in the sunlight and grabbed the gelding's reins.

"I suppose 'tis why we look to heaven for our hope." Jonas slapped his arm in a friendly manner. "We'll not find the peace we crave here on earth, no matter the state of war. 'Tis the war in our souls we truly battle. Yet faith in God overcomes."

Isaac climbed onto his saddle and faced the blacksmith, now a man he called his friend. "You are lucky, Jonas Wooding. You have a family and the faith to sustain you."

"Perhaps you shall find the same, Isaac Northrup. I pray you do."

Doffing his tricorne hat, Isaac waved farewell.

As Isaac rode down the road toward Fairfield, the sun glistened on the morning frost in the trees and grasses. A small herd of deer wandered along the path, then paused to observe him. They seemed content in being together—much like the Woodings, who supported one another and made a life together. Grief would always be a part of this world, but the love of a family and their faith brought them joy. Not to mention, 'wee babes.'

Isaac smiled when he envisioned Primrose. For the first time, after years of loneliness, his heart glimpsed something more. Hope.

LOVE'S KINDLING

DAWN OF AMERICA SERIES—BOOK ONE

1

Fairfield Connecticut, 1779

That voice again, yet no one appeared before him.

Could he be dreaming?

"Sir? How do you fare? Where is your pain?" Now he knew he heard the voice. Yet he saw nothing—and no one.

The back of his head throbbed sufficiently to keep time with a drummer boy.

Zadok Wooding's arm seared with each attempted movement. Yet the fact his eyes would not reveal the face of the woman speaking caused his greatest distress.

"Sir?"

He rubbed his eyes with the hand that moved easily.

"What?" His own voice, yet unfamiliar. Strained. "Where am I?"

Reaching to touch his eyes once again to be certain they were indeed open, Zadok fought the panic that jerked his heart rate to a gallop. Such a sudden change in pace—almost as fast as the kick he'd inflicted to the gelding's side during his frantic mission to deliver the letter.

"Sir, you've fallen from your horse. My name is Miss Whitney. You're not twenty rods from my home in Fairfield."

Her voice soothed him. Yet, why couldn't he see her?

His mouth dried so quickly, he reasoned it must be filled with dirt.

"I ... I cannot see you." His breathing raced. "I cannot see anything. Am I dreaming ... or having a nightmare?"

A gentle yet unexpected touch on his arm caused him to flinch.

"I am sorry, sir. I didn't mean to alarm you. Can you get up?" Her voice brought a measure of calm like rain on a hot summer's eve. Yet the darkness enveloped him so completely he thought he must be dead. Yet if so, why was he still breathing? He was more than aware that his chest was rising far too quickly while dizziness encompassed him like a whirlwind in his head.

He pushed himself to a sitting position with his left hand. The pain in his head and his right arm brought him to the point of nausea. He inhaled deeply, fighting back the sensation.

"Please, help me." His moistened palm groped for her hand. Finding it, he gripped her fingers as firmly as one holds onto a cliff from which they might tumble to their demise. "I do not understand why ... why I cannot see?"

He recalled his grandfather describing a darkening of the sun in London some years before. Halley's Eclipse, he'd called it. For three whole minutes, darkness enveloped the city, and many thought it was the end of the world.

"An eclipse. That is what is occurring. Grandfather said he could not even see his hand in front of his eyes." He took momentary comfort in the thought and then realized the woman hadn't mentioned any darkness. "Miss Whitney, can you see anything?"

There was a pause before she replied. "Come. You are too

weak to ride. I'll guide you to our home and tend your horse. I'll send for our physician."

"Wait. Can you?" He knew her answer before she spoke it.

"Aye, sir. I can see."

AURINDA GRIPPED the stranger's unhurt arm as she guided him to the barn. The muscles in his limb tensed so tightly, she could feel the fear in his sinews. She wished she could comfort him in this terrifying turn of events, yet words escaped her. What might alleviate her own terror if she suddenly discovered she no longer could see?

Words seemed insufficient at such a moment. She prayed Dr. Northrup might bring encouraging news to this man. She also hoped the good physician might bring medicinals for relief of the pain that elicited moans from this patient as he clenched his right arm and held it close to his chest.

"Please sit here in this bed of straw, Mr. ...."

"W-Webster. Zadok Webster." On a secret mission, he hesitated to reveal his real name. One never knew who might be a trustworthy Patriot, or a Loyalist.

He bent his knees and slowly descended onto the straw. As he thudded onto the thick, crunchy pile, she winced to see the pained expression on his face. "I shall fetch the doctor forthwith, Mr. Webster. May I first bring you some water from the rain barrel?"

"Aye." It was said with such distress, it sounded more like a cry than a word.

She nearly ran to the barrel just outside the barn door, grabbed the ladle, and brought a generous portion to the sweat-soaked man. She held it to his lips. Despite her efforts to keep it from spilling, it seemed as if half of the liquid ended up on his chin and shirt. "I am sorry, Mr. Webster."

"Thank you." His breathing came so rapidly, she feared for him.

Would he go into a stupor? Would his heart give out? She had heard of such things following a severe injury or shock.

"Let me help you lie down, sir. You must rest." She gently pulled his shoulder back onto a thick pile of animal bedding. 'Twas hardly a feather bed yet would have to do. She'd heard the soldiers often had little more than the hard ground on which to sleep. "I shall return as soon as I find the doctor."

Aurinda nearly tripped as she hurried out the barn door. She thought about stopping at the cabin to tell her father about the injured man in the barn but decided against it. No reason to complicate the situation. He might even refuse offering assistance to the patient, and she wouldn't take that chance. She'd address the situation later—after Mr. Webster had been tended.

She hoped Dr. Northrup would be easy to find in the small community of Fairfield, but one never knew if there might be another urgent need. He seemed to be busier than usual these days, especially with so many gone to war. Elderly parents who would normally be looked after by grown sons were often suffering from one health concern or another.

Even today, Aurinda had taken time from her weaving to bring soup to old Mrs. Hawthorne, who suffered from apoplexy. Dr. Northrup frequently made her aware of such needs in Fairfield. Aurinda was used to these interruptions in her already burdensome routine, and she didn't mind.

Her heart warmed at the gratitude expressed by the lonely widow when she delivered the victuals. 'Twas the least Aurinda could do for the patriot cause to free her country from the rule of England. She could not carry a musket to battle, but she could transport a warm meal to a soldier's mother in need.

That unexpected interruption to her routine this day imparted another realization: Had she not been on that back road to the center of Fairfield, she wouldn't have found the injured Mr. Webster.

Listening in to Dr. Northrup's conversation with Mr. Webster, Aurinda now knew the man to be a blacksmith from New Haven. The physician's healing hands quieted the patient as the doctor lifted his eyelids and peered into them with a candle held closely. He blew out the burning wick. She was relieved, lest a fire begin in the dry hay. The doctor moved his fingers carefully toward the back of Mr. Webster's skull. He stopped when the patient winced.

"So, you remember the horse stumbling, and then you awoke on the ground?" The doctor pulled out a bottle from his leather saddlebag.

"Aye." The patient's face paled as he slowly rubbed the back of his head.

Measuring out a small portion of the liquid into a cup, Dr. Northrup handed the vial to Mr. Webster. "Before I set the arm, take this laudanum. 'Twill take the edge off the pain."

Aurinda stiffened at the thought of this man in misery. Although her father frequently complained of one ailment or another, she'd become accustomed to his incessant grumblings, which rarely seemed serious but often prompted a visit to fetch the doctor.

Dr. Northrup, whose friendship with her father extended back to the French War, seemed as pleased with these visits as her parent. The two veterans shared tales of battle with one another, and occasionally, the physician offered medicinals. *Probably to justify his presence.*

But this was different. Zadok's arm lay in a peculiar position, and it would likely cause him very real distress when set right to heal.

"What can I do to help, Dr. Northrup?" She surprised herself with her boldness. Normally she stayed in the background during the physician's ministrations, but this time she had a desire to help. The patient was in obvious distress, and the fact he couldn't see added to her sympathy. *What would it be like to suddenly be blind?* She shivered.

Dr. Northrup raised his eyebrows at her offer. "An extra pair of hands would be quite useful. You can start by holding his upper arm while I straighten it out."

Closing her eyes tightly, Aurinda lurched at the cracking of the bone and the heartrending cry from Zadok. *Why did I offer to do this?* She swallowed the bile infusing the back of her throat.

Without thinking, she touched his other arm with reassurance. "It should heal well now, Mr. Webster."

"Thank you." His voice edged on agony, but he seemed intent on maintaining a brave front.

"You bore that with some courage, young man." Dr. Northrop closed his saddlebag. Turning toward Aurinda, he handed her the laudanum. "He may need this for a day or two while the healing begins. But not too much, mind you. Supplies are low with the war on."

"I understand."

The doctor wrapped the splinted arm and exhaled a deep sigh as he stood. "The good news, Mr. Webster, is your arm should heal well. The uncertain news concerns your sight." He paused as if measuring the weight of the words he was about to speak.

"The fact is, I have seen this before—an abrupt injury to the back of the skull leading to blindness. Occasionally, with time, the sight returns. Other times ..." His voice trailed off, and he looked toward the open door of the barn.

"Sometimes it doesn't?" Zadok's unseeing eyes widened.

"Aye, Mr. Webster. I wish I could assure you 'twill return. But I cannot. Only the good Lord knows the answer." He pushed his tricorne hat firmly onto his head. "I'll stop in on the morrow to see how the patient is faring."

"Thank you for coming, Dr. Northrup. Will you see my father before you leave?"

For the first time this visit, the physician grinned. "Aye, I shall."

While the doctor limped toward the door, Aurinda turned toward the patient on the bed of hay. Tenderness gripped her heart. If ever despair could be reflected on a countenance, it was clearly visible on Zadok Webster's face. His high cheekbones, smeared with dirt from the fall, accentuated the depth of his warm eyes and the terror they reflected. She noticed his mouth tightening as he seemed to struggle to keep his lips from trembling.

"Try not to fear, Mr. Webster. Dr. Northrup has given you hope. We must pray your sight will return."

"We must pray? Do you believe such a prayer can be answered?"

"I ... I believe it can be answered, aye. But the answering is in the hands of the Healer. I suppose He will decide."

"So then, do our prayers matter, since God has the final choice?" His words brimmed with bitterness, and his cheeks darkened to a ruddy hue.

"I know sometimes our prayers are not answered the way we would desire."

"Then why bother at all?"

She couldn't answer. Weren't her own prayers unheeded by God when she was a lass of five? When she begged God to allow her to stay with Aunt Primrose instead of being torn from her aunt's comforting arms and into the cold embrace of her father?

"I cannot say. The Good Book tells us so. Yet ..." She stumbled for a reply. "Yet, I *will* pray for your eyes to see again, Mr. Webster." She turned her attention to his horse in the stall. "I need to tend your mount."

"My mount. The papers! Miss, please bring me the haversack on the saddle."

What sort of papers would take his focus so completely from his blindness? Aurinda did what he asked.

He grabbed at the sack with a flailing arm and caught the strap. "Can you help me, miss? At the bottom of the sack are some carefully folded papers. Please tell me if they are still there."

With searching fingers, she finally felt the edges of paper below a tin cup, razor, and tinderbox. "I feel them."

He exhaled with relief. "Please, miss. This is most imperative. I am forced to rely upon your goodwill and your allegiance. I need to know if I can trust you."

Holding her breath longer than she intended, she finally let it out. "I am a patriot by allegiance, sir. But my father's favor rests with the king's army. He does not know my feelings on the matter. So, if you would be so kind—since you now owe me a debt for saving your life—please do not inform my father of my patriot leanings lest he turn me away from our home." There, 'twas said in the open, far from the ears of her Loyalist father.

"I'm so relieved, Miss Whitney. I must entreat you, 'tis of the utmost importance I deliver this letter."

She fingered the papers, tempted to pull them out. "You? Deliver this? And how, pray tell, might that be accomplished when you are so badly injured?" Not to mention his lack of eyesight.

He sat without speaking.

"Might I look at it, Mr. Webster?"

"You will not be able to read it. There is no message you will be able to discern."

"Well then, how can it be of such import?"

"Go ahead and look at it." He nodded in the direction of her voice.

She dug into the sack and carefully extracted two folded

pages. Opening them, she shook her head as she doubted the man's sanity. "There is no message here, sir, save a receipt for cornbread pudding. How can this be of such importance?"

"Miss Whitney." He fumbled for her hands with his own and gripped her fingers. "There is most certainly a message here, done with invisible ink. 'Tis written between the lines of the receipt."

"Invisible ink!" She scoffed. "I've never heard of such." She withdrew her hand from his clutches and folded up the papers.

He sought her hand again and squeezed her fingers more firmly. "You must believe me. I assure you this is an important missive on its way to the Continental Army."

"And why exactly would an invisible message be needed?" She laughed.

"'Tis not truly invisible. It merely needs a special application of something called a 'reagent' to be read. And the recipient of this message is none other than General Washington."

She paused at the name. "General Washington. And how exactly did you come by this missive?"

"'Tis a long story to be certain."

"Well, I'm awaiting the tale." She gripped the folded letter while her other hand clutched a fistful of straw.

"'Tis no tale, miss, but true enough. I run the smithy in New Haven. The original courier of these papers arrived with a horse needing shod. The lad all but fell off his mount—this gelding here—as the rider was afflicted with fever. My mother took him to the cabin to tend his illness. He was near out of his senses, but he gripped my arm and shared his urgent business with me in private.

"He explained about the invisible message and most urgently encouraged me to get this letter delivered at a certain location to a major in the Continental forces." He stopped for a moment. "I cannot tell if you believe I have lost my senses with such a story. I cannot see your expression, and you speak not."

His words faded into the recesses of her thoughts as a deeply embedded dread, born of living for so long under threat from the king's army, began to extend roots of fear. This anxiety first sprouted in her heart years ago. It twisted tentacles of terror in her mind, despite her efforts to control it.

The pounding in her chest testified to the constancy of danger, ready to leap into her life at the smallest reminder that America was at war and her world could change in a moment.

"Miss Whitney?" He squeezed her arm.

She forced her thoughts back to Mr. Webster's question. "On … on the contrary, sir, I am quite shocked by this. But I do believe you." She stood on unsteady legs and walked toward the open door of the barn. Laughter echoed from the house several rods away. Her father and Dr. Northrup must have shared something quite amusing. How absurd to hear mirthful chatter when her world was on the edge of annihilation.

What should she do? To deliver so important a message herself seemed impossible, not to mention highly dangerous. And yet, was there another way? This letter to an American major must be extremely important, or else why would it be written in ink that most readers could not see? The whole idea seemed absurd, yet brilliant, at the same time.

Thinking about her own safety, Aurinda quickly dismissed the panic, inhaling deep breaths to calm her thoughts. What did it matter if she lost her life for her country? She had no one who would care, save father, and his need for her seemed to be as his housekeeper and cook. His affection for his only child was strained, blaming her for the death of his wife in childbirth twenty-one years before.

It was a long time to carry a grudge against a helpless infant. Yet her father would never forgive her for being born.

Her resolve was set. She would deliver the letter to the major. Now she had to create a plan.

2

"Deliver it yourself? That is impossible!" Zadok Wooding forgot his physical pain at the young woman's proclamation.

"'Tis more possible than carrying the letter to the recipient yourself, sir." Irritation rang in Miss Whitney's voice.

"'Tis just ... highly dangerous, miss. There are soldiers from both sides in the woods. Women often become victims of men's baser sensibilities. Especially during war." Sweat dripped from his forehead. "Please, reconsider."

"And just who might we trust in this matter? I've already told you my father is a Tory. There are others as well. Besides, I often travel to Norwalk to deliver my weaving to customers. I am careful to stay on the roads, and my business would appear to be my usual occupation. It should not raise anyone's suspicion. In fact, it should lessen anyone's supposition I might be carrying anything other than my cloth."

Zadok could not argue with her logic. It made complete sense. Yet he could not dismiss the fear that things could go awry.

"Your father is not concerned that you travel for business by yourself?"

She harrumphed. "My father is not so concerned when it comes to my welfare, Mr. Webster."

Taken by surprise, he did not press her for an explanation. How could a father not be protective of his daughter? He remembered his own parents when his younger sister became ill with the grippe. They fretted as they tended his sibling and sent for the physician. Both sat at his sister's bedside for hours on end, applying cool linen to her forehead. Eventually, his father shed bitter tears at her passing. It was the only time Zadok ever witnessed the man cry.

Shaking his head as if he could erase the memory, his thoughts returned to the present. "What will you tell your father?"

"Merely that I am delivering the weaving to one of my customers in Norwalk. He'll be happy I'll be returning with a few shillings to buy some food." She paused. "I do not know how I'll explain the fact there is no payment." The first note of worry crept into her voice.

He reached for the haversack nearby and fumbled in a small pocket where he hid his valuables. "Here. 'Tis not much, but I hope will assuage his anger—or any suspicion."

"I'm grateful, sir."

"'Tis I who am grateful." He searched until he'd found her arm and gently squeezed it. "I promised the courier at my home I would carry out this mission. I've let him down, yet you have rescued this most urgent assignment. Thank you."

She removed his fingers from her arm, and warmth infused his cheeks.

"Forgive my boldness, Miss Whitney. I did not mean to be so familiar with you."

"No matter, Mr. Webster. I am not offended. I must needs

hurry if I am to allow sufficient daylight to carry out this mission."

Dry straw crunched as she stood.

"Fare you well, Miss Whitney. Godspeed."

"I shall need His wisdom to carry this out, but I am determined to try."

Her skirts rustled when she exited the barn. Time was of the essence, and fear clenched his spirit. He almost asked for Divine intervention for her brave undertaking, but then he thought better of it, doubting it would make a difference.

With Miss Whitney's leave-taking, Zadok was left once again to dwell in the darkness. When others were present, he could distract himself from the torment the pitch black evoked in his spirit. When by himself, the blackness became a suffocating presence, like a host of demons wrapping their evil arms around him and squeezing away his breath.

He gasped for air, body trembling, as he waged war with the sobs ready to burst from the sheer horror of the never-ending night. It was as if he'd been sewn into a shroud and nailed into an eternal coffin without hope of ever seeing daylight again. He was buried alive. Yet, this was no way to live.

He lifted his head to the heavens.

If this is to be my misfortune, then take my breath away along with my sight.

Aurinda strode into the main room of the cabin, trying to appear as casual as possible. Her father looked up from his reading.

"Where have you been? Setting your eyes on our crippled visitor? I suppose a blind man would be a perfect suitor for you with your plain looks."

She cringed at her father's cruel words while inwardly berating herself for allowing his criticism to eat away at her. She was not fair or winsome in her looks. Hadn't Father reminded her often enough? Still, his words cut into her spirit like a bayonet sharpened for battle.

Ignoring his comments, she headed for her bedroom. "I'm going to Norwalk to deliver some weaving, Father. I shan't be long."

"Norwalk? Were you not just there a few weeks past?" She tried to ignore the fact he hadn't shaved in several days. His clothes reeked of sweat and ale, despite the fact she'd delivered clean clothing to him days before.

"Aye, Father. But Sally Lyman took such pleasure with the linen, she requested more. The weather is fine, if not a bit warm, but 'tis a fine day for a walk. And I'm certain the patient in the barn will not trouble you. The laudanum should help him rest. I've left him sufficient water and food nearby, so you needn't be concerned."

"Perhaps Dr. Northrup will drop in again to attend him, and he and I might visit."

Aurinda sighed. She should be used to her father's selfish ways by now.

Slipping into her bedroom, she closed the door behind her, then found the folded length of linen she'd set on her chest of drawers. Thankfully she'd finished the weaving a few days before. She grabbed her silk sewing case and removed the scissors from the hidden inner pocket before folding the mysterious letter into a tight wad and tucking it within. The case fit into the pocket of her apron. Squeezing it with her fingers, she paused to whisper a prayer.

"Dear Father in Heaven, please give me success in this journey. Help me find this Army major and let him accept this missive from a stranger—a woman, no less. Guide my steps and protect me. Please … hide me from the eyes of those I cannot trust. Amen."

Picking up the material, Aurinda left the safety of her room and faced an uncertain journey. In this time of war, with soldiers everywhere, she knew a woman alone could become a victim. And no one would pay a penalty for the crime.

3

Aurinda swatted at the numerous flies swarming her face. This July weather was far warmer than she'd anticipated, and moisture trickled down her face and neck. This was not a casual journey. The comfort of the temperature did not matter when there were far more important considerations. The safety of the new America could be at stake.

A new America.

After so long a struggle, it hardly seemed possible it was still not resolved. Here they were, four years since the beginning of the conflict with England, still struggling to win freedom from the oppression of King George and his Parliament. It terrified her to think of the British holding New York not many miles from her home. Although much of Connecticut supported the patriot cause, there were sufficient numbers of Tories present to keep one's guard up at all times.

Even within the walls of her own home.

It was a long walk to Norwalk, and Aurinda tried to hurry while thinking of anything that would take her mind off the danger. She mused on the fiery preaching from the church pulpit in Fairfield on Sabbath Day last, as the parson renounced the tactics of English tyranny.

Father stayed at home, of course. His refusal to attend Sabbath services defied the local authorities. 'Political meetings run by insurgents,' he called them. The local sheriff let the matter drop, since no one wanted to stir the ire of the Loyalist community.

Her father's Tory leanings made her cringe with embarrassment. She noticed sometimes a group of townspeople would stop speaking when she drew near. Did they think she was a Tory as well? The thought elicited cramps in her belly.

No rain had fallen for weeks now, and the dirt swirled around her feet, filling the small crevices in her shoes. Her stockings would need considerable soaking before the stains would disappear, if they ever did.

Usually these trips to Norwalk were a day of relief away from her father and his cynicism. But today was different. Although she trod the same road she always traveled with her fabrics, Aurinda carried the added weight of a small letter. This extra burden furthered the strain. She could easily be intimidated by anyone asking questions about her business. Usually there was nothing to hide.

Today, the future of her country could be at stake. The very thought drew fresh moisture on the nearly drenched shift underneath her gown.

The appearance of scarlet-clad soldiers approaching on foot sent her heart thudding. She stepped to the roadside to allow them passage and curtsied. A corporal paused and tipped his hat, leering at her in an uncomfortable manner. She clung tighter to the bolt of fabric and held it higher against her breast.

"And where might you be heading, miss?" The soldier continued to grin, causing her to chill despite the heat.

"I have business in Norwalk, sir. As you can see, I am a weaver and have goods to deliver to my customer there." She smiled in as friendly a manner as she could muster. But she feared he would see terror in her eyes.

"I see." The soldier fingered her linen, and his hands stroked the fabric far too close to her bodice.

She stepped back, breathing so fast she grew dizzy. "Aye, I must be going, sir."

He spoke again but was interrupted by an officer at the back of the line of soldiers.

"Good day, Miss Whitney. And how be your father this oppressive, hot day?" The lieutenant wiped the back of his hand across his forehead.

Aurinda recognized the officer and nearly fainted with relief. "He is well, thank you, sir. As I told this soldier, I have goods to deliver to my customer in Norwalk." Her heart continued to thud while her knees threatened to buckle.

The officer glared at the overly friendly comrade. "Then let's allow Miss Whitney to be about her business, Corporal Botsford."

"Aye, sir." The corporal rejoined the unit of soldiers, much to Aurinda's relief.

"Good day, Miss Whitney." The lieutenant tipped his tricorne hat at her and continued on his way.

"Good day, sir." She smiled, but the blood rushed into her ears, and her heart took on an uneven beat. When they were no longer in sight, she collapsed on a large rock on the side of the road and inhaled deep breaths until her heart steadied its frantic beat.

Continuing on her way, she closed her eyes momentarily to thank the Lord for His safekeeping. Her steps hurried faster than ever. The journey to Norwalk had never seemed so long before. An eternity ensued before the first homes in the town appeared. She practically ran the final rods toward the marketplace.

In her mind, she replayed the instructions given by Zadok

Webster. 'Go to the tavern with the image of a fox on the sign and ask for Major Talmadge. The taverner will direct you.'

She could barely swallow with her throat so dry. Perhaps they had cider inside. She hoped she had sufficient coins to pay for it.

As she opened the door, a pewter bell near the wall rang, announcing her presence. The entire population within stared at her. She tried to smile, but her trembling lips prevented it. A woman approached, hands on hips. "What can we do for ya, miss?"

"I … I could use some cider to quench my thirst. I've just now walked from Fairfield. I think I have sufficient shillings. Can you tell me if I do?"

The woman glanced at the coins in her hand and nodded. Then, she stared at the bundle of folded material she carried. "Got business to attend to, do ya?"

"Aye."

The woman continued to scrutinize her but filled a pewter mug with cider.

Aurinda was never comfortable when others stared at her, assuming her indelicate features drew unwanted attention. She swallowed the cider so quickly, she nearly dribbled the liquid onto her gown. "Thank you." She handed the woman a coin.

The ample taverner grabbed it from Aurinda's hand and started to walk away.

"Please, ma'am, if I could beg your help."

The woman turned and stared at her. "What for?" The taverner cast that suspicious gaze at her again.

Aurinda cleared her throat and kept her voice low as she drew closer to the woman. "Might you be able to tell me where I can find a Major Talmadge?"

The woman's eyes blazed. "And what business might you be needing the major for?"

Aurinda's thoughts spun faster than her loom but, instead

of creating yards of linen, she wove a tale. *God, forgive me for lying.* "Well, the major ordered some material for his lady friend ... Oh, dear. Might that be you? I may have spoiled his surprise." Aurinda attempted to hide the material under her apron.

The woman's face morphed from anger to delight. "Why that Bennie the fox! Ordering something for me?" Her face turned bright red.

"Oh, please forgive me if I have spoiled the major's surprise. He told me to keep it a secret, and I fear I have ruined his plans. Please, do not tell him you know about his gift." Aurinda bit her lip, playing the role of the guilty party.

"I shan't tell him anything. I'll be as surprised as a pig on killing day."

Aurinda's eyes widened at the comparison. "Thank you, ma'am. Now, if you could just direct me to where I might deliver the gift."

THE AMERICAN ENCAMPMENT was well hidden, but the woman in the tavern had given Aurinda specific instructions to guide her way. 'Past two groves of oak trees, then look for the boulder big enough to sit on. Four more rods and take a sharp turn right. Follow the rugged pathway and...'

"Well, hello there, miss. How might I help you?"

An extremely tall man with dark hair and piercing eyes greeted her. Dressed in the blue Continental uniform, the man's presence projected strength and vitality, both charming and frightening. He'd approached her so suddenly, she struggled to put her words together and found her hands trembling as they held the yardage.

"I am looking for a Major Talmadge."

"And what manner of business do you have with the major?"

"I have an important communication to give him." Her hands moistened as she clutched the bolt of linen.

He stepped toward her. "And what sort of communication would that be?"

"A letter, sir. A very important one."

"I see. And who is this missive from, may I ask?"

"I was told by a courier that it came from a boatman on the Sound."

"Truly? And why did the courier not transport it himself instead of sending a female?"

"He became gravely ill. Then, the next courier fell off his horse and was blinded by an injury to his head. I am the only one he could trust to deliver it."

"You?" The American officer threw his head back and guffawed. "What are you? A tradeswoman? Delivering secrets?"

Just like Father. Not in his physical appearance but in his disdain for her. She raised her chin and focused her eyes on his face, wishing she could stick him with one of her longest needles, as if it were a nail thrust into his wooden heart.

The veins in her neck pulsed in rapid rhythm as she fought back the desire to loathe the man. "I imagine General Washington would be relieved to know that every loyal patriot, whether strong soldier or weak weaver of cloth, would be willing to put their life at risk for America."

His face darkened, and he reached out his hand. "Give me the letter."

"Are you, in fact, Major Talmadge?"

"No, I am his superior officer. Give it to me."

She stepped back. "I was instructed to only give it to Major Talmadge."

"You insolent …"

Inhaling deeply, she fought back a dizzy sensation. She nearly sank to the ground with relief when a tall and lean American officer appeared unexpectedly out of a grove of thick trees. His eyes were also intense but appeared to be much kinder than the first officer.

"I am Major Talmadge. What seems to be the trouble?"

"Major, I have an important communication to give you. This letter came from a boatman on the Sound."

The man nodded in understanding. "Aye, very good. I am grateful to you, miss. How did it come to be in your hands?"

"I explained to this gentleman that the first courier became dreadfully ill. The second courier fell off his horse and was blinded by the fall. Since I am the only one he knew he could trust, he placed the letter in my hands. I carried it here forthwith."

"I see." Major Talmadge glared at the other man. "As Intelligence Officer, it is my duty to receive these missives. You did correctly, miss, in handing it over to the proper recipient."

The large jaw of the other officer contorted as redness crawled up his neck. After he stared with blazing eyes at Aurinda for a moment longer, he stomped off into the woods.

Her mouth dropped open, and she stared at Major Talmadge. "Who is that man?"

"Arnold." Major Talmadge grimaced. "General Benedict Arnold."

4

After handing the letter and the yardage to the Major—explaining the ruse that it was a gift for the taverner—she curtsied to the officer and bid him farewell. She noted the amused smirk on his face before she left. So relieved that her errand was over, she covered her mouth with her hand to keep from laughing.

Soon, her mirth was replaced by fear as she noted the townspeople staring at her. She hurried her steps toward Fairfield.

Crickets chirped in the nearby grass, then quieted when Aurinda approached the barn. Limping from a sore on her foot brought on by too-tight shoes and the heat, she hobbled toward Zadok, who sat up, wide awake.

"Miss Whitney?" His voice held earnest hope.

"Aye. I've returned."

"I'm so relieved. I feared for your safety." He stuttered. "And, of course, for the successful delivery of the letter." His Adam's apple moved as he swallowed.

"I'm here—weary and needing some cool water to wipe away the dust—but I am back. And the letter is safely delivered."

His grin revealed teeth that reflected the moonlight streaming through the doorway. "I don't know how to thank you."

"Then do not try." She yawned. "I am greatly relieved I found the major and placed the message into his hands. 'Twas the least I could do for my country."

"For *our* country. And I am grateful."

She drew a cup of water from the rain barrel and sat on a mound of hay not far from Zadok. Folding her leg upward, she removed her stocking and inspected her foot while lifting her sweat-soaked shift up over her knees. There was no reason for modesty in front of a blind man, and the heat, even in the late-night hour, steamed oppressively. She inhaled sharply when she touched the painful blister.

He cocked his head. "Are you injured?"

"Just a sore from my shoe."

"Put a bandage over the spot after you have washed it." His brows furrowed. "Don't forget some slippery elm as well. Or perhaps bear grease."

Aurinda startled at his concern, not to mention his doctorly advice. "You seem well versed in medicinals."

His face softened. "I've just learned from my mother and sister. They are quite adept in dressing wounds."

The reddened area where the blister was had opened. The raw lesion would likely benefit from the medicinals Zadok recommended. Tears erupted unexpectedly, and she sniffed sharply to stem the flow from her nose.

"Are you in pain?"

"Nay. 'Tis just ... never mind."

"What?"

The tenderness in his voice was an unfamiliar balm to her wounded soul—a soothing medicinal to her spirit that she'd not heard in many years. Not since Aunt Primrose. Wiping her arm across her face to remove the flow of tears, Aurinda was grateful he could not see her.

"I shall be fine. 'Tis just a small blister I can cover 'til it heals." Suddenly feeling exposed, she drew her shift back over her legs and wrapped her arms tightly around them.

Zadok shifted his legs to change position, then winced when he accidentally used his right arm.

"You must take care with that arm, lest it not heal properly."

"I know." He hugged his splinted limb closer to his body.

"Perhaps you need more laudanum to stem the pain."

"I'd be grateful for a small amount. I did not wish to take any whilst you were gone. I feared I might not be awake when you returned, and I wanted to be certain you *had* returned."

"You mean, you wanted to be certain the letter was delivered."

"Aye … nay. I … I wanted to know if the letter made it to the major, but mostly I feared for your safety."

"My safety?" No one ever thought about that. Certainly not her father. He likely was sound asleep, even now.

"Aye. I very much wanted to be certain you made it back. Did anyone cause you concern on the road?"

She bit her lip. "Not too much. The Lord watched over me." She readied to stand, but Zadok reached toward her and held her arm firmly but gently.

"Then I am grateful to Him, if indeed He provided your protection."

A shiver needled its way up her arm as she drank in his appearance, truly seeing him for the first time. Rare was it possible to stare at a man without the hindrance of social constrictions. But his unseeing eyes that glowed pale in the moonlight made her linger a moment. Were they grey or blue in the sunlight?

His long hair was the color of his chestnut gelding; the

strands of his mane were undone from the leather ties used to pull them neatly back. No one had bothered to comb it since the fall from the horse. His lips that seemed to flow with comfort and concern nearly drew her breath to a standstill. They were full, but not overly so. They were just right.

"Aye." She shook herself to break the spell. "He indeed protected me." She paused, not knowing how else to respond to his words. "Thank you for your kindness." She stood, and his hand fell away from gripping hers. She poured him a measure of laudanum and handed him the vial. "Here, Mr. Webster. Your medicine."

Although he could not meet her eyes, he looked upward. "Thank you. And please, call me Zadok."

"Zadok. An unusual name for these parts. Was he not a mighty man of valor in the Good Book?"

He grimaced. "A poorly chosen name, to be sure."

Aurinda did not know how to respond to his thoughts. She believed his name to be well-chosen. "I think 'tis a fine name and well-suited to you." She turned and started to leave, then paused. "Good night, Zadok, man of valor."

His expression contorted as he turned away from her.

The distress she saw on his face surprised her. Inhaling sharply, she hurried toward her house.

MAN OF VALOR. *Surely she jests.* Zadok winced when he lay back on the pile of hay, cradling his right arm on his chest. He closed his eyes, but unwelcome childhood memories intruded his thoughts.

He'd long been tortured by recollections of competing with his brother while they grew up and always losing to his robust sibling. Somehow, Peter had the upper hand in everything.

Though only two years apart, Peter continued to excel in the ax throw, as well as racing for distance, even when the brothers grew into manhood. Mighty Man Zadok indeed.

Their mother always encouraged Zadok when he failed to best his older sibling. 'You just wait,' she would say. 'Your day of valor will come.'

That day had not arrived by the time their father announced he would take Peter with him to fight with the Continentals. Zadok would be needed to tend the forge at home. Being reminded the army horses needed to be well-shod for battles did little to remove the sting. Once again, Zadok was pronounced a weak failure, only fit for shoe-making.

For three years now, while Father and Peter sent home word of heroic battles in which they had fought, Zadok grew more bitter—and hated his name all the more.

A glimmer of hope appeared for the blacksmith when the courier carrying the secret missive for General Washington needed a replacement. While Zadok did not wish the man to be ill, he hoped, at last, he could accomplish a heroic deed. Perhaps that day would prove his name to be aptly given.

But that opportunity had now turned into a nightmare, far worse than any midnight terror from his childhood memories. Unending blackness surrounded him as panic gripped him once again. He struggled to breathe while praying his breathing would cease and buried his face in the straw, hoping it would smother his miserable circumstances. But his deathly hopes were disarmed by a sneeze, forcing him to turn his nose and mouth away from the dusty, dried strands.

Tears crept from his eyes. His mother's prediction of greatness appeared to be lost forever, bested by a weaver of cloth whose sight allowed her to carry out the courageous mission.

Mother always insisted God inspired her to name her

second-born after the mighty man of valor she read about when her labor pains began.

But Zadok decided if God had chosen that name for Him, the Almighty must have an ironic and hurtful sense of humor. A God like that would never heal him. Zadok would, instead, live the rest of his life in the demon-filled darkness.

5

Aurinda awoke the next morning with the dusty stickiness of the roadway still clinging to her gown. She'd fully intended to clean off the dirt from her mission to Norwalk last night but fell asleep on top of her quilt instead.

Slipping out of her clothing, she searched for a bar of bayberry soap and washed in the basin. The water turned a dark shade of brown as she removed the filth from her hands and face. Her stockings, gown, and shift would have to wait for washday. She slipped a clean gown over her head and inhaled the fresh smell of the linen. Her hair would take too long to comb out, so she covered the tangled strands with a mobcap.

Father was wide awake and in a foul mood when she entered the main room to fix his breakfast. "Were ya plannin' on sleeping away the whole day? I'm hungerin' for some victuals."

"I am sorry, Father. 'Twill not happen again." Stirring the large kettle of gruel simmering in the hearth, Aurinda plopped a goodly portion into a trencher. She sprinkled cinnamon on the hot cereal and marveled at how the spice transformed the color of the pale mixture of corn and butter. She carried the bowl to her father, who sat up in bed.

Not crippled enough to remain reclining, he still spent most of his hours with his feet propped and his arms unproductive. Occasionally, he made a great fuss about getting up and doing fieldwork before he'd ask a neighbor to assist him with his chores. And, of course, Aurinda must help at all times. He was never satisfied unless she was working.

He regularly complained with a loud voice about the lack of respect the colonists paid to veterans, such as himself, who won the colonies away from the French. He groused even more about the rabble-rousing insurgents who betrayed the king of England in their efforts to overthrow English rule. He had no sympathy for the cause.

What would he say if he understood where her loyalties lay? Aurinda did not dwell on this but continued to make him tea and offered to bring more wood in for the hearth.

Every once in a while, she caught her father staring at her in an odd manner, almost as if he were seeing someone else. When he noticed her glance his way, he quickly turned and complained about this or that. There were always things that dissatisfied Abijah Whitney, so grievances were both plentiful and often profane. When his vocalizations edged on irreverence, she hummed hymns under her breath.

"Is there anything else you need, Father, before I tend to our patient?"

"Our patient?" He nearly choked on a spoonful of gruel. "The sooner *your* patient is on his way home, the better."

"I'm certain he is anxious to return." His home. His family! "Father, I must send a post to inform his family of his whereabouts, lest they worry."

"Huh." Father resumed eating.

Without saying another word, she left the cabin and approached the barn.

Zadok still slumbered, and she shied away from touching his

shoulder to awaken him. Instead, she leaned over and said in a quiet voice, "Mr. Webster. Zadok."

Eyes startled open and he rubbed them as if trying to instill sight. After a moment, he stopped, and his countenance darkened. "I nearly forgot ..."

He tried to sit up but groaned when he moved his right arm even slightly.

"Let me help you." She put an arm around his left shoulder and supported his efforts to sit upright. "There. 'Twould be wise to give you a bit of laudanum to lessen your pain."

He squeezed his eyes shut. "That would be useful." He opened them and shook his head. Did he think the action might bring back his vision?

When she poured him a vial of the medicinal, she broached the subject of his family. "Zadok, I'm certain your parents will be concerned for your safety. May I send a post to inform them where you are?"

"Yes, of course. My mother will be frantic with worry."

"What shall I write?"

Zadok paused in thought and moved his jaw back and forth.

As he appeared to wrestle with his thoughts, Aurinda watched with curiosity.

"I don't know what to say to her. I am the son who was supposed to keep the family together while my father and brother are at war. And now ..."

"And now you have no sight. Can you not tell her the doctor holds hope for your recovery?" She hesitated a moment before touching his hand.

"Tell her ..." He inhaled a ragged breath. "Tell her about my arm, but please do not inform her about my eyes. She will find out soon enough."

"Very well. I shall send the note forthwith."

He looked toward her. "Thank you, Miss Whitney."

She started to walk back to the cabin then turned to face him. "Please. Call me Aurinda."

"Aurinda. It means golden. Is that the shade of your hair?"

Heat infused her cheeks. "Aye. I've been told that is the reason my mother named me such. Before she died."

"I am sorry. You must miss her greatly."

"Well, I never knew her, really, as she died giving birth to me. But my aunt stayed with her when I was born, and she told me my mother saw my hair and said I had a crown of golden curls. 'Aurinda' was the last word she spoke."

"And what of your aunt?"

She clenched her gown with both hands, and her eyes moistened, remembering the loving aunt who had raised her for five years. Aurinda would never forget the day Father returned from the war and took her away.

"I have not seen her since I was a lass of five. And now she is gone." She spun away and hurried toward the cabin.

ZADOK WISHED he could say words that would wash away the sadness he heard in her voice. But he knew grieving for someone you loved could not be removed so simply.

He tried to imagine the golden curls on Aurinda's head. He'd only known a few lasses with hair described in such a manner, and he'd always found the sight to be mesmerizing. It seemed like shafts of sunlight from heaven had transformed into a crown of golden hair. He sighed. What he would not give to embrace the vision with his own eyes.

6

Three days passed with Aurinda tending Zadok each day in between her chores. While his arm improved, his eyes were no better. There were moments he imagined seeing light, and Aurinda would send for the doctor. Each time, Dr. Northrup examined him, however, he could ascertain no change. Darkness still enveloped Zadok's world.

Zadok's mother replied to Aurinda's note. The post rider carried a return message that Aurinda read out loud. She wondered about the different last name of Zadok's mother but thought that might seem like prying to ask about it.

Mrs. Wooding thanked Aurinda profusely for taking care of her son. His mother looked forward to him returning to them as soon as his arm healed. Work in the smithy was getting behind, and she feared he would have difficulty catching up.

Aurinda paused in her reading and glanced at Zadok. He sat stiffly on the hay mound, chin on one knee while he gripped his left leg as though it would run away if he did not hold onto it.

Moisture from her hands dampened the parchment of the note, and she wiped them off on her apron lest the ink of the letter smear. Clearing her throat, she tried to speak, but the words seemed to be stuck. Unless Zadok's sight returned, he would never catch up on the work. One could not labor as a blacksmith in the dark of blindness.

"Perhaps I shall read the rest of the letter at another time." Aurinda folded the pages.

He lifted his chin from his knee. "No, please … continue."

"Very well."

She held the letter up so the afternoon light would illuminate the message as she read:

The man who was ill and fell from his horse recovers yet is still weakened. I imagine he may take several days yet to recover fully.

Your sister seems most anxious to spend time with him, reading and bringing medicinals when he needs them. I have listened carefully to their conversation lest I find his character at all alarming. As yet, he seems to be a good Christian man with moral principles. Time will reveal the truth of it. At such times, I dearly wish your father were here. But since I can expect you home soon, I trust that you shall be a good judge of his character.

Zadok exhaled loudly. "Shall I judge the man's character by listening to his voice? I do not think that possible." He picked up a pile of hay and threw it across the barn. It flitted through the hot air and sank far short of Zadok's thrust.

"Much can be discerned by one's voice. Perhaps you will hear more than those of us who rely on our eyes." She refolded the letter. "Is there anything I can bring for you?"

"Nay. Save a new set of eyes." His jaw clenched, and he rubbed the back of his head.

"I would give you my own if I could." Aurinda went to the rain bucket, which seemed to be running low on water.

Zadok looked toward her. "I believe you would. You have a golden heart to match your brilliant hair."

"You are too kind. And you only suppose my hair to be brilliant because you cannot see its true condition. Would you like some water?"

"Aye. Thank you. I do have something to ask of you."

"Anything."

"Is there something I can do to repay you—to help in your work on the farm? You seem to be laboring from sun up to dusk and beyond. I can even hear your weaving loom late into the night after dark. Please—let me lessen the burden for you."

Aurinda started to say no, then thought of the abundant weeds in the cornfield. If she showed him how to feel for the weeds, that would give her more time to work on her weaving and do her numerous chores. "There is one thing you could manage."

"Anything. I will go mad sitting around, doing nothing."

"The cornfield. The weeds are as plentiful as the corn this summer. I could show you how to feel for the weeds whilst avoiding the thick stalks of the crop. Would you be willing?"

"Of course. Show me the way."

"First drink this." She brought the cup of water to him. "Lest you get heat sickness from the sun."

Zadok drank every drop and stood from his bed of hay. When he tried to get his balance, he wobbled.

She grabbed his uninjured arm and steadied him.

"It will take some time to get my bearings back." He gave a laugh that sounded more nervous than amused.

"You will do well. Keep your hand on my arm, and I'll guide you to the field. There now. 'Tis easier than you thought, is it not?"

"Aye, 'tis so."

~

IT WAS NOT ONLY EASIER for Zadok to keep his balance by following Aurinda to the field, the experience proved to be a pleasing sensation as she held onto his arm. Not since childhood and under the care of his mother had he been forced to rely on a woman to guide his path. Rather than resenting the dependence, however, he found being so close to her exhilarating.

He didn't know if his other senses had sharpened with the loss of his sight, but with every breath he took, he inhaled the earthy scent of her. It was a blend of sunshine, flowers, and that feminine aroma that escaped description. Whatever the source of the aura, he delighted in it—the first pleasant sensation since he'd fallen from the horse several days before. Zadok regretted when they arrived at the field and he no longer needed to cling to her arm.

"Here we are. If you sit along the edge of this row, I can show you which are the weeds. It will take some practice to feel with your hand which are the 'evil interlopers' in the garden and which are the bean plants surrounding the corn stalks."

She took his fingers and guided them to the base of the row of corn stalks. He could barely concentrate on the task he needed to learn. Her fingers elicited another most pleasing sensation, this one flowing up his arm.

"This is, of course, the thick stalk of corn. These thinner stems belong to the beanstalks that weave their way up and around the corn. And these ..." She drew his fingers over the fuzzy weeds. "These are the nasty plants that must be removed. If they aren't, they will interfere with the growth of our food crop." She released his hand, much to his regret. "Now you try. Tell me what you're feeling."

He knew she referred to the plants and weeds. But if he revealed what he was truly feeling in his heart, she might be less gentle with him. She might slap his face and walk away in a huff. Focus on your task, Zadok. Grabbing a plant with a thin stem, he moved his hand up the shoot until he felt the beginning of an attachment to the cornstalk. "This is the bean plant."

"Well done. Now, can you feel for a weed?"

He fingered a path along the dirt, searching for a leaf or stem that felt somewhat hairy. "Here. Here is the 'interloper,' as you call it."

"You are a born farmer. And your work will help me a great deal. Thank you."

Zadok heard the delight in her voice. "'Tis the least I can do."

"I'll return in an hour or so. You mustn't overdo it, since you're still recovering." The swish of her skirt and the increasing heat from the sun on his face revealed she had stood and moved away from him.

"Aye. Thank you."

"'Tis I who am grateful."

He listened to her footsteps as she walked away and inhaled deeply. But this time, his senses were no longer bathed in her feminine presence. That loss elicited an ache, both painful and intoxicating.

REGRETFUL STEPS CARRIED Aurinda back to her cabin. She would've preferred to spend the entire day next to Zadok, guiding his strong hands in the garden, leading him through the field with his fingers gripping her arm, even just feeling his manly presence next to her. She'd had few agreeable encounters with men before.

The close interactions with her father while serving him victuals and cleaning up after his linens and clothing were far from pleasant. His revulsion for using soap added to the displeasure.

Most of the young men at church—those who were not away at war—neither caught her eye nor drew her respect. But besides the lack of acceptable suitors, what man would care to align himself with so unattractive a woman as herself? She had long ago determined she'd remain unmarried, content to weave her cloth, work her father's farm, and perhaps one day, be mistress of that homestead.

In the meantime, she'd care for her only parent out of respect and obedience to God. The parson had counseled her that it was her duty, and she would please God by honoring her father.

There were days when that task seemed far too burdensome to bear. Days when his hurtful words sapped her spirit of all joy. Those were the moments when she would pour out her sorrow to her Father in Heaven, who loved her for who she was, unsightly appearance and all.

Today had been a day unlike any other. She'd been drawn to a man whose voice echoed kindness, whose unseeing eyes reflected brightness, and whose strength lay not just in his sinews but in his courage and good character. This was a man she could admire. This was a man she could love.

But even if his sight never returned, she'd not burden him with a consort as undesirable as herself. She respected him far too much to ruin his life.

7

4 July, 1779

Z adok's attempts to lather the soap Aurinda had brought to him were awkward at best. Cleaning his face and fingers one-handed became nearly impossible, and when the bottle holding the suds tipped over onto the hay, he nearly cursed. He stopped himself lest Aurinda and her father hear him.

He was nervous enough being invited in for the morning meal—the first time her father had consented to his presence in their cabin. The last thing he wished to do was offend the people who'd provided a place for him to recover.

Earlier, Aurinda had brought him a basin of warm water and the soap, along with an invitation to breakfast. He expressed his gratitude along with his surprise at the invitation. Aurinda convinced her father, since it was Sabbath, it would be the Christian thing to do.

He could hear her approach the barn for the second time this morning, and he nervously combed his wet fingers through his hair. His hair ties had long since come out, and his locks hung down his back in what felt like disarray. Zadok dreaded the thought of his appearance. Even if he had a looking glass and could see, it would do him no good with the use of just one good arm.

Sweat soaked into the clothing borrowed from her father. Aurinda had insisted on loaning him a shirt so she could launder the one he'd worn the day she'd discovered him near his horse. When she entered the barn, her voice dazzled with vitality.

"Might I help you? I should have stayed to pour you the soap. I'm so sorry. Here is your clean shirt, and I can help you change if you need assistance."

"No need." His brief laugh rang with far too high a pitch. The thought of her assisting him made him tug at his collar. "Dr. Northrup will be here shortly and can help me."

"Very well. I'll let him bring you to the cabin when he is finished examining you. Perhaps he will join us for victuals."

"Did I hear someone speak of victuals?" Dr. Northrup gave a friendly greeting.

"Good morning, Doctor. Please join us for our Sabbath breakfast. Your company is most welcome."

"Thank you, Miss Whitney."

Dry hay crunched beneath her shoes as she left.

"She is a sweet lass. 'Tis most unfortunate she never knew her mother. Nevertheless, she bears her sweet disposition." The doctor paused. "It's too bad ..."

"What's too bad?" Zadok's curiosity stirred.

"Never mind, lad. Let's check this arm. It has been a week now, has it not?"

"Aye. The longest week I've had in my life."

The doctor gave him a fatherly pat on his uninjured arm then maneuvered his right arm with skilled fingers. "You seem to be healing well. This arm should be good as new before long."

Zadok held his breath for a moment. "And my eyes? Will they be good as new?"

"Let's take a look."

The physician pushed up his eyelids. The man was so close to his face, Zadok smelled ale on his breath. After a moment, he heard the doctor sigh.

"Still no shadows?"

"Nay. Nary a change."

"Well, 'tis still early. It may yet improve. Sometimes swelling within the brain takes its time to diminish." He heard the doctor clasp his haversack. "At any rate, let us feast on Miss Whitney's victuals, shall we?"

"First, can you help me with my shirt and hair? Aurinda ... Miss Whitney ... she offered to help, yet I feel that would be ... difficult, since she is not married."

"And likely never will if her father has any say in the matter." Dr. Northrup muttered under his breath, leaving Zadok to wonder at his meaning.

THE SMELL OF SALT PORK, biscuits, and butter wooed Zadok to the cabin. If he'd not thought himself famished before, he quickly changed his mind, and his belly growled in agreement.

Dr. Northrup guided his steps to the front door. A creaking hinge welcomed them into the house.

"Well, well, here is our Sabbath guest. Welcome." An unfamiliar voice greeted Zadok with dubious sincerity.

Zadok shifted his stance as he rubbed his damp palm on his pant leg. "Thank you, sir." He startled when a hand touched his arm.

"I'll show you to your seat, Mr. Webster." Aurinda's presence warmed him.

"Thank you."

She drew him toward a chair, and he stumbled slightly as he maneuvered his foot around the table leg. Plopping into the seat, he attempted to hide a wince. He could not see if he was successful, but no one mentioned his grimace.

"Morning, Isaac."

Must be Dr. Northrup's Christian name.

"So, Mr. Webster. What brought you to our town of Fairfield? Business? Pleasure?" Suspicion laced Mr. Whitney's voice.

"Well, sir, 'twas a pleasure ride of sorts, but mostly business." He had to think quickly. "That morning I tested out some new shoes I'd just finished making for the gelding."

Mr. Whitney smacked his lips from something he'd finished drinking. "So, you rode all the way from New Haven to Fairfield to determine if the shoes were sound? Twenty-five miles? Was that not a bit extreme?"

He imagined the man glaring at him. "I ... I suppose 'twould seem so." The heat inside the cabin grew oppressive.

"Father, please. Our injured guest does not need an interrogation. He explained why he was here."

"He hasn't, daughter. A smith does not need such a distance to determine if a pair of horseshoes is properly fit!"

"Please, Miss Whitney. Your father is correct." Zadok inhaled deeply as he concocted a lie. "There is another reason I came all the way to Fairfield."

"Well. Explain yourself." Mr. Whitney's loud and unfriendly voice filled the room.

"I came to see a lass." His breathing quickened with the statement. But he knew he had to make up a plausible reason, or the man's suspicions could lead to trouble—not just for himself but for Aurinda. He wouldn't do anything to endanger her.

"I see." Mr. Whitney's voice carried a somewhat crude tone. "A man might travel some distance indeed to visit with a special lass. And what is her name?"

"Father, please ..."

"No, 'tis all right. Her name is Annabell. But she is not from these parts. She lives in Danbury, and we were to rendezvous in Norwalk."

"Ah. She must be quite a handsome lass to lure you on such a journey. Tis a shame you may never indulge in her countenance again."

"Father!"

Dr. Northrup cleared his throat. "What Abijah means is he is sorry you are blinded at the moment, and he hopes you will indeed be able to see your sweetheart again in the future."

"If you say so, Isaac." Abijah Whitney harrumphed.

"I do." The authority in the doctor's voice commanded a change of subject.

"Might I offer you some cider, Zadok?" A hint of sadness in Aurinda's voice drew his attention.

"Aye. Thank you."

A measure of liquid poured into a cup. Zadok felt Aurinda's fingers tremble slightly as she drew his hand toward the cup. He wished they were alone so he might inquire of the cause.

"Your victuals are delightful, Miss Whitney." Dr. Northrup's change of subject brought welcome relief to the tension in the room.

"'Tis an advantage that her skills in cooking help make up for her uncomely features. 'Tis certainly your fortune, sir, that your lack of sight protects you from her lack of, shall we say, delicacy."

An abrupt feminine gasp followed by the sound of a chair pushed away from the table churned Zadok's stomach. A door flung open, and Aurinda must have left the cabin. Her muffled sobs diminished.

"Abijah, was that cruelty necessary? And to your own daughter." Dr. Northrup chastened his friend.

"Best to face her shortcomings so she won't get hurt."

"And you think your words do not wound her? Our patient

here may suffer from blindness. But the true blindness here is in your mind. Good day, Abijah."

Zadok stood. "Let me come with you, Dr. Northrup."

The man pulled on his arm and half dragged him to the doorway. The open air outside provided fresh breathing after the foul words spoken within the walls of the cabin.

"Forgive my old friend, Mr. Webster. He's not been the same since the war. And since Aurinda's mother died. Yet still, his words can annihilate with their poison. 'Tis sinfulness the way he speaks to his daughter."

Sinfulness indeed. Zadok had witnessed cruelty before, but none so painful as he'd heard today. "Where is Aurinda?"

"I think I know. Do you wish me to take you there?"

"Aye, please."

Dr. Northrup led Zadok into what seemed to be thick woods.

"Put your good arm up to protect yourself from hanging branches."

Zadok followed his instructions. Twigs occasionally scratched at his face, and he stumbled a few times over rocks. But he did not care. He determined he would find Aurinda and comfort her.

"I once found Aurinda here after a similar assault of words hurt her feelings." Dr. Northrup stopped abruptly and whispered. "If you tread carefully, you'll feel a grassy meadow beneath your feet. It is next to a lake. Walk this way."

The doctor gently pushed him in the direction he needed to go. Zadok grabbed at trees and made his way toward the water. He knew he was close when he heard ducks. He swallowed past a painful lump in his throat. "Aurinda?"

She gasped. "Who's there?"

"Zadok. Please, let me talk with you."

"How did you get here? How did you know?" Her thick voice told him how much she'd been crying.

"The doctor brought me. I asked him to help me find you."

"Why?" The word was difficult to understand with the abundance of her sobs. "Why would you want to be with someone so indelicate and horrible to look at? I suppose you can stand me because you cannot see me."

He followed her voice until he reached her. "Aurinda." Near tears himself, he wrapped his uninjured arm around her and held her close.

She wailed until she seemed unable to cry any further. She clung to him for a moment then pushed herself away. "I have drenched your clean shirt with my tears."

"No matter." He stroked her arm until she stepped back.

"You need not feel sorry for me. I will dry my eyes and get ready for Sabbath meeting."

"May I go with you?'

"I thought you were not a praying man."

"I am today. Let me go with you."

"Very well."

She took his arm and led him back through the woods to the barn. He was assaulted by small branches every few feet, despite his attempts to shield his face with his left arm. Terrified he would further injure his eyes with an unexpected encounter from a tree, he lowered his head as he clung to her arm.

At such a time when Aurinda needed him to be strong, he appeared to be the weaker of the two, depending on her ability to navigate the way home. His vulnerability angered him anew.

"We're back at the barn. I'll go wash my face and be ready forthwith. My father will not come and worship with the 'insurgents.' He is an unforgiving man."

Her skirts rustled as she left.

Perhaps he himself needed to become a praying man. Otherwise, he might never be able to forgive her father for what he said.

8

"*But I say unto you, love your enemies, bless them that curse you, do good to them that hate you, and pray for them which despitefully use you and persecute you.*"

"These words in the fifth chapter of the Gospel of Matthew should guide us in our times of prayer, lest we become embittered by the persecutions that rage around us. Lest we harden our hearts against the enemy who seeks to kill and destroy us while we endeavor to birth this new nation under God, a nation of life, liberty, and the pursuit of happiness.

"And on this fourth of July, whilst we celebrate the anniversary of the Declaration of Independence, may we never forget the sacrifice so many have endured, and continue to endure, in the travail we now face. As a mother undergoes pain when she births her child, may we recognize the need to stand firm and resolute in the sacrifices necessary to deliver this new nation. May the God of peace prevail in our hearts, despite the war that rages in our land. Amen."

The parson lifted his head. Gripping the sides of the podium with both hands, his eyes roamed the pews. "I see many of the good townspeople of Fairfield are anxious to not only give praise to our Creator but also to celebrate the birth of our new country. And for those who remain loyal to the king, you are welcome to join in our celebration as well. We shall pray for you."

Strained laughter rippled through the audience of 100 or more. While the parson tried to offer a moment of Christian peace with his remark, others frowned at his efforts to be conciliatory. Cessation of conflict between the Tories and patriots seemed as likely as a snowstorm in July.

Aurinda took Zadok's arm and guided him to the end of the pew. When she unlatched the door of the row, her neighbors, the Turners, approached from a few rows back and greeted her.

"'Tis so good to see you, Aurinda." She wondered if Mrs. Turner noticed her swollen eyes.

"Thank you, Mrs. Turner." She avoided the woman's probing gaze. "This is Mr. Zadok Webster of New Haven. He had an accident on our land, and we've been taking care of him this past week."

"Good day, Mr. Webster." Mr. Turner gripped Zadok's hand. "We heard about the injury to your eyes. Sad business."

"Aye. I'm certain I've overstayed my recovery time with the Whitneys. 'Tis near time I returned to my home in New Haven."

An unexpected ache, not unlike hunger, but worse, gripped Aurinda. The emptiness his announcement elicited felt like she'd been given a choice morsel to enjoy, only to have it removed from her plate. She hadn't even known she was starving for the delicacy—until now.

"You need not go so soon, Mr. Webster." She stumbled over her words. "Your arm must still heal before you return to your occupation."

"And what is your occupation, Mr. Webster?" Mr. Turner stared at Zadok with a concerned expression.

"I'm the blacksmith in New Haven, sir." He frowned. "At least, I used to be."

"And what does Dr. Northrup say about your sight?" Mr. Turner's words brimmed with concern.

"He is hopeful Mr. Webster's eyes will heal." Aurinda interrupted. "I am praying they will." She smiled at the Turners, but the expression on their faces nearly made her lose hope.

Mrs. Turner put her arm around Aurinda's shoulder. "Come, let's see what the town has brought for the celebration. My husband can assist Mr. Webster."

As they strode away toward the tables of food, the older woman stopped and put her arm around Aurinda. "Is there anything I can do to help you? I know things can be ... difficult in your home."

"I'll be fine." She again tried to avoid the woman's gaze. "I'm safe. Just not from my father's tongue."

"Your father is a cruel man." Mrs. Turner's face reddened, and her lips thinned. "I know you feel a responsibility to be a faithful daughter, but his words to you are a pox in your life. You must know you are always welcome to move in with our family. I could tell your father I need your help with my little ones. Please consider the possibility."

Aurinda smiled as her eyes misted. "I am so very grateful to you, Mrs. Turner, and I shall remember your kind invitation."

The ladies stopped abruptly and turned when a rider approached the gathering and reined his horse in a swirl of dirt. The mare's sides were lathered in sweat, the rider's face reddened, his expression intense.

The parson pushed his way through the gawkers and grabbed the reins of the panting steed. "I say, what is your business here? We are preparing to celebrate our country's birth!"

"I regret this intrusion, sir. But I bear news of great import. The king's ships are heading toward New Haven. 'Tis a large fleet, manned by thousands. Our scouts have been watching the frigates, led by the flagship Camilla. But there are others, and we now know they plan to debark at New Haven. 'Tis imperative you take measures to protect your town, lest you be next in line for attack."

There were gasps and cries from the crowd at the news. Aurinda's dread had returned, only this time, the reality of the fear stood at her front door. She searched for Zadok, who still stood next to Mr. Turner. His face paled.

Aurinda ran to him. "Zadok, we must return to the cabin forthwith. We must warn father."

"I must return to my home." He grabbed her arm. "My mother and sister are there!"

"You cannot. You wouldn't be able to get there by yourself."

"Then come with me. We can ride the horse after dark. Please. I must rescue my family."

Go with him? Aurinda stared at him. Could she risk the wrath of her father by so blatant a move to protect patriots? Her rapid breathing, along with the heat, threatened to make her ill. But looking at Zadok's expression with such pain at the thought of losing his family to the king's soldiers firmed her resolve to help. "Very well. I shall go with you."

He hugged her close, taking her by complete surprise, then whispered in her ear, "Thank you."

Looking around to be certain no one had seen this sign of affection, Aurinda realized the townspeople had scattered to their own homes. They were too concerned about the safety of their town to be judging a public display of endearment.

Aurinda's words caught in her throat. After a moment, she managed to encourage Zadok to hurry toward the cabin. "Let us prepare for the journey. I'll pack food and water. We can leave at sunset, since father will be in a sound sleep by then."

"Will this turn your father's wrath against you even further?" Zadok paused on the road back to Aurinda's home and looked toward her. "I fear for your safety."

She almost cried at the tenderness in his voice. Without

thinking, she took his hands in hers. "I'd rather face my father's anger than allow your family to perish. I will not let fear stand in my way of doing what is right."

A smile emerged on his face. "You are a true patriot, Aurinda Whitney. And a courageous friend."

Warmth flooded her face and neck at his words. She shifted her feet. "I'm not so courageous. I tremble at the thought of this endeavor. Yet I keep imagining your mother and sister facing the king's army with no one to protect them. I cannot let that happen."

"Nor can I."

They finally reached Aurinda's home.

"We must not stir suspicion with father. I'll spend the day with him in the cabin. I'll pretend to retire at darkness, then slip out the open window. Wait in the barn for me."

"I shall."

She took him to the barn and then prepared to leave, but he reached for her wrist. When he found it, he held tight for a moment, then found her cheek and stroked it with a solitary finger.

"I must go." She shivered at his touch and inhaled deeply. "I'll see you at sunset when the crickets begin their song."

He did not speak when she turned and left. Her heart pounded out a thousand words she'd like to say to him. Yet, every sentiment she wanted to express seemed to be overrun by one thought: She could never be pleasing enough for him.

9

Aurinda shifted slightly in the saddle, the closeness of Zadok behind her eliciting moisture on her brow. It was not just the warmth of the summer evening. Perhaps if she spoke, she could forget the feel of his arm wrapped around her. If she spoke too loudly, though, she could give away their presence to anyone nearby.

"How far to New Haven, Zadok?"

"Twenty-five miles," he whispered.

So far! Lord, help us.

Aurinda had only occasionally controlled the reins on a horse. She prayed she'd remember the technique as she gripped the leather straps with fervor. "How will I know the way?"

"If you follow the old trail through the woods as I guided you, you'll stay the course, all the way to my home."

"Very well." She shivered.

"Are you afraid?"

She wanted to appear brave, but that would not be truthful. "I'm terrified."

"I'm here with you, and I have my pistol." He hugged her briefly.

Conjuring up a courageous voice, Aurinda sat straighter in the saddle. "Aye. We shall get there together. If a king's soldier appears, I'll direct your aim by saying right, left, or straight. Will that help?"

"Aye. Just be sure to duck if I'm forced to shoot."

"I shall, to be sure." She grinned. "I cannot see you, but I sense that you are laughing."

"Only a bit." His voice whispered near her ear. "We'll get there together."

Together. If only there could be a *together*, with no war and no fear. If only Zadok's sight returned. If only she were beautiful. If only. But there were too many obstacles to the dreams that beckoned her soul. Her heart could not afford to imagine her world could be anything different than what it was. She prayed God would help her be content with what she had, as distressing as her life could be. That thought made her grateful that God promised a better world after death.

At least she'd be reunited with her mother and Aunt Primrose. No more tears. No more sorrow.

Her eyelids grew heavier as each moment passed.

Zadok startled her when he whispered, "Go ahead and sleep. I'll hold the reins for now."

HER HEAD JERKED DOWNWARD, and her eyes opened wide. "How long have I been resting?"

"Awhile."

Her back ached while her parched throat longed for water. "Can we stop for a moment?"

"Aye." He pulled on the reins with his left hand, and the well-trained horse stopped. "I'll get down first, then help you." He slipped off the horse's back and reached up with one arm.

She could not easily see the stirrup in the dark and slipped. He must have felt her falling or heard her cry of fear, because his strong arm caught her and lowered her to the ground.

"Are you all right?" His rapid breathing revealed his anxiety.

"Aye. Thank you." She moved away from his arms. "I'm quite well." She pulled the wooden canteen down from the saddle, unplugged the cork, and guzzled a long drink.

"You are parched. I'll take a drink as well."

As she handed him the canteen, she realized she had an urgent need to relieve herself. She bit her lip, wondering how she could slip away in privacy without explaining the reason. As he wiped the liquid from his mouth, she curled her arms around her waist. "Zadok?"

"Aye?"

"I ... I must slip away a moment."

His eyebrows furrowed, and he pressed his lips together. "Aurinda, 'tis not safe. Why must you ... oh ..." He shuffled his feet. "If you must go, please do not go far. And look sharp for any sign of troops."

"I shall."

Terrifying sounds filled the short distance she walked to locate a private spot. Far away, a wild animal must have found its victim and the subsequent screech sent her blood racing. An owl hooted in a tree nearby and fluttered downward with huge, flapping wings. She squelched a scream with her hand.

When she finished, she smoothed out her gown and ran back toward Zadok. Before she could reach him, a king's soldier stepped out from behind a tree. Already nervous, her level of fear now soared. Her legs shook to the point of buckling her knees. She leaned against a narrow birch tree for support.

"And where might you be going in such a hurry, miss?" The silver buttons on the soldier's red coat glistened in the moonlight while he crept toward her.

Aurinda tried to speak but could not. As he edged closer, she reached to the ground for a rock.

"Planning on killing Goliath, are ya?" He laughed. "Looks like you've not got a slingshot to help you there, miss."

"Nay. But she has a pistol-carrying companion."

Zadok!

The soldier frowned and grabbed at his sword, unsheathing the weapon with a *shashing*.

Before he could wield it, Aurinda yelled, "Left!" She ducked, and the pistol exploded in a haze of smoke. Afraid to look up, but knowing she must, she saw the soldier lying on the ground, shot through the chest.

She ran toward Zadok and threw herself into his arms.

"Did I hit the mark?" He still held the pistol.

"Aye." Tears erupted, and she clung to him.

"Is he moving?"

"Nay."

"Let's get out of here." He wrapped his arm around her. "There may be others."

After leading him back to the horse, she could barely climb into the saddle with her trembling limbs. Once they were both situated with her in front, Zadok clung tighter to her than he had before.

When they were far enough away that she felt safe to whisper again, she turned toward him. "Thank you for saving me." Without thinking, she drew her face upward and kissed his cheek.

He tightened his grip around her waist and kissed her hair.

They rode on in silence.

As dawn approached and streaks of gold and orange brightened the eastern sky, Aurinda gasped. A fleet of ships, flying the flag of England, permeated the normally scenic Long Island Sound. Larger frigates filled the deeper waters, while smaller vessels entered the harbor, carrying hundreds, perhaps thousands, of troops.

A loud explosion from a field piece on land alerted the two riders the patriots were fighting back. They both jumped, and the horse nearly reared from the sound.

"What is happening, Aurinda?"

"So many enemy ships, I cannot even count them."

Zadok's grip around Aurinda's waist tightened. "We've got to find my family." He kicked at the tired horse, and the young gelding quickened his stride.

"We must let the horse rest. Let's tie him to a tree on the edge of the woods. We'll need him to get back to Fairfield."

"You're right. Guide him to a safe place."

She grabbed the reins and led the chestnut gelding back amidst the trees. Zadok jumped off the saddle and reached upward to help her down. She trembled, and he must have felt the fear emanating from her quivering arms.

"Perhaps you should stay here."

"You need my eyes, Zadok." She touched his face.

"I'll never forgive myself if anything happens to you."

"God will watch out for us." *God, I pray you do!*

Without another word, Aurinda led the way toward the harbor. Crouching low, she observed the patriots in combat with the Regulars who had landed on the beach. She gasped at the human carnage inflicted as men in red coats impaled patriots with their bayonets, while the Americans fought back, firing their muskets and thrusting knives to counter-attack.

Blood was everywhere, and Aurinda shielded her eyes to avoid the image as nausea threatened to overwhelm her. She prayed the feeling would ebb and that God would strengthen her. She took in a deep breath.

"We need to hide on the bluff. Let's crawl there." Aurinda struggled to hold her gown while scooting across the sandy soil.

Finally, they were close enough to reach the meadow along the shore and would be able to shield their presence by hiding behind trees at the edge of it.

Zadok sniffed the air. "I smell smoke. And not from gunpowder."

Aurinda searched the horizon. "They've set fire to a large home and barn."

The cries of farm animals being slaughtered rose above the musket fire.

"'Tis not enough to burn the homes. They must kill our animals as well?" Zadok's voice shook with rage.

"Come, let's find your family." Aurinda encouraged him to move on.

More homes burst into flames while enemy troops spread out and torched whatever buildings they came to. Women and children came running from the buildings, crying in anguish.

Heavenly Father, have mercy!

Residents of New Haven threw valuables into ox carts, and one woman screamed she could not find her baby.

Occasional bursts of gunfire exploded from behind bushes and trees as patriots targeted the invaders of their town. Aurinda turned back to scan the harbor and wished she hadn't. The enemy's ships stood anchored the whole length of the bay, with huge guns at the ready to destroy New Haven and all its residents. She could barely swallow past her fear.

To her right, a band of about 40 patriots scurried behind a hedge. When the king's soldiers followed a group of Continentals up a hill, the Americans hiding behind the bushes opened fire. Aurinda covered her ears to protect them from the deafening melee.

"Zadok, we must find your mother. Can you tell me what to look for?" She had to almost scream for him to hear her.

"Look for the smithy not far from the college. Look for the tall spires of the churches nearby."

Aurinda scanned around. In sharp contrast to the horrific scenes of bloodshed were resplendent forests, meadows, and fields of grain. Barns, sporadically set afire with torches, had been awaiting the abundant crops come harvest season. The ripening grain in the fields was instead sprinkled with the blood of soldiers.

Through the thick black and gray smoke of musket fire and burning buildings, she finally saw the spires of the two churches. Grabbing Zadok's arm, she pulled him toward the buildings. She could barely breathe but kept trudging toward her destination and nearly ran into a woman carrying a baby. "Please, ma'am, can you show me where the smithy is?"

"'Tis that way." The woman's shrill voice could only be matched by the baby's ear-piercing screams. "But no one's there. Mrs. Wooding is hiding in the grasses that way."

"Thank the good Lord! Zadok, let us find her and your sister."

Zadok gripped her arm while she ran toward the location where she'd been directed. Aurinda stumbled on a rock and fell.

"Are you all right?" Zadok crouched near her.

Musket balls flew over their heads. "Let's get out of here!"

They bent low and hastened toward the grass-covered bluff, then dropped to the ground, hidden from the enemy's sight. Crawling toward the edge of the woods—made more difficult for Zadok with his splinted arm—they slowly reached about a dozen women and children hunkered down in the tall grasses.

"Zadok!" A middle-aged woman, her face covered with soot, reached Zadok and held him closely. When she pulled away, her smile faded. "Zadok? Can you not see me, son?"

Tears rolled down his cheeks. "Nay, Mother, I cannot. I lost my sight in the fall from the courier's horse. It may return, but the doctor does not make promises about it."

"No matter." She touched his face as tears escaped her eyes. "You're alive!" She held him tightly, then released him. "Your sister is here … and the courier. They are at the edge of those woods."

"We are here to take you to Fairfield, Mother."

"We?"

"Aye, Aurinda and I. She is the one who rescued me and called the physician."

Mrs. Wooding looked at Aurinda for the first time and reached toward her. "Thank you. I am ever grateful to you for saving my son."

Aurinda smiled and looked downward. She could sense her cheeks burning. Perhaps the heat from the fires brought the warmth. Or perhaps it was the deep longing for a mother's love that elicited tears as Mrs. Wooding held her close.

But as the bullets whistled overhead, they all flattened against the ground, the tall grasses hiding their presence. They lay there for what seemed like hours to Aurinda, yet it could not have been more than a few moments. She wiped the moisture away from her cheeks before anyone would notice.

In between the sounds of the weapons, she heard a haunting melody that beckoned her. She pushed upward a few inches from the ground and listened intently to hear every word sung by one of the women several yards away.

Sleep sweetly, dear baby
Stay safe in my arms,
Your sweetness, I treasure
More than riches or charms
Whilst nightfall surrounds thee
In God's tender care
Remember thy Savior
'Twill always be there.

She searched the recesses of her memory, foggy and clouded by time. "I know that song."

"You know it?" Zadok reached for her arm.

"Aye. 'Tis stirring both sadness and joy in my heart. What is that song?"

"'Tis a lullaby." Mrs. Wooding kept her voice low. "Primrose is comforting that child. Poor dear's mother was killed in the assault."

Primrose?

Aurinda swallowed with difficulty. Her voice rasped. "Who is this Primrose?"

"A friend of mine. She's never married, nor had a child of her own, save a niece who was taken from her years ago." Mrs. Wooding stared at her with an odd expression. "Are you all right, dear?"

She'd thought the pace of her rushing blood could not quicken any further, yet it now galloped faster. Dizziness nearly enveloped her. *Primrose? No, it could not be.*

The singing stopped, and the woman turned toward her. Still clutching the young child, Primrose's face contorted. "Aurinda?"

"It cannot be."

"Ye are the spitting image of yer mother!"

Aurinda crawled toward the woman, embracing the only mother she'd ever known. She began to sob and couldn't stop. Clutching her aunt, Aurinda's mind whisked back in time to that painful day when Father peeled her fingers away from Mr. Wooding. It was the final contact with those she loved. And her life would never be the same.

Clutching Aunt Primrose for several moments, Aurinda feared ever letting her go. When she finally did, she could barely speak. "Aunt Primrose, how is this possible? Father said you had died."

Her aunt's countenance darkened as she wiped the tears flooding her cheeks. "'Tis not surprising. Yer father ne'er wanted me to see ye again. I wondered why I ne'er heard from Isaac again."

"But why? And Isaac who?" Aurinda tried to wrap her mind around the shock of this reunion.

"Ne'er mind ye, lass. Yer father wanted no reminders of yer mother. And I believe he thought ye would want to stay with me."

"Of course, I wanted to. But to say you were dead?" The cruelty of the lie bore into Aurinda like a thousand nails. She could never forgive her father for stealing her away from the only love she'd ever known. Then lying to her, so her hopes of finding that mother-figure again were thwarted? That was utterly unforgivable.

"I did not know where he'd taken ye. I sent letters to him in Fairfield, but they came back unopened. If I'd known where ye were, I would have sought ye out, at least to make sure ye were well." Primrose caressed the curls escaping Aurinda's mob cap. "Such lovely hair. Just like yer mother's."

Aurinda clutched her Aunt Primrose, who rocked her as though she were a young child again. After a few moments, the little orphan, who was now subdued in her arms, squirmed.

The temporary joy of seeing her aunt again was quickly replaced by the fear enveloping the town like a shadow of death. "We must get away from these soldiers. Please, Aunt, come with me. Bring the child, unless she still has family here."

"Nay, she does not. Her mother was a widow. And Hannah, only a wee one of five, left all alone."

"We shall embrace her into our family. But please, let us hurry." She led Aunt Primrose and the child toward Zadok, who had reunited with his family and the courier closer to the woods —closer to safety.

"Aurinda, we must hurry." Zadok's disheveled hair surrounded his face covered with soot from the fires.

"Aye. We have two more coming with us. I'll explain everything when we are out of danger."

"*If* we can *get* out of danger. Hurry."

10

The sounds of the assault on New Haven faded as Zadok and the small group of survivors distanced themselves from the attack. But every scream and cannon shot still echoed in his head. Would he never stop thinking the enemy was near at hand?

"Zadok?"

Exhausted and hyper-vigilant, he nearly jumped when Aurinda said his name.

She placed gentle pressure on his arm. "Zadok, we must rest. The women may fall off the horse from fatigue. The child is asleep already."

He shook his head as if he could bring clearer thinking to his mind with the maneuver. "But we haven't gone very far. The enemy is still too close."

"We've walked several miles, and we are away from the main road. The soldiers were too busy plundering the town to follow us. Otherwise, they would've caught up to us by now. Please, think of your mother."

"Of course. We must rest." He exhaled. "Safe enough, I suppose, for now. Go ahead and rein in the gelding." He looked upward. "Mother, 'tis time to stop and rest." As he took the reins from Aurinda, he heard one of the women slide off the horse.

"Hand me the child," Aurinda said.

Sounds of the women's skirts rustling and shoes hitting the dirt let him know everyone had dismounted.

"Find a safe spot near a tree in case the enemy should show their faces." He removed the pistol from his belt. "I need to reload this."

"Aye, can I help you?"

"Do you know how?"

Aurinda sighed with impatience. "Of course, I do, Zadok Webster, else I wouldn't have offered to assist you."

"Sorry."

"'Tis I who am sorry for my sharp tongue." She grabbed his arm. "Please, forgive me."

"Of course." What was to forgive? She'd borne so much distress yet rarely complained. One outburst of impatience hardly seemed worthy of an apology.

Zadok knew it was time to give her the explanation of his name.

"About my last name, Aurinda. The reason I said my name was Webster was because of the secret mission I was on. I knew not where your allegiance lay, and I did not dare reveal my true identity."

"So your true name is ..."

"Wooding. Zadok Wooding. I regret that I lied to you."

"I understand. 'Twas a lie born of concern. There are so many fears right now and one never knows who can be trusted."

She yawned.

"Aurinda, you must rest as well."

"Then who will stand guard?"

"I shall." The courier stood with hands on hips as though he were the appointed guard of the group. "I am well enough now to help. The rest of you can sleep."

He and Zadok's sister, Mercy, drew forward from the rear of the group.

Relief flooded Zadok's weary body. "Thank you. Aurinda, please sit next to me in case I require your help. And remember to give me the direction if someone approaches."

Aurinda paused. "Very well." She led him to a thick tree trunk and they slid down to the ground, side-by-side

He re-loaded his pistol, asking Aurinda for help when he needed it. She'd become quiet. "Do not fear that I shall try anything untoward. Remember, my mother is nearby." He waited for her to laugh at him, but instead, he felt her lean into his shoulder and then heard a soft snore. Aurinda's was joined by the snores of the two older women.

The warmth of the late morning air lulled him as well. The comforting feel of her head on his shoulder, along with that feminine aura he relished, soon beckoned him to close his eyes.

UNSURE OF HOW long he'd slept, when Zadok's eyes opened, he sensed Aurinda's arm wrapped around him. He reached with his hand and discovered her head resting on his chest. Gently touching the curls that escaped her mobcap, he wrapped a ringlet around his finger, savoring the feel. He inhaled her scent that tempted him to draw the woman closer.

Yet, reason prevailed, and he berated himself for the desires that filled his thoughts. He pushed himself straighter against the tree trunk, and she stirred.

Suddenly she released her embrace. He heard her sit up and then move away from him. "I am so sorry, sir."

"Sir?"

"I mean Zadok. Please, I had no intent of giving the wrong impression. I was so exhausted ..."

"Please, Aurinda, there is naught to apologize for. We were

both bone weary." He had to admit he wouldn't have discouraged her familiarity had he been wide-awake. But this was neither the time nor place to entertain thoughts of affection, nor to be in a position as a prospective suitor. There were no assurances his sight would return. And who would desire a blind husband who could neither provide for a wife, nor see to her needs?

But he'd had a glimmer of hope the night he'd shot the Redcoat in the woods. Aurinda's directions certainly guided his dead aim, and the high-pitched sound of the sword being unsheathed helped draw him to his target. But he recalled the obscure shadowy form he thought he saw at the time. Was it possible his sight would return? It would take more than dim shadows to prove he could see again, however, so he put the memory aside and stood.

Someone approached him. "I am Caleb Beckwith, the courier you replaced when I became ill. I must thank you for ensuring the delivery of the note to the army. I only regret the effort cost you your sight."

Zadok stood straighter and cradled his broken arm. "I only regret I could not carry out the mission, Caleb."

"I understand. Our circumstances had a most fortuitous meeting for us both, however. Your sister has been most healing in her ministrations. And Miss Whitney is ..."

Aurinda interrupted their conversation. "Gentlemen, we must hurry back on the trail. We have stalled far too long as it is. Mr. Beckwith, have you noticed any water nearby? We must fill our canteens before we carry on."

"I shall locate some forthwith, Miss Whitney."

"Thank you."

After Caleb was out of hearing range, Zadok spoke in a low tone. "Was that a terse tone I heard in your voice?"

"Aye."

When she did not explain, he drew closer to her. "Are you

seeing something I cannot?"

"Aye." A pause. "He … he spends much time fawning over your sister, yet I cannot help but feel he is not sincere."

Zadok clenched his fists and heat crawled up his already warm neck. "Why is that?" *Dear God, if only I could see!*

"'Tis difficult to answer this."

"Please, Aurinda. Try. I must know. Mercy is my sister." His blood pounded in his ears at the thought of her being misused by a scoundrel.

"Because of the way he looks at me."

His rage exploded like one of the cannons in New Haven, and he turned away from her lest he curse in her face and in earshot of all the women.

"Zadok, please." She grabbed his uninjured arm. "Do not say a word. If you confront him now, he will leave with his horse. We need it to get back safely to Fairfield. Your mother and my aunt do not have the stamina to walk the distance."

He wished Caleb Beckwith stood in front of him so he could use his work skills to hammer the man. Even without the tools, his good arm could crush a few bones in the man's face. He covered his eyes and prayed for restraint.

"Zadok, please. He's returning with the water. Please do not say anything to anger him."

"You must promise me, Aurinda." Zadok spun toward her. "If he tries anything with you, you will tell me. Promise me." His voice trembled with the anger seething through his veins.

"I promise."

"I'm sorry if I upset you."

"Nay. We must end this conversation now, or he shall hear us," she whispered. Her skirts rustled away from him as she walked toward Caleb. "I see you have found water. Good. Let us be on our way, then."

His mother's voice drew near. "Zadok, what is wrong?"

"We must be on our way, Mother. But I beg you to keep an eye on Mercy. Please."

"I shall." Her skirts' swishing faded into the distance.

He heard the women mount the gelding, and then Aurinda helped the child into Aunt Primrose's arms.

"Zadok, all are mounted. We are ready to leave."

Wiping the sweat from his forehead onto his shirtsleeve, he begged God to return his sight, if for no other reason than to protect the women in his life.

He realized it was in complete desperation he'd resorted to asking God for a miracle. But he wondered if God would listen to a sinner who only utilized prayer when in anguish.

11

Aurinda wished she felt refreshed from their rest, but her fear of the king's soldiers began to compete with other concerns. Could there be a confrontation between Zadok and Caleb Beckwith? Battles on every side bespoke tension and danger.

Could she be certain Mr. Beckwith eyed her in that manner? She wished she'd imagined it—that lingering gaze where it should not be. No, she hadn't mistaken his intent. She'd seen it before, and she knew it well. All she could ascertain was that men in Fairfield and New Haven must have been desperate to hope for an alliance with such an unappealing woman as herself.

Although, where he'd gazed far too long was perhaps the only thing Mr. Beckwith was interested in. She crossed her arms tightly across her chest as she let go of Zadok's arm.

"Your arm must be tired of holding onto mine. Just don't let me lead the horse astray so we can stay on the trail," Zadok said.

"Aye. If I see we are going astray, I shall set the course right again."

"Are you well? Is anything—or anyone—troubling you?"

"Nay. I'm careful and stay far away from him." So far. But the man's eyes could molest a woman with their vile intent.

Zadok kept his voice low. "Remember, I am armed."

"Aye. And 'tis a relief."

By the sun's slanting rays, it was late afternoon, yet the heat grew worse. Aurinda glanced up at Aunt Primrose and observed her flushed face. Mrs. Wooding looked as if she might faint from the scorching temperature. Her forehead dripped with sweat.

"We must stop and rest. And we all need more water," Aurinda said. She took the reins from Zadok and led the horse under the shade of a large maple. Usually a breeze brought coolness through the woods, but the air lay heavy and still today. Aurinda found breathing was even difficult.

She helped the child down, her small body frail and her clothing covered in sweat. Mrs. Wooding attempted to dismount on her own but nearly lost her footing. Caleb Beckwith hurried over and assisted her.

"Aunt Primrose, let me help you." Aurinda stood next to the horse, arms stretched upward.

"I can do it." Mr. Beckwith appeared all gallant and noble as he reached up for her aunt. Primrose's knees nearly buckled when he set her on the ground. "There now, allow me to help you find a cool spot under a tree." His gaze met Aurinda's as he assisted Aunt Primrose.

Aurinda turned away.

"Thank you, young man." Aunt Primrose expressed her gratitude, seemingly unaware his chivalry masked devilry. His loyalty to his country notwithstanding, Aurinda didn't allow his political allegiance to the patriot cause to overshadow his tainted character. One had naught to do with the other.

With the older ladies settled in the cooler shade along with the orphan child, Mercy Wooding slowly made her way to the group.

"So pleased we're taking a rest." Her fair skin had turned beet red, and she breathed rapidly.

"Do sit down, Mercy." Aurinda brought her the canteen. "Have some water. We've not met before, but I feel I know you a little since I've made acquaintance with your brother."

Mercy had the same slate eyes and chestnut hair as Zadok. She appeared a few years younger than Aurinda, but womanhood had fully bloomed in her figure.

She smiled at Aurinda but kept looking around. "I wonder where Caleb has gone."

"I believe he is looking for a stream, so we can replenish our canteens."

"He's always keeping busy since he's recovered from his illness."

I imagine he is. Aurinda bit her tongue before she spoke those thoughts. "I imagine Mr. Beckwith will be leaving soon now that he is better." Aurinda hoped so.

Mercy bent her head slightly toward Aurinda and whispered, "Nay." Her gray eyes glistened with excitement. "He says he would like to stay in New Haven, where he can see me every day!"

"Did he?" Aurinda attempted to sound pleased but worry prickled up her spine. "And does your mother know?"

"I think she suspects, but we are waiting to tell her. After all, we've only known one another such a short time. Yet I know I love him already. And he loves me." She giggled, leaned back on her outstretched arms, and closed her eyes with a dreamy look on her face.

"Truly, 'tis a very short time. Are you certain about his character, Mercy? Perhaps before deciding if you love him, he should prove himself worthy of your affection." Aurinda bit her lower lip.

Mercy opened her eyes wide in disbelief. "His character is impeccable!" She turned away in a huff. "He says he attends

Sabbath meeting when'er he is in his hometown of Hartford. And besides, he would never kiss me the way he does should he not intend to make me his consort."

Aurinda squinted her eyes shut and prayed she would keep the tone of her voice even. Opening them, she leaned in toward Mercy. "Mercy, please believe me when I say men sometimes desire things from women that have nothing to do with honorable intentions. I do not wish you to get hurt."

"Mayhap, you are jealous of me?" Mercy backed away from Aurinda. "Wishing you were fair enough to attract such a handsome man as Caleb and that he'd set his eyes upon you instead?" Zadok's sister stood up in a snit, her face reddened, and stomped off into the woods in the direction Caleb had gone.

Oh, Mercy, if you only understood.

Despite her hurtful words, Aurinda truly did not wish any harm to befall Mercy. Yet still, hearing the young girl's undisguised abhorrence of Aurinda's lack of beauty stung nearly as painfully as similar insults from her father. Perhaps they seared into her heart more deeply because they were from Zadok's sister.

12

By the time Aurinda and the refugees from New Haven reached the edge of the Whitney farm, darkness enveloped the landscape. The horse limped from the long journey, and Aurinda fared little better. She had removed her shoes long before arriving home and knew her feet must be bleeding by now. She'd experienced the stab of more than one sharp pebble on the way.

"I'll lead you all to the barn where you can rest. We have water in the rain barrel, and I'll fetch food from the cabin."

The women and the orphan child, Hannah, collapsed on the mounds of straw. Caleb brought the exhausted gelding into a stall and provided oats and water for his mount.

Aurinda brought cups of water to everyone. She first handed some to Zadok, but he held up his hand in protest. "Give it to the women first."

It seemed everyone's thirst was unquenchable. Lest anyone become ill from drinking too much liquid, Aurinda asked them to stop after two cups each. When they were finished, Aurinda carried a ladleful to Zadok, but he tipped it toward her instead and said, "Please, drink."

The liquid coated her parched throat when she guzzled the offering. "Now 'tis your turn."

He readily gripped the cup offered to him. "Thank you."

"When shall my thirst be quenched?" Caleb seemed to inflect dual meaning in his question.

"Here." Aurinda handed him the cup. "I am certain you have the strength to procure your own."

He gripped the cup, making sure he stroked her fingers as she offered it to him.

Aurinda drew her hands away and wiped them on her apron. *If only Zadok could see what he's doing.* "I'll go get victuals now." She spun toward the open door of the barn and saw a light burning in their cabin. She prayed the encounter would not turn unpleasant—or worse. "Father is still awake."

"Aurinda, let me go with you." Zadok stepped carefully toward her.

"Very well." She walked back to meet him and guided him toward the cabin.

Lord, please protect us from Father's anger.

When she opened the creaking door, her father shouted, "Who goes there?"

She cleared her throat. "'Tis I, Father. Zadok and I."

"And just where have you two been these last two nights? Your wanton behavior has besmirched your character, daughter. I ought to use my whip on you."

Zadok's face blazed red. "No one will be whipped, sir. And your daughter's behavior has been far from wanton. She has helped me rescue my family from the barbarous behavior of His Majesty's troops, who have plundered my hometown and inhumanely killed innocent people!"

"Innocent? Insurgents deserve such condemnation and reprisal for their treason." Aurinda's father spat while he spouted his hatred for the patriots.

"It did not seem the Regulars paid any regard for who they

killed or burned out of their homes. All were victims." Zadok's voice seethed.

"Not so, you insolent Whig. The Regulars would spare all who are loyal to their mother country, as you yourself should be." His eyes burned with fury while he threw off his bed covers and started to stand.

Fearing her father would look for his pistol, Aurinda placed her feet firmly in front of him, standing between him and Zadok. "We found someone else in New Haven, Father. Perhaps you remember her." Aurinda glared at him. "Aunt Primrose. She is in our barn, even as we speak."

Abijah Whitney's face turned ashen. He fell back onto his bed, the steam of rage vented in mere seconds. He stared at his hands that clung together.

An inner flood of heat rose in her breast—a smoldering rage that had simmered for many years. "How could you tell me she had died? I thought I'd never again see the only person who'd ever loved me. You could not have hurt me more if you'd cut my heart out! And to find the story to be a lie? How could you?" She sobbed out the words, squeezing the back of a chair she stood near.

Zadok reached toward her, but she pushed his hand away. Uncontrolled furor filled her soul, and there could be no room for solace, not even from Zadok.

"You have been a constant source of pain to me my whole life. Your actions and words have hurt me to the core. But this ... this is the worst of all injuries to my soul."

Father's frame appeared to shrivel in front of her eyes. "I ... I was so lonely for your mother. Then when I saw how attached you'd become to your aunt, I could not bear one more loss. I wanted you for my own."

"You mean you wanted me as your servant, to cook and clean. Little more than a slave. You never wanted me to be your daughter. You never loved me." She gritted her teeth, afraid she might say more.

He lay back down on his bed and turned his back to them.

Aurinda stomped over to the pantry and grabbed food supplies for the refugees. She thrust several items into Zadok's arms so she could carry more. When their arms were full, she held onto him, leading him out the door and back to the barn. Her breathing came in fits and starts. Staring straight ahead, she could not look at her companion.

After delivering the victuals, Aurinda snuck out of the barn to find a quiet spot to be alone. She'd never confronted her father in such a manner before. But she'd never before discovered such a hurtful deception. The cruelty of it had impacted her life in such a dreadful manner.

How might her life have been different with Aunt Primrose? To feel her love through childhood and her encouragement as she became a woman? Those moments could never be replayed. They were lost forever in the painful years of growing up with a cold and distant father bent on using his words more like weapons.

Aurinda sat in the dark for what seemed like hours. She did not want to pray. Indeed, she could not pray. Her God had forsaken her as her earthly father had done. This could not be undone. She grew too exhausted to sit up anymore and, with aching limbs, made her way back to the barn.

All were asleep save Zadok. "Aurinda?"

"Aye." Her voice sounded as cold as her heart.

"Can you sit by me?"

"Why? I've nothing to say."

"You do not have to say a thing. I ... I just need you beside me."

Walking stiffly toward Zadok, she slumped onto the straw next to him. She sat silently. Soon, she could feel his hand covering hers. She did not move.

Then he put his uninjured arm around her and slowly drew her head onto his shoulder. He said not a word, just stroked her hair.

But his gentle affection melted the anger in her heart. Tears flowed from her eyes and soon poured from them. She clung to him and wept until there were no more tears.

13

A gentle hand nudged her awake. "Aurinda." The voice was the one she'd longed to hear through the years. Eventually the longing had turned into grieving, since she knew her aunt would never come back. Yet now, as if resurrected from the dead, Aunt Primrose's voice soothed her once again with its comforting tenor.

Aurinda opened her eyes and looked into her face. The years seemed to melt away, and she was a girl of five once again. She lifted herself from the hay, then glanced at Zadok, sound asleep next to her.

"'Tis a miracle ye've been reunited with yer old friend, Zadok." Aunt Primrose's mischievous grin brought back many a memory.

"Old friend?" Aurinda's jaw dropped open.

"Aye. Ye both played together as wee ones. Zadok loved to wrap dandelions—dirty roots and all—through yer golden curls. Ye'd get so angry with him. Until he handed ye a bouquet of flowers to make up for the mess." Aunt Primrose grinned. "So many memories."

"I'd no idea. Zadok never mentioned it." Aurinda stood, dusting off the hay from her gown.

"He likely did'na remember. He did'na know 'twas ye who rescued him. Even if he could see, he might not have known." Primrose put her hands on Aurinda's arms. "Come, walk with me."

Glancing back at the still-sleeping Zadok, Aurinda followed her aunt. They sauntered toward the fields ripe with growing corn.

"Zadok wanted to help on the farm, despite his blindness. I showed him how to feel for weeds and pull them out. 'Twas an unexpected gift from someone who is blind." She looked back toward her aunt. "I still cannot believe you're here." She stopped and hugged her for a long while.

"I heard ye arguing with your father last night." Aunt Primrose leaned away from her. "Ye sounded sore vexed, ye did."

"I've ne'er spoken like that to him before." Aurinda released her and stared at the ground. "Something deep inside … I cannot describe it … seemed to pour from the depths of my soul. An anger I did not know possible." She looked at her aunt from under her eyelashes. The venting of that rage had been honest, yet ugly. She meant every word of it, but it still tormented her spirit.

"I do understand that vexation. 'Twas how I felt when yer father took ye away from me. I took out my hurt on others around me. Even the man I decided to marry. When my anger seemed greater than my love, he left me." Tears welled in her eyes.

"Aunt Primrose!" She hugged her again. "I ache for you, for this sad loss. I am so sorry."

"'Tis in the past now. But I know what bitterness can do to one's soul. When ye can'na forgive someone—anyone—not only do ye displease God, ye spread that bitter spirit to yer world around ye. 'Tis like a poison that slowly spreads and kills where 'er it goes. I know. I learned the hard way and paid a painful price. Do ye understand?"

She looked away. "Aye. Yet, I still cannot imagine forgiving Father. He ruined my life."

Primrose tilted her head and drew her brows together. "Did he, now? He changed yer life, aye. But 'tis not ruined. Ye have much to look forward to."

"Look forward to? There's a war at our doorstep." Aurinda spat out the words like they tasted of bitterroot.

"Aye. Even in war, God is very much alive and work'n in your life. Tell me somethin'. Were it not for the war, would ye have met up with Zadok again? Would ye have found me again? As terrible as this conflict is, I always try to see the small miracles in the midst of the pain."

"Then you must be looking harder than I, Aunt Primrose. All I can see is the suffering." She started to walk away, but her aunt stopped her.

"Look deep in your heart, Aurinda. Stay true to the faith yer mother longed for ye to have. Forgive yer father. I know ye may not feel the desire. But forgivin' is not about the feelin' of it. 'Tis about obeyin' God."

Aurinda pulled her arm from her aunt's grip and stumbled back toward the barn. She stopped a moment and turned to face her again.

"'Twould take a miracle to bring me to forgive him. And I see no miracles today."

14

The closer she came to the barn, the louder the men's voices became. Furor had broken out between Zadok and Caleb.

"I told you she wanted me to kiss her."

"I may be blind, but I heard you trying to persuade her to do something she did not wish to do. I heard her say 'nay.' Do you not understand when a lady is refusing you?"

"We've done far more than that before." Caleb huffed.

Mrs. Wooding ran into the barn. "Mercy! What is this about? What, pray tell, have you and the 'patient' been doing whilst he healed?"

Aurinda rounded the corner of the barn door in time to see Mercy straightening her hay-covered clothes and her face a bright shade of red. She spoke through taut lips. "Nothing, Mother." She looked upward, defiance evident in her upturned chin. "He loves me, Mother. We did nothing wrong. He wishes to marry me."

"I never said we would marry, Mercy." Caleb combed his fingers through his undone locks. "At least, not soon." He shifted his legs.

Inches from Caleb, Zadok's face contorted. He lunged toward his adversary while guarding his own broken arm as best he could and thrust his left fist repeatedly into the man's face.

The courier swore at him and leveled several punches back at the enraged brother. "Caleb, stop!" Mercy tried to intervene.

But Aurinda pulled her away. She searched for the pistol belonging to Zadok, made certain it was loaded, and fired it into the air. The horse bucked in the stall at the sharp sound echoing inside the walls of the barn.

Both men, now bloodied, stopped.

She held the smoking pistol in both hands. "Caleb Beckwith, your presence is no longer needed on this farm. Take your mount and leave."

Mercy burst into tears, and Caleb stopped on his way out, whispering something in her ear. She cried even harder. Mrs. Wooding moved to stand in front of her and wrapped her arms around her daughter.

Wiping the blood off his mouth, Caleb went to the gelding, saddled him, and rode off without a word.

The orphan girl, Hannah, wept with a heartbreaking cry and Aunt Primrose, who had just returned, swept her up in her ample embrace.

Aurinda hurried toward Zadok and crouched next to him. "Look at you, Zadok Wooding. We just get you a little healed, and you go and get yourself injured again." She stroked the blood off his face. "Let me dress your wounds." As she ran to get water and bandages, she nearly bumped into her father.

"I heard a gunshot."

Aurinda ignored him and walked past him to get to the house.

Forgive the man? She could barely abide his presence.

~

ZADOK SAT on the straw and rubbed his sore jaw. His whole body hurt from the altercation. He only hoped his foe hurt as badly. Perhaps even more. If only he could've seen the damage he'd inflicted on Caleb Beckwith and hoped it was sufficient to keep the man far away from Zadok's family. If he showed up again, he had every intention of killing him. Zadok was not a bloodthirsty man, but he wouldn't allow his sister to be trifled with.

As he rubbed his jaw, he overheard Primrose engage Mr. Whitney in what sounded like an intense conversation. He would have enjoyed the satisfaction of hearing the aunt's verbal assault, but their voices faded. *They must have walked away.*

The aching in his head and jaw intensified.

Aurinda arrived with a basin and bandages.

"How bad do I look?" He allowed her to wipe the blood away from his face.

"Bad enough. What were you thinking, starting a fight when …" She stopped.

"When I'm blind? They say justice is blind. I carried it out."

"I believe justice does not bleed—but you do." Aurinda harrumphed.

Her hands, which occasionally made contact with his skin, were soft when she wiped the linen across his cheeks. He winced when she touched a bruise on his jaw.

"Sorry."

She finished far too soon.

"I need to fetch Dr. Northrup to examine your arm. I fear it may have been injured in the fracas."

"Must you go?" He surprised himself with the question.

She stood to leave, then paused and crouched back down, leaning in toward him. She kept her voice low. "Did you know we were friends when we were little?"

Did she jest? "Nay, 'tis not so."

"Aye. You can ask your mother. Aunt Primrose told me as

much when we walked this morning. Is that not strange?" Her voice had the lilt of a young girl.

"I think 'tis quite a coincidence. I am beyond surprised."

"As was I. Aunt Primrose said you used to put daisies in my curls with the dirty roots attached." She laughed. "Sounds like a boy."

The golden curls. Of course. He remembered the girl with the golden hair who lived there one day, then disappeared the next. He'd never understood the why of it. He just remembered he missed her. Even if she did get angry when he put dirt in her hair. An intense sadness nearly overwhelmed him. His face must have shown his melancholy.

"Are you well? Perhaps you were injured badly in the fight." Her hand touched his arm, sending ripples of pleasure through him.

"I'm certain I shall be fine. But perhaps 'twould be best to have Dr. Northrup visit."

"Aye. I'll fetch him forthwith." She squeezed his arm. He heard her stand and hurry away.

Footsteps approached him. "Son, are you all right? I heard Aurinda say she would fetch the physician."

"Aye, she'll get him." He paused. "Mother?"

"Aye?"

"Did you remember Aurinda?"

"I didn't remember her name from the letter she wrote after you were injured. But when Primrose saw her and reunited with her niece, the memories flooded back."

"What do you remember?"

"Many small things. Her hair. Her laugh. The way you two played together." His mother paused. "You were both so young when her father took her away. But I shall never forget you weeping when you realized she was gone. You told me you wanted to marry her someday, and you'd ne'er be able to. Your words nearly broke my heart, as I know her absence broke yours."

He swallowed back tears. "Thank you."

"Can I get you anything, Zadok?"

"Nay, I shall rest a bit."

Zadok lay on his side so no one could see him. He struggled to recall the young Aurinda, but it seemed a blur in his mind. But he did recall the closeness he felt toward her—the closeness he still felt. The tragedy of it all was, after so many years of being apart, they were finally reunited, only to be thwarted by circumstance once again. For no one would marry a blind man who could neither provide for a family nor care for a wife.

The malicious irony of their reunion only reinforced his belief that the God so many worshipped must not be kind or loving.

His life bore living proof.

15

Aurinda met Dr. Northrup at the barn door when he arrived late in the afternoon. His dirty clothing and slowed gait were an unusual sight for the usually energetic man who normally dressed impeccably.

"Dr. Northrup, are you well?"

He wiped his moist brow when he accepted the cup of water she offered.

"Aye, well enough. I've just come from New Haven after helping the wounded there. An abysmal sight." He swigged the contents of the pewter cup, then requested more.

"We came from there ourselves last night. 'Twas horrifying." Aurinda took the cup from the doctor and refilled it.

His brows drew together. "Why were you there?"

"Zadok and I rescued his family and mine from the attack. We found an orphan child there as well."

The doctor looked up and noticed the other women and the child in the barn.

"Evening, Dr. Northrup."

The doctor focused on her aunt and gave a slow, disbelieving shake of his head. "Primrose? Primrose Allan? Abijah said you'd succumbed to fever."

"'Tis I to be sure, Isaac." She focused an unblinking gaze at him. "And now ye know yer friend lied through his teeth. I am very much alive and well and grateful to see my niece once again."

Aurinda's eyes widened. "You know my aunt?"

"Aye." He took a step back. "I accompanied your father to New Haven when he went to take you home."

"Ye mean when he stole my niece from my arms." Primrose lowered her chin and glared at him.

He spun his tricorne hat a few times in his hands. "Now, Primrose, you know I had no say in the matter. Aurinda rightfully belonged to her father."

"'Twas right by the law. But there was no heart in the takin'. He stole her and ne'er allowed her to see me again. I waited, ye know. Yet you ne'er kept your promises to let me know how the lass fared. I waited for ye. Yet ye were as silent as the grave."

Aurinda's eyes widened at her aunt's tears. What did they mean?

"I'd no idea …" Dr. Northrup dropped down on the hay and rubbed his forehead. His face paled to a ghostly shade.

"Perhaps you should rest a bit." Aurinda interrupted. "I'll serve you some ale and tell father you're here."

"Nay." He spoke quickly. "Nay, do not tell him I'm here. Tell him the ale is for the patient."

"Very well." Aurinda walked back to the cabin. She sighed with relief her father wasn't there. She'd no idea where he'd gone. After grabbing the pewter mug from its peg on the wall, she filled it with the golden liquid, then carried it back to the physician.

He improved after sitting for a time. "Primrose and Aurinda, from the bottom of my heart, I am sorry. I knew naught of Abijah's deception."

"'Tis not your fault, Dr. Northrup." Aurinda placed her hand on his shoulder. "We know where the guilt lies."

He patted her hand with a fatherly gesture, then squeezed it briefly. "So, where is Mr. Webster? Why cannot that man stay out of harm's way?"

"Over here, Doctor." He'd taken up sleeping quarters in the stall where the gelding had been.

"I placed fresh straw in here for Zadok so he could rest with less disturbance." Aurinda sat next to her childhood friend while the doctor probed his facial injuries.

"It seems to just be bruised, nothing broken that I can feel." The doctor good-naturedly punched him on his good shoulder. "Is it askin' too much for you to stay out of trouble, lad?"

Zadok did not grin. "I defended my sister."

The doctor met Aurinda's eyes. "I see. And is this scoundrel gone from here?"

"Aye, Dr. Northrup. He has gone." Aurinda touched Zadok's splint lightly. "I am concerned about Zadok's arm. He took a few blows before I intervened."

"*You* intervened?" The doctor raised his eyebrows.

For the first time, Zadok grinned. "She is quite skilled with a pistol, Doctor."

"I didn't shoot him," Aurinda said, "lest you think I killed a man. I merely shot upward to end the brawl."

"Well done." He focused his examination on Zadok's arm this time, gently squeezing the limb and watching for a response. Zadok winced a few times, but the doctor seemed satisfied. "I believe there is some bruising but nothing further broken. And the limb seems to be healing soundly."

She exhaled. "That is wonderful news."

"I do suggest, Mr. Webster, that you protect that head of yours from further injury. If there is any chance for your sight to return, you must guard it most carefully."

"Aye, doctor. I understand. Although 'twould not be likely now, would it?"

Dr. Northrup held his chin and stared into the distance. "I seem to remember some years ago, a lad lost his sight in much the same manner. He was blind for many weeks before his brain healed enough. Then one day, he opened his eyes and saw shadowy figures moving about. Within a few days, his sight had returned. Do not give up, Mr. Wooding. There's still hope."

Zadok sat without speaking.

"Thank you, doctor," Aurinda said. "You have given us hope. And, about Zadok's name, he is actually Zadok Wooding. He gave another name because of a secret mission he was on. He did not know who he could trust at the time."

"Ah, that all makes sense now."After a moment, Dr. Northrup stood. "Miss Whitney, I think I'll take my leave and get some rest. There are troops guarding the beach here at Fairfield, just to be certain the Regulars do not attack our town after they leave New Haven."

"Here?" She blinked rapidly while pounding blood coursed through her veins. "They could land here? Please tell me, Doctor, what have you heard?" Her hands turned clammy, and she forced herself to take deep breaths.

"'Tis just a precaution." He placed his hand on her arm. "The troops will likely head toward New York. Please do not fret." He turned to leave, and Aunt Primrose met him at the door. They engaged in earnest conversation as if they were old friends. For the first time, Aurinda understood that they apparently were.

She turned back and caught Mrs. Wooding's eye.

"We must pray for protection, Aurinda." The woman breathed rapidly as she stroked the hair of the sleeping orphan.

Without a word, Aurinda spun around to leave the barn. Her terror had escalated while her faith had shattered. Others would have to do the praying. It was all she could do to breathe.

16

Aurinda gasped as she awoke from a fitful slumber. "What was that?"

Had she dreamt the loud explosion? Nay, there it was again. Then silence. But the blast echoed in her ears, propelling the rhythm in her heart to bounce out of control. Where had the detonation come from? And what did it mean? She crawled through the straw in the barn until she came to the horse stall where Zadok lay.

He seemed wide awake when he reached out for her. "Aurinda?"

The tightness in her throat choked off any answer. Instead of speaking, she took shelter in his unsplinted arm and buried her face against his chest. She counted the beats of his speeding heart and felt his uneven breathing as its rapid pace vied with her own. Fighting back tears, she sobbed, "Zadok!"

"I'm here."

She could not miss the trembling in his hands as he held her close.

As the moments passed with no further sound of cannon fire, the crickets resumed their chirping. Although Aurinda struggled to stay alert, the utter weariness of the last few days weighed upon her eyes until the heaviness of keeping them open became too great.

~

AURINDA THOUGHT she imagined earnest voices nearby. She sat up next to Zadok and touched her hair that had fallen from her mobcap. She searched for her cap and found it in the hay. Pushing her long locks over her shoulders, she inclined her ear. There were the voices again. She hurried outdoors, where she found Aunt Primrose speaking to Dr. Northrup. They paused when they saw her.

"What is it? Why are you here, Dr. Northrup?"

"He's come to warn us, Aurinda." Aunt Primrose stood straighter. "The same fleet that attacked New Haven is now anchored in our harbor, near Kinzie's Point." Primrose covered her mouth with both hands held tightly against her reddening cheeks. Tears escaped, despite her efforts to prevent them.

Aurinda threw herself into Aunt Primrose's embrace, and they clung to each other.

"I would have come sooner." Dr. Northrup placed a calming hand on their shoulders. "The militia saw the frigates passing by and thought they were on their way to New York. But when the fog cleared, their location to debark became clear. They are landing troops in Fairfield even as we speak. We must get everyone ready, and you all must go into hiding."

"What about Father?" Aurinda's mind swirled with the news. "Shouldn't he come with us?"

"Come." Dr. Northrup led her toward the cabin.

Blinded by terror, she stumbled as she ran.

When she opened the door, her father stood, dressed and readying his pistol and musket. "Well, Isaac, which side will you fight on?" Abijah Whitney checked his supply of lead balls.

"I'm not fighting, Abijah. Remember, I'm the physician. I don't inflict musket balls into flesh, I remove them."

"Father, you must come with us." Aurinda interrupted. "The troops are armed and will destroy our town like they did in New Haven."

"They will not harm those of us loyal to the crown. I've naught to fear, daughter, unlike your rebel friends. I spoke with my comrade last night. We've been assured all of us Loyalists will be spared. If you've a particle of sense in you, you'll stay here where 'tis safe from the onslaught."

She couldn't believe her ears. "Father, 'tis not so. I saw what happened in New Haven."

"Daughter, I know I've been a poor excuse for a father." He laid his weapons down and walked slowly toward Aurinda. "But I do want you to be safe. Please, stay with me." He awkwardly placed his hands on her shoulders.

Could he not have been so gentle for all these years?

Her lips quivered. "Father ..."

"Abijah, this is foolishness. I heard from the residents of New Haven themselves how the Regulars dragged women and children from their homes and torched their belongings. There was no thought for their allegiance. 'Twas savagery, I tell you!"

"I'll not leave my home." Abijah removed his hands from Aurinda's shoulders and walked away from them both.

"But Father ..."

"Aurinda, there's no time. We must get you and the others away from here." Dr. Northrup drew her forcefully toward the door.

She pulled back on his grip. "Father, please. You could be killed. I may never see you again." She inhaled a jagged breath and fought back a sob. Why did this hurt so much? All the man had ever done was cause her pain. Yet, in that moment when he begged her to stay with him, a bond had stretched a thin strand from his heart to her own. It confused and troubled her. And dug a deep trench of loss at the thought of losing him she could not explain.

Dr. Northrup gripped her arm more firmly and nearly dragged her out the door.

Once they were outside, Aurinda ran. Even now she could hear gunfire in the distance.

"Zadok!"

"The others have run for the woods." He stood in the doorway of the barn. "I waited for you."

She grabbed his good arm and clung to him with trembling fingers. The three raced toward the trees, led by the doctor.

"I told them where to hide." The doctor gasped for air when he spoke.

They continued to climb upward into the thick forest. Zadok's face, already bruised from the fight, was now covered with scrapes from tree branches.

Aurinda suddenly stopped. "I forgot the pistol."

"I sent it with Primrose." Dr. Northrup's reddened face dripped with sweat.

"Are we nearly there? My head is about to burst." Zadok let go of Aurinda's arm and clenched his hands against his head while he squeezed his eyes shut.

"We can stop for a moment," said the doctor.

"I'm so sorry you are in pain." Aurinda reached up to stroke Zadok's head and nearly wept.

"Your cool fingers are soothing." Zadok clung to her hand.

"There is a cold stream of water near the grove where you'll be hiding. Bring him linens soaked in the water."

"Aye, Doctor, I shall."

Cannon fire from the center of town caused Aurinda to jump. She nearly screamed but covered her mouth lest anyone hear her. "Let us move on."

Dr. Northrup paused. "I'll leave you two here. The people in town will need me sooner rather than later. Keep on this path until you see the thick grove of pines. The others will be inside it."

"Please, Dr. Northrup." Aurinda sensed she might be saying goodbye to him for the last time. "Be careful."

He forced a laugh. "I'm getting too old and wise to let a musket ball find me. Take care, Aurinda and Zadok. Godspeed."

Her lip quivered as she mumbled her farewell. After he left, she turned toward Zadok. "He's been good to me all my life. More like a father than my own." Another explosion of fire. Was it getting closer? "Let us hurry."

17

Would the fear never cease? Just when Aurinda had recovered from the New Haven attack, she now faced the even more frightening prospect of her hometown invaded by the king's troops. She'd known the Regulars could be bloodthirsty, but having seen the merciless plunder that took place in New Haven, she knew firsthand the terror they brought with their military presence.

She tried to forget the images of Americans sliced with bayonets and shot down with muskets. The memory of women who screamed and ran away, not just for their lives but for their virtue, sent shivers of terror throughout her body.

Lord help us!

Although Fairfield had a small number of militia, what strength could that be against thousands of England's well-trained soldiers armed with multiple weapons? She tried to control her tremors, but to no avail.

Zadok must have felt her trembling as they almost reached the grove of pines, their refuge in the impending destruction. He paused their walk and placed his left hand on her. "Aurinda,

I want you to know I shall do everything in my power to protect you and the others."

"I know." Her voice sounded more like a hiccough.

"I want you to know something else. The other night, when I shot the king's soldier in the woods, something strange happened. At first I did not know if 'twas real or not. But it has happened again. I ... I am seeing a few shadows."

"Shadows? Zadok!" For just a moment, her own dark mood experienced a glimmer of hope.

"I still do not know if my sight is truly coming back or if this might be as clear as it gets. But I am telling you this so you know I can see a few clouded images at times, which may help me to protect you." He reached up and stroked her hair. "I do not know how I could stand the pain were anything to happen to you.

"Even if my sight does not return, if I can at least use my pistol and hit the mark, I'll be forever grateful." He touched her lips with his finger, drew her chin upward, and leaned down to kiss her.

Her heart raced as she briefly accepted his show of affection, but then she turned away. If his sight returned, he would know how unseemly her appearance was. She mustered every ounce of strength and pulled away from his arms. "We must find the others and hide."

She tried not to notice the look of hurt that clouded his face when she turned away. It only reflected the deep anguish that ending that kiss had caused her. She grieved the loss more than he would ever know.

THE BATTLE BEGINNING on the beach in Fairfield rivaled the conflict raging in Zadok's mind. While the militia faced wounds in their body, Zadok's pain stirred in his heart with unfulfilled longing for Aurinda. Had he misread her affections? Had he thought she would refuse him, he would never have kissed her. Even in those first glorious seconds of feeling her lips on his, it seemed his passion had been returned.

Until she pulled away, casting doubt on her devotion to him. Would he be able to conceal his affection for her when they were forced to share a hideout while emotions ran high? If he thought they were going to die, could he keep himself from expressing his feelings to her? He had no solution for his dilemma—or for his pain.

"Here, Zadok. Here is the grove Dr. Northrup found. Put your arm up to keep the pine branches out of your face."

He did what she suggested yet still felt further scrapes tearing at his flesh.

"Zadok!" His mother's voice drew him into the shelter. "Thank God you are here."

"I was about to say the same. Is Mercy here? And Primrose and Hannah?"

"We're all here. And I have the pistol and bullets should we need them," Primrose said. "Aurinda? Are ye well? Ye're as pale as a ghost."

She paused. "I am well, aunt."

"Why don' ye come hither so I can visit a spell with ya?"

The rustling of Aurinda's skirts moved toward Primrose's voice. Their hushed mutterings were barely audible with the increasing echo of gunfire coming from down the hill.

His mother put her arm through Zadok's unbroken one. "Come, let us sit and pray." She drew him toward Mercy and Hannah, and they all sat on a bed of soft evergreen needles.

When his mother lifted her petitions to heaven, he imagined he was a boy again, and his parents were praying God would guide him as he grew and provide him with a faith that would see him through life's trials. He'd weathered many a storm so far, yet this day challenged that prayer in so many ways.

Not only was his life—all of their lives—in danger, but he was in peril of losing the love of the woman who'd captured his heart so many years before. He was not certain which loss would be more agonizing.

∼

AURINDA BARELY KEPT her tears at bay. Primrose's soothing embrace tore away at all the shields that imprisoned the closely guarded fortress of her heart.

Her aunt squeezed her shoulder as they sat side by side. "Tell me, love, what ails ye?"

She glanced at Primrose, no words needing to be shared.

"Dr. Northrup told me all about yer father and his wretched words, making ye feel like an old horse in the barn. How black is that man's heart? Could he not have loved ye and made ye feel like the treasured gold that ye are?"

Aurinda stared at the copse of trees surrounding their group like a redoubt against the enemy. Tears rolled down her cheeks past her silent lips. Occasional bursts of cannon fire caused her to jump, reminding her that enemies inhabited their town. Not that she could forget. But today, another enemy aimed at her spirit—the words her father had been inflicting upon her for sixteen years.

Words of insult and abuse. Words meant to hurt and tear down her ability to see any value in herself. Indeed, insidious phrases that made true love from a man of good character seem insincere and false. Love out of reach though mere inches away, a chasm never to be overcome. She closed her eyes and clung to Primrose while the screams from Fairfield grew louder.

∼

ZADOK SAT OUTSIDE on the hill, staring at glimmering, unformed images in the distance. He sensed night had fallen, but the odd patches of light in the distance confused him. He could only assume it was bad news for Fairfield.

Mosquitos buzzed around his face, an annoyance with one arm splinted while the other held a weapon. At times, he set the pistol down and swatted at the blood-sucking insects.

He clutched the pistol with moist hands and occasionally wiped the sweat from his palms onto his breeches. Although he still could not see clearly, his gaze riveted on the light that seemed to dance among shadows.

The women inside the hideout had fallen asleep—at least for now. A rustling of the branches behind him prompted him to face the sound and hold up the pistol.

"Zadok, 'tis I." Aurinda's voice shook.

"I apologize." His cheeks burned.

"'Tis understandable. I should have told you 'twas I."

His arm muscle twitched, and nausea crept into his belly. *I could have shot her.* He set the weapon down and reached toward her. "Come sit by me. You can hold the gun and tell me if you see anyone." Immediately, her aura immersed him. He breathed in her scent as deeply as he could. When her leg accidentally touched his as she sat down, he shivered.

"I ... I wanted to see how you were." She paused. "Oh my ..."

"What?"

A convulsive sob burst from Aurinda. "The town is set ablaze. The troops are destroying buildings. I know not which ones. Dear Lord, please stop them!"

He drew her close and held her. An unusual flash of light illuminated his sight for a brief second, followed by a sharp crackle of thunder. "The lightning. 'Tis difficult to know which is brighter—the oncoming storm or the fires burning the town."

"You can see the fires?" He felt her turn toward him.

"I can see the light of them. Nothing is clear."

"Can you see me?" Her voice was an anxious whisper.

"Nay. I only dream of seeing you, Aurinda. I can only imagine your hair, your eyes, your sweet lips." Before he could think clearly, Zadok kissed her.

This time she did not pull away but returned his affection. She seemed as anxious as he to linger in the satisfaction of the embrace.

Crying from within the grove of trees shortened the tender moment, much to his regret.

"'Tis Hannah," Aurinda spoke close to his ear. "Poor child is fraught with fear."

"Aye, 'tis no wonder." He brushed his lips against her cheek and longed to kiss her again but drew away. "Perhaps you should see if there is anything you can do to help her."

"Aye." She placed the weapon back into Zadok's hand and stood. Her footsteps returned to the pine enclosure but, in a few moments, her skirts rustled toward him again. "I have Hannah here. I'll hold her, and perhaps she'll sleep. The others are all slumbering."

She plopped onto the ground next to him, and he could hear the soft whimpering of the child.

"Ho there, Hannah. Aurinda will care for you." He reached toward the orphan and stroked her arm.

Hannah pulled her arm away and cried in fright.

"I fear she might believe you are one of the soldiers." Aurinda's voice carried sympathy in the message. "'Twill take time for her heart to heal."

As long as it will take for yours to recover? Or will you never heal from your father's wounds? He wanted to say these words to her, but he dared not.

Mesmerized by the dancing beams in the distance, he stared at the glimmering light. The unexpected flashes of lightning added sudden bursts of illumination, both frightening and beautiful. But it was the sharp burst of thunder that drew Aurinda to lay her head on his shoulder, clutching the whimpering Hannah. It could thunder all night if it meant Aurinda would remain close to him.

For the first time in his life, he thanked God for a storm.

18

A s dawn approached, Aurinda awoke and stared in the
distance. Smoke still drifted into the sky, but it appeared
the conflagration might be over. "Zadok, I think the troops may
have stopped setting fires. I need to see if Dr. Northrup is well
and if he needs help."

"Aurinda, nay. The Regulars are likely still there. I beg you,
please, do not go there yet."

"I feel I must. I can shoot a pistol, and I can see clearly to
defend myself."

"Nay, you cannot imagine how dangerous this could be.
Please ..."

"I know, Zadok. I saw New Haven, but they have ceased
setting fires in Fairfield. I need to check on my friends to ensure
their safety." She rose from the ground, still holding Hannah.

"Wait." His earnest expression pleaded with her. "If you
won't be dissuaded, then let me go with you."

"You?" Although he still could not see well, she thought
about his presence and how she might be safer. "Very well. I'll
bring Hannah into the grove with the others, and we can leave
together."

Upon entering the haven in the trees, Aurinda told them their plans.

"Zadok, nay!" Mrs. Wooding covered her mouth with her hands. Her eyes widened. "If the soldiers are there, you could both be killed!"

"Mrs. Wooding, I only see smoke coming from the buildings that were burned evening last. I feel I must help my friends."

"And what do you think, son?" She turned toward Zadok. "Is it safe? I fear for you both!"

His Adam's apple rolled as he swallowed. "I will carry the pistol, Mother, and be on the alert. I cannot allow Aurinda to go alone."

"And I shall go with them both." Primrose stood and straightened her shoulders. "Another set of eyes to look for danger and a pair of hands to help the wounded canna' hurt. Mrs. Wooding, can ye watch wee Hannah here?"

"Very well, then." Mrs. Wooding's shoulders slumped in defeat. "Mercy and I shall watch Hannah."

"I'm hungry." Hannah's small voice sounded pitiful.

"Of course, ye are, lassie. This kind lady will find ye some victuals." Primrose squeezed the girl's shoulders.

"Yes, of course, Hannah." Mrs. Wooding looked toward Aurinda. "May we go to your cabin—provided it is safe there— and gather some food?"

"Aye, of course. 'Tis likely to be safe by now."

The threesome turned to leave. "I'll pray the Lord watches over you."

"Thank you." Aurinda hadn't known the concern or prayers of a mother since she'd come to live in Fairfield. It was both comforting and grieving, as the loss of it dug deep into her heart.

"Let's hasten." Aurinda led Zadok through the trees out toward the edge of the bluff on which they'd watched the fires and lightning last night. She searched the town in the distance from this high point and saw nothing further of concern. All seemed calmer.

Their footsteps slipped at times on loose stones and dirt as they traversed the steep hill. Undaunted, the three slowly made their way toward the center of town, keeping their voices low and conversations to a minimum.

"Wait." Zadok pulled back on Aurinda's grip. "I hear marching."

Primrose paused and listened. "Aye, 'tis so."

"Let me get a bit closer to get a better view." The trees were so thick, Aurinda had trouble finding a place where she could be both hidden from the town and able to get a clear image of the activity. Sure enough, British troops marched in formation, back toward the ships in the harbor. Excited by this discovery, Aurinda scurried back toward Zadok and Primrose. "The Regulars are leaving!"

"Then we'd best give them a bit of time to depart from their wretched pillaging." Zadok's nostrils flared as he tightened his lips.

"Aye." Aurinda walked toward him and, without thinking, took his hand. She knew she should discourage his affections, yet her heart seemed to make decisions that conflicted with her better judgment.

Aunt Primrose gave a mischievous grin and spoke in a low voice. "Does me heart good to see ye together again."

Aurinda's cheeks burned, and she quickly dropped her hand to her side. "How long do you think we should wait? I fear for Dr. Northrup. And the Turners. And all my friends." She bit her lower lip.

Primrose tiptoed toward the spot where Aurinda had snuck a peek and viewed the scene. "Let us at least wait 'til those black-hearted soldiers have gotten closer to the beach."

"Wise words, Primrose." Zadok gripped the side of a tree he leaned against, breaking off pieces of the loose bark.

Sauntering back toward the view, Aurinda watched a while before speaking. "I believe 'tis safe now. Shall we go?"

"Sweet Jesus, protect us." Aunt Primrose seemed adept at sudden, unexpected outbursts of supplication to God.

Although grateful for Primrose's fearlessness, Aurinda could not be so bold in her heavenly entreaties.

Without speaking, the three of them used trees to hide behind as they slowly made their way toward the center of town. Zadok clung to Aurinda's arm. At times, his grip made it appear he wanted to force her along faster than she was willing to go.

The smoldering smell of smoke drifted everywhere, burning the inside of her nostrils. Aurinda covered her mouth and nose to keep from coughing. There were still many buildings left standing, and she was relieved the meetinghouse still stood.

When she neared one home whose windows were broken, she paused. Someone cried within. "Step carefully, Zadok. Glass is everywhere." Stepping over the shards, they entered the opened doorway. A mother sat on the floor, an infant at her breast, the child barely clothed. The woman stared as if unseeing.

Aurinda released Zadok's grip on her arm and hurried toward the young mother. "Mrs. Moore, are you well? Are you injured?"

At first the pale woman did not answer, then slowly turned toward Aurinda as if hearing her for the first time. "My wee babe. They stripped him of his clothes. They … they held a bayonet to my breast and threatened to kill us both." At this, the mother's eyes welled, and she gave a bizarre sob—more a spasm than a cry.

Aurinda saw bloodstains on the mother's bodice and carefully removed the sleeping baby from her arms. "We shall watch your little one for you. Let me dress your wound, Mrs. Moore."

She handed the infant to Aunt Primrose and fought back tears. Stepping over broken furniture and shattered plates, she located a basin and filled it with water from a bucket nearby. She tore off a piece of her petticoat as she returned to Mrs. Moore's side then gently cleaned the blood from the woman's chest. Aurinda sniffed hard.

"This should heal without much of a scar, Mrs. Moore." She knew she lied but felt the need to somehow comfort the woman whose distraught expression reflected the horror she'd endured.

Footsteps entered the house. Aurinda jumped up in alarm. Mrs. Moore sat without a sound as if the lifeblood had been drained from her.

Dr. Northrup stood in the doorway, his gaze bouncing from her to Primrose to Zadok. "What in heaven's name are you doing here?" Sweat and grime covered his face while he hurried to check on Mrs. Moore. "'Twill be all right, Maggie. Your babe is being well cared for." His soothing voice returned to suppressed rage. "I told you to stay in the grove."

"I thought the troops were leaving, are they not?"

He stood and glared at her. "The Regulars are, aye. But the worst are yet to come."

"What do you mean, the worst?" Zadok rubbed the back of his neck.

"I mean the Jagers—the Hessians. Better known as the sons of plunder. You'd best get these women away from here. Pirates and looters are burning the buildings still standing. What's left of them anyway."

Aurinda put her hand to her throat.

"Aye. Aurinda, help Mrs. Moore. And Primrose, bring the baby." Zadok's voice sounded strained.

"Please, Mrs. Moore. Come with me." Aurinda helped the terrified woman to her feet.

Dr. Northrup led Zadok as they hid behind houses in an effort to make their way back to the woods.

Dozens of Hessian soldiers plundered houses even while colonials, unbeknownst to Aurinda, took torches and set homes afire. She gasped when she saw the meetinghouse go up in flames. "Nay!"

"Come on." Dr. Northrup hurried the group along.

"Who are these colonists? They are not from Fairfield."

"Loyalists from elsewhere. Traitors to their neighbors!"

A small group of Hessians plundered a nearby dwelling. One of them saw Dr. Northrup and directed his small rifle toward the physician. Aurinda grabbed the pistol from Zadok and pointed at the German soldier. *Dear God, help my aim.* She fired. When the smoke from the pistol cleared, Aurinda finally opened her eyes to see the Hessian on the ground and Dr. Northrup's pale face.

The doctor wiped his brow. "I shall thank you properly later. Come on."

Aurinda paused in horror at the awareness of what she'd done. Sweat emerged on her face while the words "Thou shalt not kill" played over in her mind. *I have killed a man.* The terrifying realization paralyzed her, despite the voices that entreated her to keep moving.

Dr. Northrup grabbed her arm and led her, along with Mrs. Moore.

The group hurried behind a building but soon had to move their hiding spot when they realized that house burned, as well.

"Dear God, help us."

Was that Zadok praying? Aurinda didn't have time to contemplate the plea to heaven but instead focused on helping Mrs. Moore and the others to safety.

Smoke gagged them as they fled for their lives. Primrose covered the infant's face to protect his lungs, and Aurinda handed a piece of her petticoat to Mrs. Moore, who covered her mouth. The acrid smoke brought tears to her eyes, while nausea accompanied the taste. Or was it the thought of killing the Hessian that made her want to retch?

By the time they reached the edge of the woods, she limped and, one by one, the members of the group collapsed onto the ground behind the trees. She tried to inhale deeply but started coughing until she vomited. As she wiped the spittle from her mouth, a hand came to rest on her shoulder.

"Are you all right, Aurinda?" It was Zadok.

"Aye. Nay." She shook her head as tears erupted, forced from her by the inferno she'd witnessed in Fairfield. She sobbed until they dried up. When she stopped, she realized Zadok had wrapped his unbroken arm around her, trying to shelter her from the horrors around them. Although she would never feel safe again, his comfort abated the terror, if only for a few moments.

19

The walk back toward the Whitney cabin sapped what little strength remained in Aurinda. Few words were spoken by the exhausted group as Dr. Northrup walked with Zadok, Aurinda supporting Mrs. Moore, and Aunt Primrose carrying the infant trudged back uphill toward her home.

Her eyes still burned from the intense smoke. She craved cool water to wash them. Indeed, she longed for an entire bucket of water to cleanse away every bit of dirt from her clothing and her body, as if washing away the filth could remove the painful memories of the firestorm in Fairfield.

Images of the Hessians shooting at anyone in their path and delighting in the terror on their victims' faces gripped her mind. One woman had been forced to endure the hands of a lustful miscreant. Aurinda squeezed her eyes shut for a moment while she tried to remove the scenes from her memory. She wondered if they'd ever cease plaguing her thoughts.

As the group approached her cabin, she grew uneasy. Something was not right. Her tired eyes tried to fathom the scene around her. Broken glass lay everywhere. "Father?"

The door flung open, and Mrs. Wooding came out, her face

pale and anxious. "Dr. Northrup, thank the Lord you are here. Come quickly." Her gaze took in the small group of refugees. "Perhaps the rest of you should take shelter in the barn with Mercy and Hannah."

Pushing past Zadok's mother, Aurinda gasped when she entered her home. It had been pillaged by soldiers loyal to the same king as her father, yet that common fidelity had mattered little when the plunderers destroyed much of her home. Broken pottery, upended table and chairs, feather beds emptied of their goose down—there was little left in usable condition. She shivered.

"Where's Father?"

She hadn't noticed Dr. Northrup bending over him in his bed. Her head dizzied. The meager life she once had now lay in shambles. She stumbled toward her father's form, partially hidden under a blanket, and covered her mouth. The quilt was drenched in blood. *What had the soldiers done?*

The doctor's ashen face turned toward her. "Aurinda, go get me a bucket of water so I can cleanse his wounds."

Her limbs refused to move. She could not prompt them to work, even as her mind told her she must.

"Aurinda!"

"Aye." She shook herself. "I shall get it forthwith."

She ran out of the cabin toward the rain barrel and grabbed a bucket to fill. Leaning on the edge of the barrel, she tried to erase the memory of her blood-soaked father lying on his mattress. *Dear God, give me strength.* She fought back the nausea that rose in her throat, then felt comforting arms around her shoulders.

"There now, sweet one. God will see ye through this task. What can I do to help?" Aunt Primrose stroked a loose curl away from her face.

She slowly stood away from the barrel, inhaling deep breaths. After a moment, she met her aunt's eyes. "Can ... can you help Zadok and the women in the barn? They all must need water. And victuals. Dr. Northrup and I will tend father."

Tears welled in Aunt Primrose's eyes. "Ye're mother would be so proud of the strong woman ye've become."

"I'm not feeling strong." Aurinda's hands trembled.

Primrose hugged her. "Yer courage is not in the feelin' of it but in the doin' of it, despite yer fear." She released her niece. "Now don't ye fret about Zadok and the others. I'll take fine care of them."

Aurinda smiled her thanks. After filling up the bucket with rainwater, she lugged it back to the cabin. Each lumbering step, made awkward with the weight of the sloshing water, drew her closer to the nightmare within the cabin. She paused at the doorway and inhaled deeply. *Father in heaven, strengthen me, I pray.*

Her father moaned. As she poured water into a ceramic basin that had survived the destruction, she listened as the doctor spoke with him.

"Abijah, you'll need some stitches in these wounds. 'Twill not be pleasant, but I'll do it as quick as I can."

"Do what you must, Isaac." He looked up at her when she brought the water. "Aurinda. You're safe." Tears welled in his eyes, and he reached for her arm.

Unused to affection from him, she balked at his touch. It burned like scorching fire on her skin. She rubbed at the spot where his hand had made contact with her arm. "Aye, Father, I'm quite safe."

"You'd be quite proud of your brave daughter, Abijah. She saved my life." Dr. Northrup worked as he spoke, wiping the blood from each wound before preparing his needle to close up the lacerations.

Father did not speak but kept his eyes focused on her. When the needle pierced his skin, he inhaled sharply and clenched the mattress underneath him.

Aurinda swallowed with difficulty. "I'll see if we have more rum in the storage."

"'Tis none left." Her father gasped. "The Regulars took it all." He winced and moaned from the doctor's ministrations.

Did she have sympathy for him? He'd never shown an ounce of it to her, yet here she stood, wishing she could ease his pain. "I'll find you something to bite down on, Father."

The pile of wood near the hearth had been dismantled by the plunderers, but Aurinda found a suitable piece to bite down upon. She wrapped a strip of her petticoat around it to protect his mouth from splinters. "Here. If you bite on this, 'twill help the pain be bearable."

He clenched his teeth around the large twig, and, at times, he struggled not to scream.

She couldn't watch and turned away. "I'll change the water in the basin." Outside, she threw the bloody liquid onto the ground, refreshed the supply from the bucket of rainwater, and returned to the cabin. She stood at a distance.

"No need to stay, Aurinda." Dr. Northrup glanced her way. "I'm managing on my own. Get some fresh air to clear the smoke from your lungs."

"Aye, thank you. I'll be outside if you need me." She practically ran outdoors, grateful to get away from the horror in her home. What was left of her home. Treading carefully around the glass shards, Aurinda walked toward the barn. She prayed the pillagers had left it intact. For the first time ever, she felt grateful there were no animals within that might have been killed.

As she drew closer to the outbuilding, her pace quickened. The group inside looked up. Each face appeared paler than usual and filled with both exhaustion and fear. "Dr. Northrup is tending father. He said I could wait 'til he's finished dressing the wounds."

"And well ye should." Aunt Primrose stood. "Sit yerself

down, Aurinda, and get the rest ye deserve." Her aunt guided her by the shoulders and pushed downward on them until Aurinda sat next to Zadok. "I'll see if I can assist the good doctor." She left the barn with firm footsteps.

A grin emerged on Zadok's face. "I may not have my sight, but my ears tell me Primrose has motives to see Dr. Northrup other than helping with a patient." He chuckled.

"Zadok Wooding…" She started to berate him then paused. A grin emerged on her own face. "My Aunt Primrose. Who would have imagined? I thought they seemed quite—familiar— with one another."

She looked around at the group of women and children. Mrs. Moore lay asleep in the hay with her nursing infant by her side. Mercy lay next to Hannah, who sucked her thumb while she dozed. Mrs. Wooding yawned.

"Has everyone had some victuals and water, Mrs. Wooding?"

"Aye. All save you. You'll need to keep up your strength for the road ahead." She nodded toward the cabin.

Aurinda looked down and snapped a dry piece of hay with far more force than was needed to break it. "Aye, 'tis true enough."

"I can hardly keep my eyes open." Mrs. Wooding slumped onto the straw and fell immediately asleep.

"I saved you some bread. 'Tis dry, but 'twill strengthen you." Zadok handed a chunk to Aurinda.

"Thank you." She pulled off a small piece and savored the doughy taste. "Bread has ne'er tasted so sweet."

Zadok looked at the ground as his hands searched for a piece of straw. He placed a long stalk between his teeth, appearing preoccupied as he methodically chewed on it.

After a moment, he removed it from his mouth and looked toward her, his grey eyes filled with warmth despite their lack of sight. "My mother says you will need to tend your father for some time. Is this so?" His jaw contorted as he awaited her answer.

She turned away. "I suppose 'tis so." She bit her lip as unexpected tears welled.

"I ... I must go back to New Haven with my mother and sister. There is much work to be done to repair the smith." He cleared his throat. "Dr. Northrup says 'tis looking hopeful my sight could return. We spoke about it as we walked to your farm."

"That is wonderful news." She was grateful he could not see her face contort, because her cheeks burned and flooded with moisture.

"I ..." He swallowed with difficulty. "I had hoped you might come with me to New Haven. Yet I see you are needed here."

"Aye. 'Tis so." She struggled to keep her voice steady.

"Can you walk with me outside?"

"Aye." She stood on unsteady legs and helped him stand. Instead of holding onto her arm, his hand curled around her waist and drew her close as they exited the structure. Her breathing increased while her heart hammered against her breast. Her knees might have buckled except for his support.

They walked several rods before he stopped. "Aurinda, I know I still do not have my sight back, and I have many responsibilities at my home, but I shall burst if I do not declare my love for you."

"Zadok ..."

"Please, hear me out. You were taken from me once before many years ago. I do not wish to lose you again. You do not have to answer me just yet, but I want you to know my heart's desire is to make you my wife. And as soon as your father is recovered, I long for you to come to New Haven and marry me."

How she yearned to throw herself into his embrace and agree to become his consort. It would fulfill her deepest longings. But when his sight returned, like the doctor predicted it would, could he tolerate a wife whose countenance revolted him every time he looked her way? Would he resent her for entrapping him before he knew better?

"I ... I do not think this is possible." She could hardly breathe.

His hand gripped her waist tighter. "Not possible? Why, pray tell?" His hand shook as he held onto her.

She pulled back and looked up at his handsome face, which elicited fresh longing whenever she stared at him. "You do not know me. You do not know how I look."

"I do not care how you look. How can you think that would matter?"

"My father has made it quite clear how uncomely I am." She stepped back a few feet. "And you ... you are far too handsome for someone such as I. I could not—I would not—allow you to align yourself with such a one like me. I have long since decided my fate is to be without a consort. And that is how it must be."

She placed her shoulders back with resolve. Her stance remained forceful and determined, but her heart shredded into a thousand fragments, like someone had torn apart a piece of her woven linen and destroyed all hopes of it ever being repaired.

"Let us move on." She swallowed back a sob. "I must check on my father."

ZADOK'S THOUGHTS shot through his mind like a bullet ricocheting in a cave. She would disappoint him? Is that what she said? If either of them was a disappointment, he was. He'd never made a difference in this world as he hammered out horseshoes. His courage had been relegated to lifting the legs of a horse who might or might not try to avenge his shoeing tactics. Some hero.

Did she truly believe her father's hurtful words? Had his barrage of insults taken root in her mind to form this image? Even if his daughter were not a beauty, no woman deserved the contempt he abused her with—especially not a daughter.

He longed to actually see Aurinda, to assure her that he knew exactly what she looked like and would always love her sweetness and caring spirit—not to mention her amazing bravery—no matter what her appearance was. He despaired she wouldn't allow him to prove his love for her.

Yet the canyon separating their affections could not be bridged by any assurances he offered. The damage by her father had gone on for too long. And her ability to trust another man had been destroyed as completely as the homes in Fairfield were charred to ruins.

As he watched her shadow leave his side and return to the cabin, his hopes for happiness in this world departed with her.

20

Instead of going back to the cabin, Aurinda veered toward the forest and ran back to her lakeside refuge. Hurrying toward the water, she paid no mind to the pine branches thrust into her face and side while she forced her way through the boughs. So intent was she to reach her retreat, she nearly forgot what —or who—she was trying to escape.

Not until she felt the coolness of the lake enveloping her toes did she look down at the lapping water and try to imagine what her true reflection was in the swirling pool's edge. But the ripples dallied with her desire to see her features. If anything, the distorting movement of the small waves caused her to turn away from the reflection, confirming the image her father had created in her mind.

He must be right.

Father had never allowed a looking glass in their home, claiming he was fearful if she ever saw her image, it might terrify her from ever going out into town. She never pursued finding a clear reflection of herself, preferring to remain ignorant of the nightmare lest she become a recluse.

But now, a blind man expressed his affections for her. He

wanted to marry her. But she knew his sight would soon return, and he'd see the truth. The irony of it all tore into her breast like a dozen stab wounds.

Dear God, why did You let this happen? Had he not been blind, he would have known he should stay away.

She lifted her gown higher, then walked out into the lake, the chilled liquid calming the heat in her frame. She closed her eyes and let the sounds of the water envelop her. The lapping of gentle waves—minuscule in comparison to the powerful surges that foamed and roared along Long Island Sound—lulled her thoughts with their rhythm.

The sound of quacks forced her eyes open. A mother duck swam by, followed by several ducklings intent on keeping up with her. She watched them for a moment, mesmerized by the fluid movements of the larger bird and the frantic swimming of the little ones as they struggled to keep up.

Leading them across algae-covered rocks in the shallow water, the mama took her brood to the edge of the lake, where they pecked and ate whatever nourishment could be found in the damp soil. The mother duck remained on constant alert, listening, watching for any signs of danger to her fledglings. The ducklings were unaware of any jeopardy around them. As long as they focused on their parent, they felt secure.

How different her life was from theirs. The ducklings trusted their parent to watch out for their every need, to keep them safe from life's perils, to avoid any threat to their wellbeing. Instead, she faced insecurity. She was unprotected from life's crises, vulnerable to the pitfalls most fathers would stand against to protect the fledgling under their care. If they loved that offspring, that is.

"As a hen doth gather her brood under her wings ..." The verse from the book of Luke leaped into her thoughts, bringing an unexpected outpouring of grief from her eyes.

"Oh Father, could you not have gathered me in your arms

even once? Even a farm hen shows more love for her little ones." The delicate breeze drifting across the lake swept away her soft words. Aurinda wiped the moisture from her face, then noticed one of the ducklings had drifted away from its mother. It panicked until the parent swam faster toward the lost one and guided it back to its fellow hatchlings.

"Doth He not leave the ninety and nine and seeketh that which was gone astray?" She stared at the lost duckling, now safe back within the flock. *As God does for His children.*

When my father and my mother forsake me, then the Lord will take me up.

The Psalm, memorized by Aurinda so long ago, wove its message into the now-grown child who craved the comfort of her earthly father yet found compassion in her heavenly one. Peace nestled its way into her heart, even though her arms would never find the solace she craved.

Returning to New Haven on foot became a slow and silent walk. Zadok barely noticed the light in front of his eyes getting brighter, it so sharply contrasted with the darkness in his spirit. Aurinda had rejected him, and even the realization his eyesight grew stronger was not enough to overcome the deep pain of her rebuff. These last weeks with Aurinda had served to nurture a desire for her presence.

"Zadok, you must eat something." His mother stood before him as he sat on a large boulder covered with lichen.

"Please give it to Mercy." He'd spent the last several moments running his hand over the crusty plant growing on the granite. "I've no appetite."

"Zadok, she's already eaten. Please."

He wiped his hands on his breeches and accepted her offering of pemmican. After eating a few bites, he placed it back in the cloth Aunt Primrose had wrapped around it back in Fairfield. His stomach churned from the dried meat he'd ingested so unwillingly. The taste of it threatened to expel the contents from his gut. In hopes the gesture would prevent its regurgitation, he wiped fiercely at his mouth. The effort seemed to be rewarded when the nausea ceased.

As he stood and held his hand in front of his eyes, the vague outline of his five fingers appeared. His heart leaped at the vision, yet soon returned to its slower, steady rhythm—a dull thudding more reflective of numbness than excitement. Without Aurinda, he felt not joy but apathy to the world around him. She'd brought life and vigor to the stalwart blacksmith, who worked hard with little pleasure. And now she was gone.

"Let's be on our way, if you're both ready."

"I am." Mercy came and touched his arm. "We are both alone once again, are we not?"

"Aye." He wrapped his arm around her and hugged her shoulder. "Once again."

They shared a brief moment of sibling affection, made stronger by their loss of love from ones who they'd both hoped would bring passion into their bleak existence. Their lives— filled with war, hard work, and loss—provided little in the way of tenderness or affection. Intimacy had eluded them both.

Zadok wondered if it had evaded his life forever.

21

Aunt Primrose and the orphan child, Hannah, moved into Aurinda's bed. She had willingly given up her now-repaired mattress, preferring to sleep in the barn in the warmer weather. She also hoped the scent of the hay might yet contain a few particles of Zadok's presence. Even a few whiffs of his being could be a comfort to her.

Although fully aware she could have accepted his proposal and gladly been a recipient of his companionship until death would they part, she loved him too dearly to take advantage of his ignorance. The thought of him awakening to her ugliness each morning was too dreadful. She would not do that to the man she loved.

When Zadok left the previous day, she had hidden in the woods, afraid to say goodbye, afraid she would change her mind and agree to go with him after her father was better. But now, she regretted she'd missed one last opportunity to take in his strong face with the lips that once met hers in tenderness and a passion she'd never known before and would never know again.

Aurinda wiped away her unbidden tears with brusque fingers. Bits of straw covered her gown as she stood on unsteady legs. It seemed thoughts of Zadok always brought weakness to her knees. Brushing away the fodder, she strode with heavy steps toward the cabin.

She dreaded, once again, helping Aunt Primrose change her wounded father's dressings. The gaping lacerations from the enemy's sharp bayonets had been delivered with ferocious thrusts.

The thought of the excruciating horror her father endured during the attack was only matched by the consternation she would face as she watched her father's face twist in pain while his wounds were cleaned and recovered. She was grateful Aunt Primrose's skilled hands managed to accomplish the task with speed.

Aurinda was unaccustomed to seeing her father in actual pain. His frequent complaints in the past seemed more dramatic than real. But the depth of agony the king's soldiers had inflicted on this man, who'd been loyal to the very ruler behind this vicious attack, was undeniable. She cringed at the brutality, as well as the disloyalty. Despite the intensity of her feelings toward her father, she wouldn't wish this pain upon any human.

She took his hand while her aunt worked. "Would it help if you squeezed my fingers, Father?"

"Nay, daughter." He jerked his head from side to side as he released her hand. "'Twould only cause you pain—far more pain than my words have inflicted upon you."

"Then I shall fetch a stick for you to bite on." She shifted her legs and touched his face.

Aunt Primrose stared at her for a moment then returned to her task.

After searching for the right size stick in the kindling, Aurinda brought one to the patient. She wrapped it in cloth and placed it before her father's mouth. "Open your teeth, Father."

He clamped down on the thick twig with a desperate bite.

"I'll fetch some clean water, Aunt." She left the cabin, leaving the door partly open. Relief replaced anxiety. Refilling the basin from the dwindling supply in the rain barrel, Aurinda shaded her eyes and stared into the distance. Not a rain cloud in sight. She exhaled and shuffled her way back to the house, careful not to spill the basin's contents.

She backed into the door she'd left ajar and nearly dropped the bowl when her father moaned loudly. Apparently, even the rum Aunt Primrose had medicated him with hadn't diminished enough of the pain. She could not imagine the depth of discomfort he might feel had Dr. Northrup not brought another bottle of the medicinal.

"Thank ye for the water, Aurinda. Perhaps ye could read to Hannah in your room. She might be blessed with the distraction."

She covered her mouth in shame. So consumed with her own trials, she'd ignored poor Hannah. *Lord, forgive me.* "Of course, I'll see to her, Aunt Primrose." She ambled toward the door and knocked lightly. "Hannah, 'tis Aurinda. I'd like to come in." It seemed strange to tap on her own door, but she didn't wish to frighten the child with a bold entrance. When Hannah didn't reply, she carefully opened the creaky-hinged portal.

With her eyes wide open, Hannah sucked her thumb while she lay curled up in the middle of Aurinda's bed.

She tiptoed toward the bed and spoke in a quiet voice. "Dear Hannah, may I sit with you for a bit?"

The child nodded her head.

"Thank you." Aurinda sat on the quilts covering her mattress, folded her hands on her lap, and prayed for wisdom to say the right words to this terrified child. "Have you had some victuals this morning?"

The child nodded.

"So, you're not feeling that growling in your tummy."

Hannah shook her head.

"Very good."

Something about the vacant look in the girl's eyes transported Aurinda's thoughts back in time—sixteen years before, when another desolate child lay on this very bed. That feeling of abandonment, a bleakness so powerful it overwhelmed the young Aurinda, nearly thrust her into withdrawal from the world.

She remembered Aunt Primrose's words to her when her father gripped her across his saddle and wouldn't let her return to her aunt's embrace. 'Remember, Aurinda, I'll always love ye and so will God. Pray to Him in yer need.' The words echoed through Aurinda's mind like a soothing balm in the midst of her darkest hour.

Empathy flooded her for this young orphan who must be feeling the terrible grief of being forsaken by the one who loved her. She couldn't possibly understand why she'd lost her mother. How do you explain death to a five-year-old? Then again, had she seen her mother killed by the soldiers? The thought was a sickening one, too terrible to imagine. Aurinda took a deep breath and prayed for wisdom.

"Hannah, I am dreadfully sorry your mother could not come."

For the first time, Hannah unplugged her thumb from her mouth. She furrowed her small brows. "Why could she not? I want her here with me."

"I know you do, and you must miss her terribly."

Tears emerged in Hannah's eyes.

Aurinda continued. "You know your dear mother would be here with you if she could."

"Then why is she not?" Hannah's voice quivered.

"When … when the soldiers came to your home in New Haven, your mother was hurt. So badly hurt, she could not get better. She died, and that is why she cannot be with you. I know she wishes she could be here, holding you and taking care of you."

"My dog died. A long time ago. We buried him in the yard, and I brought him flowers." Hannah's eyes widened. "Is Mama in the ground now, too?"

Tears threatened to choke Aurinda. "Yes, little one. Perhaps we can bring her flowers when we visit your home."

Hannah's eyes bulged, and her whole body shook. "I don't want to go back home! The soldiers, the soldiers ..." She cried.

Aurinda cradled the trembling child and rocked her in her arms. She kissed the top of the girl's head, smoothing her silky brown hair back from her face. The words of a lullaby crept their way into Aurinda's thoughts, and soon the melody flowed from her lips:

Sleep sweetly, dear baby
Stay safe in my arms,
Your sweetness I treasure
More than riches or charms
Whilst nightfall surrounds thee
In God's tender care
Remember thy Savior
'Twill always be there.

22

The smell of burned wood greeted Zadok when he and his family drew closer to New Haven. By the time they reached the edge of town, the pungent odor singed the insides of his nostrils and stung his eyes. He used to view the smells from his forge as overpowering at times, but the remnants of New Haven were beyond the assault of the forge on his senses.

While his vision slowly cleared, blurred outlines of what used to be homes lined the streets. The effect was both surreal and nightmarish, as ghostlike skeletons of buildings emerged through his hazy eyesight.

It had been a week since the attack by the British, but the destruction of so many buildings and the hazy smoke still clinging in the air made the assault on his hometown seem as if it had just occurred. The only thing missing was the plundering army.

Through her tears, Mercy said, "Mother, look what they've done."

His mother's voice echoed her pain. "We will just have to build again. Let us find our home."

Zadok followed a few feet behind the women, taking in as

many images as he could discern. But the irritating soot clung to his eyes, making it more difficult to see clearly.

His mother rested her hand on his arm. "Are you all right, Zadok?"

"Aye, 'tis just the smoke burnin'."

"I'll fetch you cool water when we get home."

"Mrs. Wooding? Zadok? Praise be, you've survived the pillage. And you, Mercy. You are all safe." The hazy image of the parson stood in front of him.

"Aye, Parson. We took refuge in Fairfield, only to find that town was next in line for attack. Even more homes were burned in that village. A conflagration of the worst kind." Zadok rubbed his eyes.

"'Twas an abomination." Mrs. Wooding's voice rang with outrage.

"True enough, Mrs. Wooding. All we can do now is rebuild— and stock more arms in the event that rabble ever returns."

The thought of another attack evoked nausea in his gut. Zadok wiped his hand across his mouth as if it could obliterate any further assaults. He drew his shoulders back. "Let's get to work." This time he led the way, only occasionally bumping into small items that still evaded his sight.

It had been many days since he'd felt the ability to change his circumstances. With the return of his vision—however weak it seemed at the moment—renewed determination energized his steps.

When the trio arrived at their homestead, he refused to be discouraged by the broken windows, overturned household goods, and their missing food confiscated by the king's army.

"I'm grateful the walls still stand." Mrs. Wooding picked up broken dishes and set them in a pile in the corner.

Mercy began to do the same as they sought to bring order into the chaos of war's aftermath.

"I'll check the smithy." With determined steps, he marched

around the back of their home and stopped short. Little damage had been inflicted on the anvil and bellows, but the iron supply had been confiscated. His jaw clenched as heat climbed up his already warm neck. *What is a smith without his iron?* He picked up a horseshoe the plunderers had missed and threw it as far as he could.

Sitting on the tree stump he used when he needed a break from work, he pulled the splint off his right arm, stretched out his weakened limb, and held it in front of his eyes. He knew it was too soon for his arm to be healed all the way, but anger prompted him to rebel even from a doctor's simple instruction. Pulse pounding, he stopped himself from screaming. Instead, he looked up at the sky. Hot tears poured down his face.

"Zadok, what can I do to help thee?"

He stood up so fast, he nearly lost his balance. "Parson. You startled me."

"I can see that, and I apologize."

Zadok rubbed his aching eyes to clear his view. Parson Stone's face appeared before him in detail. "Parson, I can see you!" Gripping the man's arms, Zadok burst out laughing.

"Well, aye." He scratched his cheek and blinked. "I did not know 'twas unusual for thee."

"Did my mother not tell you? I became blind in a fall, but just today, my sight is clear. I can even see the breadcrumbs on your lips."

Parson Stone quickly wiped the food from his face. "Aye, well," he cleared his throat, "certainly a miracle of God."

"Aye, I suppose 'tis so." Zadok stopped smiling.

"Does it disturb you?" Parson Stone tilted his head and drew his eyebrows together. "That God gave you your sight back?"

"No, not exactly." Zadok folded his arms together and looked past the parson's shoulder. "I've just not been on the best speaking terms with God as of late."

"I see." Parson Stone tried covering a smirk.

Zadok's brows furrowed. "I don't know why you would find that amusing. Being a man of God and all."

"It's just … you remind me of someone from a long time ago."

"Who?"

"Thy father." He grinned.

"My father? Why, I know of no other man who has a faith in God any stronger than he has."

"That's true, but 'twas not always so. Thy father struggled with many precepts of faith. He would not come to God without a fight." The parson grasped Zadok's upper arm. "And I see much of that fight in thee." He turned toward the parsonage. "And I think that flying horseshoe ended up in my garden. Or what's left of my garden, after the Regulars did their 'plowing.'"

Zadok's face burned with heat. "I'm sorry, Parson."

"So tell me, what is eating away at thy soul?"

"Well, I suppose we could start with my name, for one thing." He placed both hands on his hips and exhaled. "'Mighty man' indeed."

"Mighty man of valor. Aye. 'Tis a heavy load to carry such a title. But a name is not always aptly given at the start. 'Tis the finish to the race that can bring the silver through the flames."

He huffed. "The only flames in my life either destroy the homes around me or make horseshoes."

Parson Stone folded his arms and gazed at Zadok. "And ye think there is little valor in thy craft and in overseeing this home? Ye've been here to protect thy mother and sister—with hindered eyesight. And thy job as smith? How would our army do with poorly shod mounts to take them into battle? Ye've been part of their victory with your hammer and forge."

"I have to stay home and watch the women and the forge whilst Peter gets to fight the enemy." He squinted his eyes and tightened his fists. "He's always carried the upper hand, even though I can fire a musket same as him."

"So, ye think thy father chose Peter to go with him because he's a better aim with a musket?" The preacher looked amused.

"Why else would he have chosen my brother?" He tilted his chin upward.

"Did it not occur to thee, that ye were the better smith and thy father could entrust thee to keep the army's horses better-shod?"

The words dropped into his heart as though an anvil had crushed him. He looked at the parson from the corner of his eyes. "The better smith?"

"Aye, lad. Heard it myself from thy father."

He blinked several times. Finally, he blurted out his frustration. "Well, why did he not tell me? All this time, I've thought Peter could best me at everything."

"I know not. But I do know life's answers are not always handed to us on a platter. Sometimes we must delve a bit deeper so we can know God better—and understand ourselves more. How many years have ye thought you knew the reason why ye were left home? You couldn't see thy own strength in your God-given skills. 'Twas not about being better than Peter nor worse. Just that God had His place for each of you."

The parson shifted his stance. "I must be on my way. I need to feed the whole flock. They're in great need of a shepherd these days. But remember, Zadok, I'm always available for the lambs feeling lost." He patted him on the shoulder and left.

Zadok watched him saunter down the road toward his next needy ewe. Scratching his cheek, Zadok plunked back onto the tree stump and rubbed his head. He was not sure what had just happened, but one of the weights dragging his spirit downward had just become less of a burden.

23

W hile she prepared for the Sabbath meeting, Aurinda absentmindedly twirled her curls around her finger. Two weeks had passed since the Fourth of July. The mere fourteen days had been filled with fear and comfort, pain and joy, secrets and revelations.

Staring at the unopened letter on her dresser, Aurinda did not have to unfold it to know it was from Zadok. It bore the same writing as the previous missives she'd received from him.

Aurinda had only opened the first one to discover his sight had returned, and he begged her to see him. Afraid she might be tempted to dismiss her fears about her appearance, she couldn't bear to read his continuing pleas.

While his essence permeated the parchment, Zadok's strength seemed etched in the heavy scrawl written with his smith's fingers. She'd inhaled his scent from the moment the letter arrived from the post rider. After staring at the unrevealed message one last time, she turned toward her bedroom door and exited.

"Well, what did the lad have to say?" Aunt Primrose placed

her sewing on her lap and looked at Aurinda above her spectacles.

"Nothing of import, Aunt Primrose."

"Ye n'er did open it, did ya?" Her aunt pulled off her glasses and sighed with exasperation. "Because if ye had, ye'd be red as a rosebud. Open it, lass!"

Heat burned her cheeks. *Now I surely am red as a rosebud.*

Hannah stared at her from the tableboard, eyes wide as a full moon. "You got a letter?"

"Aye, she did, Miss Hannah, but do ya think she's goin' to open it? Nay, 'tis Sabbath and it might bring her some pleasure." Aunt Primrose shook her head slowly and returned to sewing the new dress for Hannah.

"'Tis not that, Aunt. I ..." Aurinda smoothed the wrinkles on her gown. "I fear if I read it, 'twill break my heart." Her eyes moistened.

"Well, is not that somethin'. You go and break the lad's heart, and now ye say he'll break yours. Tsk." Her aunt gazed at Hannah. "I'll let ye in on a secret, Hannah. When love from a man 'o character comes yer way, snatch him up and don't let go. When yer older, of course."

She tried to ignore her aunt's words. "Can we start our walk to the meet ... I mean, the place of gathering?" It was still difficult to believe the meetinghouse was reduced to ashes and gone from their lives.

"Aye, of course. Hannah's dress is complete." Aunt Primrose tore the dangling thread with her teeth and held up the new gown for the child. "How do ye like it, dear Hannah?"

"'Tis lovely." The child's grin was a bright spot on the cloudy day.

"No lovelier than you, Hannah." Primrose grinned as she slipped the gown over the child's head.

An ache gripped Aurinda at her aunt's words. Had anyone shared words like that with her when she was a child? Not since she'd been brought to her father's home. She had a vague memory of the phrase—probably from Aunt Primrose—said to her a very long time ago. So very long.

She trudged over to the bed where her father lay. "We're leaving for Sabbath meeting, Father. Dr. Northrup will be by to check on you whilst we're gone."

Father reached for her hands, and she stiffened. By the time he touched her fingers, they were as unyielding as stone. She allowed the contact between them but fought back the discomfort his skin elicited when it touched hers. He must have sensed her repugnance, because he slowly withdrew his hand.

"Godspeed, Daughter."

Had his voice trembled? She avoided looking at him when she turned to go. "Goodday, Father."

"Fare thee well, Papa."

Aurinda turned to see the orphan lean over her father and peck his cheek with a kiss.

"Fare thee well, Hannah." Her father's voice was high pitched and sweet.

How dare he show affection to that child? Aurinda gritted her teeth.

Her thoughts reeled while she all but ran out the door, followed by Aunt Primrose holding Hannah's hand.

"Do ye have to be in a race, Aurinda? Slow down."

It was all she could do to lessen her pace and await Primrose and the child.

"Hannah, dear, why don't ye look at that butterfly over there?"

The orphan raced toward the orange-and-black-winged creature and stared at it with awe. She lightly touched it with her finger, then it flew away.

"See that?" Primrose pointed toward the fleeing butterfly. "Sometimes ye can chase away what ye want the most by not appreciating the moment. By not allowing the beauty bein'

201

offered to you for what it is." She turned toward Aurinda and held onto her arms. "Nothin' can change what has happened between ye and yer father. But if you can see the beauty of what he's tryin' to offer ye now, ye'll know the love of yer father, even for the time he has left on this earth."

Her eyes widened. "Is Father dying?"

"Nay, I did na say that. But no one knows, lass, the moments we are offered on this earth. If we don' treasure the beauty of those moments—like that butterfly resting on a flower—we'll chase them away forever."

Tears etched a familiar path down Aurinda's cheeks. "But every time he touches me, I feel pain."

"Then we must pray that pain away, pray for healing." Primrose hugged her closely.

Aurinda felt a small tug on her gown and looked down to see Hannah. "Can I sing you the lullaby? 'Twill help you feel better."

A laugh burst from Aurinda while she wiped the tears from her cheeks. "Aye, Hannah. I would treasure hearing the lullaby."

The threesome walked together toward the meeting place, arm in arm. As Hannah's small voice sang the lullaby, Aurinda felt the healing presence of her Savior, Who would always be there for her.

ALTHOUGH SABBATH SERVICE was now held outdoors next to the burnt-out meetinghouse, Aurinda marveled at the larger number of Fairfield residents who had come today. Even the Tories, who'd never shown up to listen to the patriotic pastor prior to the attack, wandered into the group of residents. Some had visible scars, and some—like Mrs. Moore and her infant— also carried the scars of a wounded heart. Her sister from Hartford stood next to her.

Since the Moore's home was lost in the fire, Mrs. Moore

planned on moving to the city with her sibling. Her husband was still in the militia, so there was no one to help rebuild the cabin.

Watching the mournful expression on Mrs. Moore's face brought back the memory of the day when they'd rescued her and the baby. She'd always be grateful they'd arrived in time to save them. In her mind, their plight was a stark reminder of the devastation wrought by the king's army. Aurinda would never forget it.

The Turners' little ones clung to their parents. Aurinda was relieved they had survived. She just wished there wasn't a need for their fear. Would the town ever recover from this nightmare of memories?

She glanced sideways at another neighbor with burns on his face. She knew him to be a Tory—a faithful follower of King George—yet here he was, wounded and, perhaps, without a home. Aurinda imagined the sting of betrayal by the king's troops must feel like Judas's kiss upon Jesus. Empathy for this former loyalist unexpectedly flooded her spirit. She smiled at him.

He looked at her for just a moment then stared at the ground.

It was the same expression she'd seen on her father ever since the attack. Was it truly easier to forgive a stranger than her own father? Yes. It was far more than her father's abhorrence of the patriot cause that troubled her. There was so much more.

The parson ended his sermon by requesting all bow their heads for prayer.

Prickles of guilt climbed into her heart, along with the words that had nagged her spirit since the attack: *You must forgive your father.*

She knew the truth of the command. But she knew it would take a miracle.

24

Late July, 1779

T he news could not have come at a worse time. Zadok had seen the arrival of the post rider and intercepted the letter from the Army, lest his mother or sister receive ill tidings before he did. This was woeful news indeed. Peter was badly injured at the Battle of Stony Point, and he'd requested leave to come home. Zadok stuffed the note inside his shirt.

This was the first day he'd been able to return to work at the forge since the king's troops attacked. Although the rabble had taken most of his iron, neighbors had brought in scraps from their homes and barns. A few bars of the wrought iron had even been discovered throughout the town, where the stolen pieces had been dropped by the scavengers. It had begun as a day to celebrate the return of the smithy fire. Instead, dreaded news had stolen the victory.

The initial news from Stony Point had been triumphant. In a daring nighttime campaign, the American troops had seized the outpost thirty miles north of New York. But dozens of

Americans were wounded, and Peter was among them. Now Zadok faced the painful prospect of informing his mother.

When he walked in their front door, his expression must have communicated the message because his mother's face blanched, and she began to shake. She reached for a chair and collapsed onto the wooden seat.

Mercy's eyes widened. "Mother, what is it?"

His mother's lips trembled when she said, "Peter or your father?"

"'Tis Peter. Father is bringing him home."

"Is he ...?"

"Nay, not dead, but ill from his wounds. He was injured at Stony Point."

Her eyes darted from one room to the next as she fussed with her cap. "I ... I must get his bed ready." She stood and swayed. If Zadok and Mercy had not caught her, she would have fallen to the floor.

"Mercy, get a cool linen." He guided his mother back to the chair, then picked her up and carried her to her room.

Carrying a basin and cloth, Mercy followed him. Their mother's face flushed, and she struggled to withhold tears. But the moisture erupted despite her effort. "My son ..."

"Mother, we shall take care of him, and he shall recover." Mercy's words were firm and reassuring. When had his little sister grown up?

"We must pray." The words erupted in fits and starts from their mother.

"Aye, we shall. Right now." Mercy gripped her mother's hand with her own and prayed with fervor.

Zadok shut his eyes and listened in awe at his sister's requests to heaven. He had never heard such a powerful petition to God come from her lips before.

When she was finished, she stroked her mother's burning brow. "Rest now, Mother. I shall prepare everything."

His mother's eyes now closed, Zadok hurried out the bedroom door and closed it quietly behind him. He reached his sister as she gathered linens to wash. "Mercy, what's happened to you?"

"What do you mean?" She continued to gather sheets and blankets.

"I mean that prayer. I've ne'er heard such a one from you before."

She paused in her cleaning and looked at the floor while holding a bundle of linens. She glanced up at him and smiled in such a peaceful way, he scratched at his cheek.

"'Tis true I've changed. But I pray 'tis a good change." She dropped the bundle in a pile on the floor and sat in a chair. "When we returned from Fairfield, there was something troubling me. I'd become so rebellious toward Mother, so free with my affections toward Caleb Beckwith." Her face flushed. "'Tis a wonder I do not carry his child, but we never quite went that far."

"Mercy!" Zadok gasped and collapsed in another chair near the table.

She looked straight at him. "I am not proud of my actions, Zadok, and I've begged God to forgive me." Her eyes moistened. "And I've asked God to help me be a true Christian in my deeds, as well as my words."

"I can see you've changed, Mercy." He stared at his hands then raised his eyes to hers. "And I'm glad. Mother needs you now more than ever."

Her face contorted and turned bright red. "Is Peter badly wounded?"

"I fear so." He stood and walked to her side. "We will get through this together."

"And we shall get through this with God's help." She sniffed loudly and stood again. "Thank you, Zadok."

"What for?"

"For being my faithful brother. You've always been my hero." She kissed him briefly on his cheek and took the linens outside.

He stared after her while speech eluded him.

ZADOK AWAITED his father's arrival from the army encampment. Peter Wooding was returning to his home to die. He might have survived the bayonet wounds he'd received in the decisive American victory, but infection had set in. The camp physician said there was no hope for him. It would be the kindest act of mercy to let him die among his loved ones.

Accompanied by two guards, Peter was transported by wagon. After his fevered form was lifted out of the wagon and carried inside the Wooding home, the guards saluted his father and returned to their camp.

Weariness marked his father's every movement. He held the horse's reins, and Sergeant Wooding dismounted, wincing with the effort.

"Welcome home, Father."

His parent hugged him long and hard before releasing him. "Where's your mother? Is she well?"

"Aye, Father. She's inside with Mercy."

With his back bent, his father trudged up the three steps to their home, grabbed the doorknob, and pushed the portal open. "Esther?"

His father closed the door, and Zadok led the army horse to the barn. The poor animal appeared as weary as its rider. He unsaddled the mare and stroked her sunken back. "Won't be long before you must retire as well, old girl."

She whinnied her satisfaction at the offering of fresh water before guzzling down a measure of oats and hay.

"That should hold ya for a bit."

Approaching the house, Zadok could hear the conversations inside.

"Esther, I did all I could to protect the lad."

"'Twas not enough. Look at him."

"We are at war. Not a one of us is out of danger at every moment."

A heartrending wail prompted Zadok to pause.

"But he's my son."

"He's mine as well, Esther."

His mother's words morphed into muffled sobs.

Father tried to comfort her, but she would likely never feel comforted again.

WHEN HIS MOTHER and Mercy had finished changing Peter's dressings, Zadok approached his brother's door. "May I come in?"

Peter grinned, his reddened gums from the fever obvious. "Since when did you have to ask?"

"Since you became a soldier in General Washington's army." He gave an awkward salute and smiled.

"Some homecoming, huh?" He struggled to breathe. "The victorious soldier." Peter coughed—a raucous and painful sound.

Zadok cleared his throat. "Seems to me you are the hero in the family."

"Is that so? Mercy has shared otherwise."

He furrowed his forehead. "I don't follow you."

"You were blind for a time, then shot a lobsterback, then beat up a scoundrel who was after our sister? Sounds quite valiant to me. Not to mention headstrong and stupid!" Peter tried to laugh but had to stop for all the coughing.

Zadok cringed at his brother's obvious weakness but tried to act normal. They were still brothers, after all. "If you weren't lying there with a fever, I'd take you on."

"Aye, I'm sure you would. And after years of workin' the forge, your arms look strong enough to beat me, even if I were well."

"Well then, you'll just have to get well enough so you can try. I'll be ready." Zadok grabbed at Peter's arm and squeezed it. He balked at the thin muscles he felt.

Peter's face paled, and his breathing was labored. "I think I'd best rest for a bit."

"Aye." Zadok rubbed his hands against his cheeks. "I'll be back to visit."

He turned to leave, but he stopped to stare at the emaciated soldier on the bed. The man lying there was not the brother he remembered. It was a man who'd fought for his country and helped win a victory. A man who was about to give his life for a new nation.

More than that, it was a man Zadok loved. He would always be a hero to Zadok, and the realization he would no longer be alive left a deep hole of sorrow and regret. Why had he spent so many years competing with his sibling rather than appreciating him for the faithful brother he was?

"I love you, Peter."

His brother slept soundly. Zadok left the room and slipped outdoors to the forge. He pumped the bellows, grabbed a hammer, put a piece of iron on his anvil, and beat it with angry swings, relieved the smoke hid his tears.

25

P eter died two days later. Although it was excruciating to see him suffer, Zadok was grateful for the time together, however short it turned out to be.

The army physician had sent laudanum to make Peter's final hours more tolerable. Zadok wished there was a medicinal to take away the pain of grief, but that was a suffering with no easy cure. Watching his stricken parents mourn their oldest child only added to Zadok's sorrow. While his mother and father sewed a shroud around Peter's body, Zadok escaped to his room.

Although Aurinda had never answered one of his letters, he nevertheless poured his heart out onto a piece of parchment and begged her to come. *Dear God, please let her come.* A knock on the door caused him to hurriedly sign his name and fold the message up tightly. "Who is it?"

Mercy entered the room, her eyes swollen from crying. "Zadok, the men need you to help dig the grave."

"Very well." He swallowed back his sorrow and looked at the letter. "Mercy, can you give this to the post rider?" He dug in the pocket of his work apron and pulled out a couple of shillings. "This should cover it."

"Of course, Zadok." She took it from his shaking hand.

"We shall get through this." He leaned over to peck her cheek.

"With God's help, we shall." She grinned through her quivering lips.

He rushed toward the church cemetery while trying to focus on anything but the loss of his brother. After picking up a shovel, he dug along with the other men who had volunteered to help. He ignored the looks of sympathy on their faces, preferring to expend his energy on work rather than succumb to the pain eating away at his heart.

In his anger, he prayed. *If you are a God of miracles, then bring Aurinda here.* He wiped away the dirt that had collected on his face and kept digging.

~

"POST RIDER." Hannah made the announcement while she gripped the windowsill. She had to stretch her short legs to look out the twelve-paned window.

Though her heart skipped a beat, Aurinda pretended not to hear. Aunt Primrose's stare could pierce through steel, so she refused to look at her.

"Thank ye, Miss Hannah. I wonder who might have written?" She glared an accusatory look at Aurinda while drying her wet hands.

Aurinda continued to work on her weaving. Aunt Primrose spoke with the post rider, but she tried not to pay attention. Yet she raised her eyes to glance at him through the window. Did he say he was from New Haven?

As Aunt Primrose returned to the cabin, Aurinda again

focused on her work. When her aunt remained silent, her curiosity grew.

Finally, she could not stand the wait. "Who has sent a letter?" She attempted to keep her voice level, but she knew she couldn't fool Aunt Primrose. She never could.

"Ah, so yer curiosity has got the better of ye?"

Aurinda rolled her eyes. "Very well, who sent a post?"

"I think ye know who has done so."

Exhaling louder than usual, she set her weaving paddle down and stood. Aurinda held out her hand to take the letter.

Aunt Primrose just glared at her. "If you ne'er mean to answer the lad, would it not be kinder to tell him to stop sending posts? To stop spending money on his missives?"

"Very well. I shall write to him and tell him to stop." She reached for the letter.

"Be careful, lass." Primrose looked at her sideways. "Do 'na write words ye may regret."

Aurinda bit her lip, took the letter with moist fingers, and stomped toward her bedroom, now used by Primrose and Hannah. Slamming the door shut, she plopped onto the quilts and stared at the message in her hands. She started to place it in the drawer with the other unopened letters but paused. Aunt Primrose was right. It was cruel to lead the man on. Inhaling deeply, she scanned the letter. There were two messages, one from Zadok and one from Mercy.

She first read Zadok's message. His brother was dead!

Through tears, she read Mercy's note. Her jaw opened wide.

Dear Aurinda,

My heart is breaking at the loss of our brother, Peter. He was wounded in the battle of Stony Point and succumbed to his injuries here at home. We are all heartsick.

Seeing Zadok in such misery only adds to my sorrow. He has never forgotten you, and I know he loves you with all his heart. I've seen him send posts to you, but we've not received any other posts, save the news about Peter from the army. I must say, I do not know why you have not responded to his letters. I thought that you truly loved Zadok.

Forgive me if I write out of turn. 'Tis my affection for my brother that prompts me to do so. I beg of you, please consider coming to New Haven to see him.

And I apologize for my behavior on the journey from New Haven to Fairfield. I know that God has forgiven me, and I pray that you might see fit to forgive me as well.

> *With deepest regards,*
> *Mercy Wooding*

Aurinda dropped the parchment on her lap and stared at the wall. Mercy had indeed changed. She'd become more mature, and her words reflected wisdom and concern for her family—something sorely missing just a few weeks past. Her faith and humble spirit had come at a most-needed time for her family.

And Zadok. Aurinda's heart bled for his pain. Since she'd never had a sibling, she could not imagine the pain of losing one. Yet his words dripped with sorrow at the loss of his brother, and his description of the despair in his family prompted her to summon courage.

Perhaps she could attend without him seeing her among the mourners. After all, he did not know what she looked like. She feared even the slightest glimpse of her features might be reflected in the consternation she would see in his eyes.

Yet she needed to attend his brother's burial. She could write him later to tell him she was there but had to hurry home. After all, her father needed her. He would understand that. But attend the funeral, she must. She cared so much for his grief that his mourning became her own.

After a moment, she'd made a decision. But she would need Dr. Northrup's help.

~

THE GATHERING of mourners at the graveside was larger than Zadok expected. Besides his family, many neighbors came, along with members of the local militia. Because he had been wounded in battle, Peter was considered a hero, and many came to honor him.

Near the open grave, Zadok stood at attention. His father held his weeping wife in his arms. Zadok reached over to comfort Mercy and handed her a linen kerchief to blot her tears.

Parson Stone gave a moving eulogy. He'd known the Wooding children since they were young, and he shared many a memory of the mischievous Peter who grew up to be a soldier and gave his all for his country.

It was near the end of the graveside service that Mercy tapped his arm. "Zadok, look. 'Tis Dr. Northrup."

"Where?"

"That man over there."

When the eulogy was complete, the mourners took turns putting a shovelful of dirt over the casket.

Zadok walked toward the unfamiliar face. "Are you Dr. Northrup?"

"Aye, we meet face-to-face without the cloud of darkness over your eyes." The physician shook his hand heartily. "I am sorry 'tis under such sad circumstances."

"Aye." Zadok glanced away. "But I am grateful you've come. How did you know? About my brother, that is?"

The doctor cleared his throat. "Aurinda shared the news."

At her name, Zadok's heart leaped. He scanned the mourners for her.

"Umm, she is not here but wished me to share her condolences with you."

A weight smothered the excitement in Zadok's chest, and he could barely breathe. He'd known it was too good to be true. He swallowed past the dryness in his throat. "I'm ... I'm grateful you came, Dr. Northrup. And thank you again for helping me when I was injured." He rubbed his hand through his hair. "Forgive my manners. Would you stay and share supper with my family?"

"That is kind of you, Zadok, but I must be getting back to Fairfield. I have many patients to attend to."

"I'm certain you do. Thank you again."

Tipping his tricorne hat to Zadok, Dr. Northrup walked toward his horse.

Weariness tugged at every muscle of his being as he shuffled away from the cemetery and headed toward home.

Parson Stone strode toward him. "Zadok. How are ye farin', lad? Ye look to be carryin' the weight of the world on thy heart. I've been prayin' for ye since that day we spoke. And I'm greatly sorrowed about your brother. 'Tis another huge loss from this war, and I pray the fightin' is over soon."

Zadok rested his hands on his hips, then removed his hat and wiped the sweat from his brow with his sleeve. He squinted at the sun and stared at the minister. "'Tis a funny thing about prayin'. It does not seem to reach the ears of a God Who cares for His sheep, as you say. So why do we bother?"

"I know our prayers do not always get answered in the way we like. But—"

"But what if we're askin' for something so simple? So easy? Not even a miracle ... yet, it's still not answered?" His intense gaze focused on the parson. He was on the verge of tears but too angry to give in to them.

Parson Stone's brows drew together. "I don't have all yer answers, Zadok."

"I thought not, Parson." He harrumphed. "But thanks for tryin'." He turned and nearly ran into Mercy.

"What were you talking to Parson Stone about?" She grabbed his bent elbow and walked back to the house with him.

"About how God can't even answer a simple prayer." He pressed his lips together and focused on the house in the distance.

"What prayer was that, Zadok?"

"All I prayed was for Aurinda to come." He stopped quickly, nearly causing Mercy to stumble, then steadied her. "It would not have even required a miracle." He grabbed her elbow and pulled her toward their home.

Mercy stopped short. "Zadok, Aurinda did come. I was hoping she would come see you, but perhaps she couldn't stay."

His eyes widened. "She was here?" He scanned the crowd near the church for any sign of her then realized he didn't know what she looked like. He caught sight of Dr. Northrup on his horse, and a woman, whose golden curls bounced with the motion of the galloping horse, sat behind him.

26

"Aurinda, that was a cruel plan." Dr. Northrup swatted at the mosquitoes landing on his face and hands. "I thought you were at least going to greet the man."

Tears streamed down her cheeks. They had been, the entire ride back to Fairfield. While they rested the horse by a stream where he could drink much-needed water, the doctor paced back and forth, waving his hat to cool off his skin.

"I wanted to say something to him, but I lost courage. Terror gripped me. I could not face him." Aurinda dabbed at her eyes with a kerchief.

He placed his hands on his hips and stood in front of the rock she sat upon. "Why could you not greet him? I cannot fathom your thinking. Had you angered him in some way?" Dr. Northrup's features turned redder by the moment.

"Nay, I feared ..."

"You feared what?"

"I feared what he would think about my appearance. There, I have said it. Why do I need to explain that to you? You have eyes to see how uncomely I am." Tears emerged again.

"Un… Aurinda, what are you thinking? Do you truly believe your father's words about your appearance?"

She drew her lips taut and stared at him.

"You do." He shook his head. "Surely you must know he has misled you all these years."

"How could I know any such thing, Dr. Northrup? All I have heard my whole life is how repulsive I am. Why would I think otherwise? Do you think I would inflict my repugnant face on a blind man, especially knowing he would get his sight back? How cruel do you think I am?" She shuddered.

Dr. Northrup strode with weary steps toward a boulder a few feet away and sat down with stiff movements. "Nay, Aurinda. You are not the cruel one." He placed his hands on his knees and paused. His eyes embraced her with kindness. "Aurinda, your father did not used to be this way. Things happened in the war. Things I dare not discuss with you and your tender sensibilities.

"Suffice it to say, your father never fully recovered from the wounds—those in his body, as well as his spirit." He inhaled deeply before resuming. "When he returned home to find you with Primrose and your mother gone, something even deeper happened in his heart. 'Twas a cruelty in him I'd not seen before." Moisture filled his eyes. "I should have stopped him from taking you from your aunt."

"Why did you not?"

"I thought I didn't have a ghost of a chance to keep you from him. The law would be on his side. So, I decided I'd keep watch out for you and, if I saw him injure you, I'd bring in the law to protect you. The trouble was, there were no laws about abusing someone's heart. And … I fear he injured you greatly in that way." He wiped his face with his kerchief, then blew his nose and stood from the rock with weariness.

"And so, my dear Aurinda, anything your father has said to you about an 'uncomely' appearance is nothing short of a lie. In fact, the exact opposite is true. You are a lovely and enchanting young lady who any man would be proud to call his consort."

She fixed her eyes on him. "I'm not certain I believe you."

"Well then, ask your Aunt Primrose. She will tell you the same. Ask your friends in Fairfield. But most importantly, Aurinda, ask God to reveal to you the true beauty that is yours, both on the inside and the outside."

"I … I don't know what to believe."

"I cannot convince you. But I pray God—and others—will do so." He untied the horse's reins from the tree branch. "Now, let us be on our way. We still have several miles to go."

She climbed onto the saddle behind the doctor and held onto his coat. She clung to him and his words like they were a lifeline to her happiness. Could he possibly be telling her the truth?

27

E xhaustion wrapped itself around Aurinda like a blanket dripping with rain. She greeted Aunt Primrose, Hannah, and her father, then washed her face. The sun was just rising, but after riding the mare all night, Aurinda could barely keep her eyes open.

"Can I get ye some victuals, lass?" Aunt Primrose placed her arm around Aurinda's shoulder.

"Nay, Aunt. I need to sleep."

"Then go rest on yer bed. Hannah and I've no need of it."

She had a vague recollection of hearing Dr. Northrup engage her father in earnest conversation. Closing the door, she collapsed on the quilt-covered mattress that beckoned her. She thought she heard Dr. Northrup raise his voice, but she soon drifted off to sleep.

Aurinda awoke with a start. Where was she? Shielding her eyes from the sunlight streaming through her window, it took a moment to grasp her whereabouts. Accustomed to sleeping in the barn, the softness of the feather mattress and the lilac-scented quilts had encouraged her to sleep far longer than she'd intended.

When she sat up on the edge of the bed, her muscles informed her she'd been riding on horseback all night. It was not a pleasant reminder. She stretched her arms above her head then strode with stiffened steps toward the door. No voices in the other room. The door creaked open, and she tiptoed into the main room as if she were an intruder. Somehow the cabin no longer felt like home.

"Aurinda." She jumped at the voice of her father. It was not harshly spoken, merely unexpected.

"Aye, Father. I'm awake." She stepped toward the hogshead of cider and filled a tankard full. She guzzled the sweet liquid then wiped off the dribbles on her chin.

"You are much athirst after your ride to New Haven."

She'd already erected her defenses against an expected onslaught of hurtful words. She imagined such phrases as 'Why would anyone want to see you,' or 'Why bother with the man? He can see your face now.'

Instead, there was a gentleness in his tone when he invited her to pull a chair next to his bed. "Come sit with me, Daughter. I've much to say to you."

She glanced sideways at him, set the tankard on the tableboard, and drew a chair to his bedside. "What can I do for you, Father?"

His eyes were moist, and he reached for her hand. She pulled it away.

"Please, sit Aurinda. I know you don't trust me, and I carry the blame for that."

Curious, she sat on the edge of the chair as far away from him as she could get.

It appeared he had difficulty beginning, since every time he opened his mouth, he choked on his words. Finally, he coughed and cleared his throat. "I wish to tell you a story. 'Tis not a tale, but true."

She tilted her head and listened.

"Many years ago, 'twas a young man who fancied the sweetest lady you could ever imagine. Not only did she dazzle him with her beauty, but her kind spirit so pleased the man's heart, he became smitten with her. He longed to marry her." He paused.

"Well? Did he?"

"Aye, but not without vying for her hand. She had many a suitor who longed for her besides this man. Including Dr. Northrup."

Her jaw opened. "Dr. Northrup? This lady—do you speak of my mother?"

"Aye." He closed his eyes. "'Twas to her detriment your beautiful mother chose me over him."

Dr. Northrup wanted to marry her mother? Aurinda's thoughts spun faster than her weaving loom. A deep desire to have the physician actually *be* her father nearly overwhelmed her senses. Why had her mother chosen her hateful father? What was she thinking? As she mused on this, guilt infused her. How traitorous were these ponderings? Despite the wounds she endured, he was still her father, flesh and blood. She stared at her hands while he continued.

"I knew your mother was with child before we left for war. Her younger sister, Primrose, promised me she'd take care of you both. I know she tried her best, but Eliza ... your mother ... didn't survive the birthing." Tears erupted, and he sniffed sharply before he continued the story.

"After years away at war, something happened in my heart. I grew cold. Life no longer seemed so easy to understand, and I became bitter. I began to experience hatred, and I often embraced it in my words and my actions.

"When we finally came home, and I saw you and your love for Primrose, I was jealous. Not only had I been denied love from my wife, now my own daughter preferred her aunt to me.

225

In a fit of rage, I took you from her arms and thought I could force you to love me. I was so wrong."

Hot tears worked their way down Aurinda's cheeks, yet she was too numb to lift a finger and wipe them away.

"Dr. Northrup seemed to be the only man with his wits about him." Her father continued. "He told me I was making a mistake, but I ignored him. I just thought he was jealous because Eliza had married me instead of him. I was a fool. I am a fool.

"In my desperation to keep you for myself, I wanted you to think you were not handsome to look at. I didn't want you being taken from me by a suitor who would win your love. So, I ... I lied to you and told you how unpleasant your appearance was. In fact, you look just like Eliza—your mother. Beautiful and pleasing in every way."

He sobbed so hard, Aurinda found a linen cloth to blot his tears. He took it from her and kissed her hand. For the first time, she did not pull away.

"Please, Aurinda. Please forgive me."

Shock permeated her being, and she questioned everything she knew. How could she be beautiful? And even if she were, could she ever believe others saw her as alluring? Her negative self-image had become so firmly entrenched that to think otherwise challenged her identity. Could her whole life be a lie?

"Excuse me, Father." She stood and raced out the door without closing it.

Blinded by her tears, she tripped over rocks, both small and great, as she ran to her lake for solace. She took off her shoes and stepped into the water but refused to look at her reflection. Despite the ripples, she feared she'd see enough of her true image to confuse her even further. Unaware how long she stood there, she startled when she heard someone approach.

"Aunt Primrose. How did you know you would find me here?"

"Isaac—Dr. Northrup, that is—told me where you were."

Primrose removed her own shoes and stretched out her toes before approaching the edge of the lake. "This water looks fine and cool." She closed her eyes and sighed as the liquid enveloped her feet.

Turning away, Aurinda stared toward the far side of the lake. "So yer father told ye the whole story."

She sniffed. "Enough of it."

"Enough to know the truth."

"What exactly is the truth, Aunt Primrose?" Aurinda spun around and glared at her aunt. "My whole life has been a lie."

Primrose frowned and looked down at the water. "Not all of it 'tis a lie, lass. The love we all have for ye is not a lie."

"What kind of love makes one hate who they are?" She sobbed.

"Is that how ye feel? Ye hate who ye are?"

She could not answer.

"Have ye hated the good ye've accomplished in this world? The love ye have shared when ye've helped others in need? Made beautiful linens? Taken care of a hateful father?"

At this, Aurinda cried and couldn't stop.

Aunt Primrose wrapped her arms around her. "Aurinda, I've never stopped loving ye, all these years we were apart." Now Primrose wept. "Dr. Northrup kept a watchful eye out for ye to be sure ye were safe. The minister shared God's love with ye. And Aurinda ..." She held her away until she caught her attention. "Aurinda, ye are lovely to look at and lovely in your soul. Can ye ever come to believe that?"

"I don't know."

Primrose hugged her again. "Then I'll pray God reveals the truth in His good time."

At the moment, she wanted nothing more than to feel Aunt Primrose's comfort. She was the one person who had always loved her. That was a truth she believed.

28

August 1779

It was time for Zadok's father to return to the war encampment. It would be yet another loss after so many others.

Sergeant Wooding held onto his only living son's arms. "Take care of your mother and Mercy. I need you now more than ever." His father's voice grew husky, and he hugged Zadok with a firm grip. The parting would not be easy. He finally released his son and attempted a smile edged with sadness.

"I shall, Father." Zadok's heart had been at battle for serenity ever since his brother's death. When he found out Aurinda had come to the graveside meeting yet had ignored him, despair had made its home in his spirit.

Encouraged by her visit yet confused by her actions, Zadok could only assume it was her Christian duty prompting her to attend the service, while she had no intentions of responding to his affections. *It would have been better if she'd not come at all.*

His father waved a final farewell, and Mercy comforted their mother before taking her inside.

Striding toward the smithy, Zadok pushed away thoughts of Aurinda. But that was made more difficult when he saw the post rider arrive. *What now?*

The sweat-covered rider handed him the sealed note. "Can I get a drink from your rain barrel?"

"Aye. And water your gelding while yer at it."

With heavy steps, Zadok strode toward the forge and sat on the tree stump. He did not recognize the writing in the missive, so he glanced at the signature.

"Dr. Northrup?" The words escaped his lips while he scratched his face. He went back to the heading and read:

Dear Mr. Wooding,

> *Please accept my sincere condolences concerning the death of your brother. No words can express the sadness I feel, especially in regard to the fact he gave his life for his country. I pray this horrible business will be over soon.*

> *I wish to apologize for two things: First, that I had to decline your gracious invitation to share supper with you and your family. Second, that I told you Aurinda was not in attendance at the burial. In fact, she had accompanied me but became nervous and frightened and could not bring herself to face you.*

> *You may wonder at the reason for this, and I hope to explain to you, so you will understand the situation.*

ZADOK CONTINUED to read about Aurinda's father, his lifelong lies to his daughter, and the resulting pain it had continued to cause Aurinda. Her reasons for not staying had nothing to do with him, except she was trying to protect him from her perceived appearance. The final paragraph gripped Zadok's attention.

I beg of you to allow Aurinda the time she needs to let the wind of truth be carried from her head to her heart.

The letter dropped to the ground. He stared at the steadily burning coals on the forge. The flame ... barely visible ... still appeared a pale orange, glowing so slightly as to nearly be imperceptible. But Zadok knew when the bellows blew across the coals, the fire would roar to life once again.

The wind of truth. He played the words over and over in his mind. Like the bellows that kindled the fire to life, he imagined their love growing with the flames of truth. This would, he hoped, remove all doubt in her mind about his feelings for her. And he prayed, her feelings for him would grow into a flaming passion of love and trust. He'd have to be patient—and pray. Pray God would quicken the truth to her heart.

Please, God, kindle her love for me. He closed his eyes and, for the first time in many days, felt peace in his spirit.

DR. NORTHRUP VISITED the cabin the next day, and Aurinda observed how he smiled at Aunt Primrose. She also took note that her aunt blushed brighter than she'd ever noticed before. Aurinda nearly laughed.

"I like to see you smile, Miss Aurinda." Hannah grinned with a mouthful of gruel on her face.

"Aye. 'Tis a blessing to see that lovely face." Aunt Primrose winked at her.

"Then she must take after her mother, as well as her aunt." Dr. Northrup's face took on boyish charm.

Aurinda looked away before she burst into a fit of giggles.

Hannah was not so shy in her response. "Dr. Northrup likes Aunt Primrose." Then she covered her mouth and laughed.

"Well, I should hope he likes me, as I like him." Primrose stood straight and smoothed her apron, then turned toward Aurinda and put her hands on her hips. "And what do ye find so amusing, Miss Aurinda?"

"Nothing, Aunt Primrose."

"Be gone with ya lass, I've work to do." Primrose waved her hand. "Unless ye'd prefer to dress those wounds?"

"Nay. I must do laundry today."

Dr. Northrup interrupted. "Aurinda, I stopped by to ask you if you could spare some time to help me? There are many families in town trying to gather what they can of their belongings. Or what is left of them."

"Of course, Dr. Northrup. I can leave the washin' to soak and work on it tomorrow." He so rarely asked help of her, so she knew he must truly be in need of assistance. She tried not to think about what she might face when she went through the burnt-out homes.

"Thank you for helping, Isaac, Aurinda." Her father's weak voice met her on the way out the door.

"Of course, Father."

Was it just yesterday she'd sat and listened to him tell her about her mother and him? It seemed a lifetime of hurt enveloped in one day of revelations. Discoveries that had upended her beliefs in so many ways continued to haunt her. Yet the truly haunting phrase that played over and over in her mind were his last words: 'Can you forgive me?' Could she?

"You seem deep in thought." She'd almost forgotten Dr. Northrup walked beside her.

"Aye. I am sorry for my silence."

"There is nothing to apologize for. Primrose said your father spoke to you yesterday."

"Aye." She did not wish to talk about it.

"She also said he told you I had wanted to marry your mother before your parents wed."

A volcano of emotion erupted from somewhere deep. "Why did she not? Marry you, that is?"

Dr. Northrup looked at the ground for a moment while they walked. "I would have liked nothing better at the time. But your mother chose the right man."

"The right man?" Aurinda stopped abruptly. "How can you say that?"

His eyes crinkled as he thinned his lips. "Because 'tis true. I was a young and rash man, more caught up in the ways of this world than studying at college. Your mother was wise enough to see my true character. I've changed over time, but your father was the far wiser choice. And he loved Eliza enough to give her a proper home." He put his hands on his hips and gazed at the blue sky.

"But what happened to father to change him so?"

Dr. Northrup removed his hat and rubbed his hand through his hair, hesitating before answering. "Suffice it to say, he saw terrible things happen in battle. Colonists on the frontier savagely brutalized. Women with infants torn from their arms and then ... I cannot say any more." He spun his hat in circles with his fingers. "A soldier with a wife at home, he took it very hard and began drinking. He developed an iron edge to his heart just so he could survive."

Her lips trembled, and she tried to swallow the tears away. "How horrible."

"I'm sorry I told you this, Aurinda." He put his hand on her arm. "I should not have said those things."

"Nay, I do not hold that against you. It helps me understand."

"Let us be on our way." He pushed his hat back on. "I know there are many who could use our help."

They said little on the rest of the journey to town. And though only a few rods in distance had been traversed, it seemed to Aurinda like a world of understanding had been traveled.

～

AURINDA WAS NOT PREPARED for the devastation in the center of Fairfield. Her town appeared unrecognizable, as chimneys rose from the ashes like tombstones in a cemetery. So many homes, once filled with joy and laughter, were now decimated. Dry dirt swirled around the streets, adding an eerie, otherworldly fog of ash and filth. She stared with her mouth agape until she closed it when she began to cough from the dust.

"Here, Aurinda. Take this kerchief, get it wet in that rain barrel, and place it across your mouth and nose."

She did what the doctor instructed.

"I started going through this house over here yesterday to be certain there were no bodies of animals and such." He cleared his throat. "Go ahead and look for valuables you think the owners may wish to recover. You're likely to find them on the floors since the troops did more damage than just burning the houses down."

She nodded while she tied the dampened linen across her face.

Entering through the doorway out of habit—though no doorway was needed, since all the walls had gone to ash— Aurinda searched the floor. *'Twas not enough to break everything, they had to burn it all as well?* Bitterness arose in her breast, and she prayed it would not reside there.

Her eyes watered when she found a rag doll under some books. It had mostly escaped the flames, so she placed it in a pile of things to save. An old family Bible with scorched edges survived. She smiled. *The 'sword of the Spirit' still lives.* Little could be found worth salvaging, although here and there she continued to find items the family would likely treasure.

An unfamiliar item caught her eye when a ray of sunlight reflected off something shiny. She brushed off the ashes and blew away the rest as she picked up the large, heavy piece of glass with a silver backing. A gasp escaped when she saw her reflection, her face covered by the kerchief. She slowly pulled the cloth downward, exposing a perfectly straight nose, luminescent brown eyes, and lips that turned upward at the corners.

Golden ringlets were so abundant, they snuck out of her mobcap every which way. Her smooth cheeks grew pinker the longer she stared, then changed to red as she observed her face contort, and her eyes shed tears. Placing the looking glass down on the floor, she sat in the midst of the ashes and leaned on her clenched hands.

Gentle hands touched her shoulders and lifted her up. Dr. Northrup held her as she wept. "I knew you would discover that large looking glass—I left it here for you to find. And now you know the truth, Aurinda. You dazzle with your beauty, both inward and outward."

29

September 1779

It was Sabbath, and the forge stood cold and still. It was the only day of the week the fires did not burn, and Zadok could call it his own to do as he pleased. In the late afternoon, he strolled to the vacant beach and removed his shoes and stockings. Kneading the sand between his toes, he recalled feeling that sensation years before.

The lulling swish of the waves moving in and out of the Sound soothed his mind with its mesmerizing rhythm. He plopped onto the edge of the shore, enjoying the occasional ripples of water soaking his breeches when the tide rolled to and fro. When he closed his eyes, he imagined he was a lad of eight again, searching for shells, tossing rocks, and racing in and out of the salty water with his brother.

Seagulls cried their mournful tune overhead. Farther up the beach, two of them played tug-o-war with a crab. The winner flew away while its opponent flapped its wings in frustration.

"You'll have to find yer own food."

The loser ignored his loud remark and flew away looking for its own delicacy.

He let the sun bathe his face until the heat began to scorch his skin, feeling more like working the forge than enjoying the day off. Standing upright, he stretched his arms, grabbed his leather shoes and silk stockings, and walked barefoot through the sand back toward his home. He'd enjoy the warm granules as long as he could.

An unfamiliar man approached in the distance. With the war still on, any stranger became a person of suspicion. Since Zadok was in his hometown, he greeted the man first. "Ho there. Where go ye?"

At first, the stranger lowered his brows and backed away a step. After a moment, he grinned and tipped his hat. "Name is Jonas Strickland. At your service, sir."

"And what is your service, sir?"

"I am a fisherman by trade—a fisherman without a boat to work on. That's why I'm here, looking for a vessel. I worked on a whaler in Greenland for a time but decided that was not the life I favored. Any ideas where I could find work?"

While Zadok didn't recognize him, something about his voice seemed familiar. "Have you ever been to New Haven before, Mr. Strickland?"

The man wiped sand off of his hands onto his breeches. "Nay, I hail from Boston but was told there were plenty o' boats in Connecticut."

"Is that so?" Suspicion crept in. Surely word had spread about the destruction in New Haven and Fairfield. "Well, perhaps they meant Wethersfield. Better chances there of finding a fishing vessel. Are you sure you've never been to New Haven before?"

"I'd swear on my mother's grave." The man slapped Zadok's arm, tipped his hat, and made an about-turn. "I'll check out Wethersfield. Not too far from here. Grateful, sir."

He stared after the stranger when he headed back the way he'd come. His clothes were filthy and ill fitting, more suitable to a farmer than fisherman. While most sailors wore pants, the man sported breeches and stockings.

"Zadok!" Mercy ran toward him. Her eyes were wide and her breathing rapid. "Zadok, what were you talking to him about?" She tried to catch her breath.

"He was looking for a job on the boats. I sent him to Wethersfield."

"What?" Mercy shook her head and narrowed her eyes. "What are you talking about? Why would Caleb Beckwith be looking for a boat?"

"Caleb ..." He turned on his heels to look back at the man who'd nearly disappeared out of sight. "He said he was Jonas Strickland and was looking for a boat." Although he'd had an altercation with Caleb Beckwith, he'd still been blind at the time. And the fevered man falling off his gelding before Zadok was blinded looked little like the healthy man who'd engaged him in conversation just now. "That snake!"

"Why do you suppose he's here?" Mercy's face turned ashen, and her chin trembled. "He whispered to me the day he left Fairfield that someday, he would have me—all of me." Her whole body trembled.

"I've no idea why he's back here." Zadok narrowed his eyes and glared at the man in the distance. "But I know one thing. He'd best stay away from you."

Mercy clung to her brother, and he put his arm around her shoulder.

"Do not fear. I'll watch out for you." *God, help me protect her.*

ANOTHER STRANGER on horseback appeared at the forge two days later. *Too many strangers for one week.* Zadok grimaced.

"Goodday, sir. What can I do for you today? Need some shoes for your mount?"

"Nay, I'm looking for someone. Used to be a courier of sorts."

The hair went up on Zadok's neck. "A courier?"

"Aye. Seems he visited here for a bit, according to my sources."

"Your sources?"

"Aye. Military sources."

"You are not in uniform, sir." Zadok folded his arms and stood with his feet apart.

The man pulled out a parchment and showed Zadok. "I've strict instructions from General Washington to detain a man who's been working as a double agent. Goes by the name of Jonas Strickland of late. He's had other aliases as well."

Zadok tilted his head after reading the note. "Would Caleb Beckwith be one of them?"

The rider sat higher in his saddle and tightened the reins. "Might be. Where is he?"

"He was here just before the attack on our town. He actually fled the city with my family until he attempted to toy with my sister's virtue."

The rider leaned forward. "Do you know where he is now?"

"Nay, last I saw him a few days ago on the beach. Said he was looking for a fishing boat, and I told him to try Wethersfield. I didna' recognize the man as I'd had a head injury that took my sight for a time. But my sister came to the beach as he was leaving and identified him."

The rider's brows furrowed. "Your sight seems adequate now."

"'Tis so. The physician who tended me informed me some who have an injury like I had get their sight back. I'm grateful I did, sir."

"Hm." The rider looked toward the beach in the distance.

"Let the militia here know if you see this scoundrel again. They can keep him detained until we can deal with the traitor. Thanks for your information." Without another word, the horseman cantered away from the forge and took off in a gallop when he reached the road.

Zadok stared after him. A traitor? He knew the man to be a cad ... but a traitor? He did know one thing. Mercy would not stray from home until the man was caught. And Zadok would keep his pistol close at his side from now on. This war made him realize something. He would not be able to trust anyone until they proved themselves loyal to the patriot cause.

30

"Remember, Mercy. Stay close to home until that scoundrel's been caught. I'll be at the forge, but I'll check on you at noonday."

"I know, Zadok. Thank you."

"Mother, keep the firelock handy. It's loaded with ball and powder, so you can be ready."

"I shall, Zadok." Sitting in the chair near the window, Mother seemed paler and more fatigued of late. He feared for her health as she'd not been the same since Peter's death.

"Are you well, Mother?" He bent and kissed her briefly.

She smiled tightly. "Well enough, son." She patted his cheek.

"Perhaps you should rest today. Mercy can do the cleaning."

"Perhaps. You needn't fuss over me, Zadok. Your work awaits you."

With regret, he left through the front door and walked out back to the smithy. He had numerous work orders to fill for residents and militia. Knives and bayonets needed sharpening. Broken ax heads needed repair. He pumped the bellows and fired up the coals. Whenever he did so, he thought of Aurinda.

Did she still think of him? Or had her feelings for him died like the coals whose flames had ebbed?

Grateful he could expend his frustration by hammering the iron over the anvil, he imagined he swung blows at Caleb Beckwith. Or was it Jonas Strickland? Whatever his identity, Zadok was more than willing to connect his fist with the man's face and teach him a lesson about respecting women. The fact the man had turned traitor to his country only served to instill more pleasure in the desire to beat him senseless.

When the noonday sun bore straight down on Zadok's forge, he knew it was time to break. He wiped the soot and sweat from his brow and washed his hands in the basin near the front door. Entering the house, Zadok wondered at the quiet. An uneasiness worked its way into his senses.

"Mother?" He looked through her open door and found her resting on her bed. Rather than disturb her, he closed it, then tiptoed down the hallway to Mercy's room.

Her Bible lay on her bed, still open, as though she'd just finished reading it. Tension creased the muscles in his jaw, and his head began to ache, a frequent occurrence since his injury.

While he continued to search, his heart raced. "Mercy?" He couldn't find her anywhere. Returning to his mother's room, he shook her awake. "Mother, where is Mercy?" He made every attempt not to share his panic, but she sat up suddenly when he awoke her.

"Mercy? I know not where she is! Mercy!" Mrs. Wooding screamed for her daughter.

Zadok raced out the front door, licking his dry lips and scanning the horizon. Laundry lay in a heap on the ground, and the huge kettle of water sat over the open fire. She would never leave the fire unattended. *Dear Lord, no!*

He ran to the home of the minister and found the man working in his garden. "Parson Stone, have you seen my sister?"

"Nay, Zadok. What is the matter?" The parson's eyes widened, and he gripped Zadok's arm.

"I fear she has been abducted. Please, we must find her." Zadok's mind raced from one possible scenario to another. Where might he take her? They must gather the men and spread out to search. How long ago had she left? Was she alive? This last question brought the greatest pain.

Word spread quickly, and the town selectman gathered the men. Women showed up, one by one, to stay with Mrs. Wooding. One of their neighbors took over doing the laundry. Everyone wanted to help, especially when they understood the danger Mercy could be in.

The town selectman called in the militia to assist. Zadok explained the rider's visit and how he was looking for Caleb Beckwith, and the soldiers added their numbers to the search. The parson and one other neighbor accompanied Zadok as they headed west through the forest. Other groups of searchers spread out in different directions. The instructions were that anyone who found her should fire their musket into the air.

Zadok searched for any sign of Mercy. A piece of her clothing. A ribbon. Any hint she might have been there. The thought of his sister being taken against her will was too horrible to imagine. He almost would have preferred her going with Caleb Beckwith of her own free will. Yet, he knew that wasn't what happened. He knew Mercy had changed too much, and that knowledge dug the pain even deeper into his belly.

WITH THE DIMMING light of sunset, could Zadok's sister still be alive? He couldn't think of anything else. His energy was spent from searching all day, but he wouldn't give up until she was found. He'd already searched several wooded areas to no avail.

Just as he was about to head back into the woods, he heard the first report of musket fire.

Someone had found her. With renewed vitality, he raced like one possessed and headed straight for his home, where a group of men stood watch over his mother and the women with her. Two of the men carried a limp figure into the house while members of the militia held a squirming Caleb Beckwith.

Zadok didn't stop in his frantic race but lunged at the man, fists flailing, as he screamed curses at the prisoner. It took three soldiers to tear him away from his prey.

"Let me kill him!"

One of the officers held his hands firmly against Zadok's chest. "You'll be first one invited to his hangin'."

Rage soared through his veins. "Kill him now!"

The soldier got in his face. "You will see him die, rest assured."

Zadok stopped screaming and gasped for breath. He swallowed with difficulty then said, "Is my sister alive?"

"Aye, she's inside." The soldier released him.

He pushed the man away and ran inside the house. Neighbors swarmed around his mother, who wept pitifully.

"Where's Mercy?"

The parson's wife touched his arm. "She is in her room. Don't go in there. They've called the doctor."

Zadok sank into a chair and covered his face with soot-covered hands.

The parson came through the door, struggling to catch his breath. Zadok looked up. Mrs. Stone gave her husband a nod, and he stood near Zadok's mother to pray.

For the first time since Mercy had been kidnapped, the depth of pain at what his sister must have endured crushed his heart with unimaginable torment. And he'd not been there to protect her.

Zadok crumpled into a chair and cried bitter tears.

31

The next morning, he overheard some of the neighbors whispering about Mercy being despoiled. He wanted to physically throw them outdoors on their ears. Instead, he walked out of his room and said, with as much self-control as he could, "If you ladies cannot speak in a Christian manner about my sister, perhaps you had best take your leave."

The women's eyes widened, and they turned and hurried out the door without closing it. He stomped to the portal and slammed it shut.

His mother tiptoed down the hall toward the kitchen carrying a basin filled with bloody water. The sight sickened him, and he turned away.

With his back to her, he asked, "Is anyone with Mercy?"

"Aye." She sighed. "The doctor is there."

"What about her friends?" Zadok turned to capture her attention. "Have they all deserted her when she needs them the most?"

His mother looked at her hands as she busily cleaned out the basin. "I'm certain their mothers do not wish their daughters tainted by being in her presence." Both sadness and bitterness mingled in her voice.

Zadok glanced at the ceiling and covered his eyes with his fingers. He abruptly slapped his hands on his thighs and hurried toward his room. Closing the door behind him, he sat at his desk, took out a parchment, and began to write a note. The message said two words: *Please come.* He folded the missive and addressed it to Aurinda Whitney, Fairfield.

Hurrying outdoors, he ran to the home of the post rider and handed it to the young man. "Please, I'll give you an extra shilling if you can get it there today."

The rider looked at the extra coin and grinned. "Very well." He slapped a hat on his head and went to his barn. Within moments, he'd saddled his mare and taken off down the road.

Zadok waved at him and started back toward the house. The sun became intensely bright, and he squinted against it. Rather than going to the forge, he headed indoors.

When he walked into the kitchen, his mother's eyes narrowed. "Zadok? Fare you well?"

Lights had been dancing in front of one eye ever since he'd visited the post rider, and now his head throbbed. "I think I shall lay down." He stumbled toward his room and collapsed on his bed, gripping his head. He vaguely heard his mother bring the doctor into the room. He wished he could make the pain in his head stop. Hammers on an anvil could barely compete with the pummeling in his brain.

The physician forced him to sit up and drink something. He balked at the burning liquid that made him nauseous, but his stomach soon settled. The last thing he remembered was praying his headache would cease.

～

Coolness wrapped around his forehead. Gentle hands wiped against his face, and a calming voice prayed his pain away. It was *her* voice. He struggled to open his eyes, but grogginess won the battle. He reached for her hand. The wrist was small and delicate, the fingers long and gentle. He knew these hands. Did he dare hope? "Aurinda?"

"Aye, 'tis me."

Her voice could cure any pain. With a soothing tenor of devotion, the utterance of the woman he'd come to know when surrounded by the darkness of his blindness evoked healing with her very presence.

His desire to see her triumphed over the oppressive demands of his foggy brain. He willed his eyelids to part. In so doing, he was rewarded with a vision of loveliness that matched the beauty of her heart.

"Aurinda." A single tear escaped his eye when he took in her smooth face, her lips, her golden hair. He reached up to touch the locks that had lived in his memory since childhood and wrapped a finger through one of the curls.

"You may touch them so long as you do not wrap dandelion roots in them." She smirked at the recollection of playing together when they were children.

He struggled to sit up, but she pushed back on his shoulders. "The doctor said you must rest."

Drawing her to him, Zadok met her lips with his own. They were as sweet as he remembered. After a moment, she pushed away, moisture still clinging to her mouth. Aurinda smiled, and his heart yearned for more as he attempted to pull her close again. She shook her head.

"Nay, you must rest."

"I am wide awake now."

"I see 'tis so. But I must bring you some victuals so you can regain your strength."

"Why? I feel quite content here with you. You are my sustenance."

She looked at the quilt on the bed then raised her eyes. "I believe you will wish to get up soon. The court has made their decision."

"And?" His heart jerked into an odd rhythm.

"He will be hung for treason forthwith."

"When?" He sat up, holding onto his head lest the pounding begin again.

"In one hour."

He inhaled and closed his eyes for a moment. "I want you to stay here with my mother."

"Nay." She stood and glared at him. "I'm going with you."

"Have you ever seen a hanging?" He took her hand in his as he stared at her in earnest.

"Aye. Once."

He pondered her decision and could find no reason to deny her. Most of the men and women in the town would attend. "Very well." He pushed up from the bed, and she steadied him. He wrapped his arms around her waist and drew her close. His gratitude for her presence overwhelmed him. "Thank you for coming, Aurinda. I needed you so."

"I could no longer stay away."

THE MILITIA ERECTED the gallows near the meetinghouse before they accompanied Caleb Beckwith to the death arena. When all was readied, the magistrate read the document that declared Caleb guilty of treason, and for this, he would hang until dead.

No mention of plundering an innocent woman?

Anger surged through Aurinda, her blood racing into her ears. She supposed she should be glad he would at least pay the ultimate penalty, but the injustice of the ruling that left out the charge of rape left her cold. Mercy would never be the same. Would justice turn its back on her?

The executioner wrapped a thick rope around the prisoner's neck as he stood on the gallows. The eyes of most of the townspeople were riveted on the condemned man. At the signal from the magistrate, the drop door opened below Caleb Beckwith, and his body dangled, held only by the rope that choked him.

Aurinda looked away. No matter the horrible crimes he'd committed, seeing a man swing from a rope and die a slow and painful death sent chills through her spine.

Zadok stared at the man but placed his arm around her and drew her face against his chest as if to shield her from the dreadful image.

In a matter of moments, death visited the traitor and rapist. The crowd slowly dispersed, and the soldiers took the body down from the gallows.

The corporal who'd arrested Caleb stood in front of Zadok. "There. Justice was served for your sister this day." He saluted Zadok and returned to the militia unit.

Tears streamed down his face. "Justice was served. But nothing can change what happened."

"I know." Aurinda took his arm. "Let us return to your home."

They walked back to the Wooding house. Justice could not remove the pain, only serve to prevent the guilty from repeating the crime. Aurinda prayed it would be comfort enough for Zadok. And for Mercy.

32

Aurinda knocked on Mercy's door as gently as she could. It took a harder rap on the wood to receive a reply.

"Who is it?"

"'Tis Aurinda. May I enter?" She heard no reply.

Zadok stood next to her in the hallway, then motioned her to enter. His earnest expression encouraged her to go in without Mercy's permission.

She closed the door behind her and looked at her friend. Her heart leaped with pain when she saw the girl's bruised face. *How many other bruises does she bear?* Nausea gripped her belly. She tiptoed across the wooden floor and placed a chair by the bed.

"Mercy, you need not speak unless you wish to. I'll just sit here with you, if that is all right."

The seventeen-year-old held her discolored hand against her face while lying on her side. Her eyes moved to and fro as if looking for something but never finding it. Pulling the covers a little higher, Mercy kept looking at the door, then back at the window, then at nothing at all.

Like a lost child.

Aurinda prayed silently for the lass, caught between the joy of budding womanhood and the pain of that flower being abused and ravished. The deflowering never should have taken place, save in the gentlest of ways on her marriage bed by one who loved her.

Instead, her broken spirit was left to survive in the midst of shame. And to face the ridicule of a town that considered her damaged and unworthy of second chances. Not that she'd had a first chance. She alone would face the shame, through the sin of another.

"'Twas my fault."

Had Aurinda heard her correctly? "What?"

Frequent bouts of crying thickened Mercy's voice. "If I'd ne'er encouraged him to feel so free with me, this wouldn't have happened. I am to blame."

"Nay, Mercy." Aurinda took her hand. "You never encouraged him to steal you away, to bruise you and force himself upon you. You never gave him permission to do this."

"God must be so angry with me for my sins." Mercy looked at her for the first time. "And now I must pay. No one will ever look at me again. And you warned me about his character. I thought you were jealous. I should have listened to you." Fresh tears of regret poured out.

She drew the sobbing girl close and held her.

Mrs. Wooding must have heard her daughter's wails, because she came into the room.

"My poor lass." She sat on the other side of the bed and held onto her.

The three women sat together, holding onto each other, and Aurinda didn't know for how long. But the sun's morning rays sifted through the window when Mercy finally closed her eyes in sleep. Mrs. Wooding laid her daughter's head on the pillow and drew the quilt over her shoulders.

The two women tiptoed across the floor and out of the room.

Mrs. Wooding turned toward Aurinda. "I cannot thank you enough for coming—for being a friend to Mercy. She needs that now more than anything."

"I'm grateful I could come, Mrs. Wooding."

"I believe Zadok is waiting for you and has something to ask you. I think he might still be outside. He can be quite patient in his persistence." She smiled.

Aurinda's cheeks grew warm. "I shall see if he's still awake."

She exited the front door and breathed in the cool morning mist. It surrounded the buildings and trees, giving New Haven an otherworldly atmosphere. The fog from the Long Island Sound swirled in a mysterious and frightening way.

Perhaps even a bit romantic, because when she saw Zadok walking toward her, unshaven and his hair in disarray, he had never looked more handsome. She shivered in the chilly air and hugged herself. As he approached her, he unfolded her arms and embraced her with his.

"I thought you'd never finish."

"Did you want me to leave her before she slept?"

"Nay." He kissed her cheek. "I was willing to wait." He kissed her other cheek, more tenderly this time.

"Wait for what?"

"For your answer." He kissed her on the lips.

"To what, pray tell?" Her heart fluttered.

He stopped kissing her and held her face close to his. "Will you be my wife?"

How many times had she longed for this moment—to be held by him, to be loved by him ... to feel worthy of him?

"Aye, Zadok Wooding. I shall be your wife, and gladly so."

He kissed her with such passion her knees buckled.

She pushed him away. "But only ..."

"Only what?" His eyes narrowed, and his moist lips tempted her.

"Only if you promise to place *clean* flowers in my hair from now on."

"I promise." He grinned.

This is how love should be. She reveled in his tender embrace and prayed it would feel this joyful forever. And that someday, Mercy would know true love where a couple shared both passion and respect.

33

Aurinda awoke to a loud rapping on the door of the Wooding home. She heard Zadok answer and then another male voice speaking.

Mrs. Wooding slept next to her in the larger bedroom. Aurinda sat up slowly so Zadok's mother could rest longer. Wrapping herself in a shawl, she stood quietly and tiptoed to the door. When the hinge creaked a little, she held her breath until she stood in the hallway and the door had been closed behind her.

"A message for you from your aunt." Zadok strode toward her.

He handed the missive to her, but she hesitated to open it.

"Why do you not open it?" He tilted his head while furrowing his brows.

"Because I … I fear something is wrong." Ignoring the letter would not change the contents of it. It would be either a positive message or a difficult one. Aunt Primrose would not pay for a post rider without good reason.

Unfolding the parchment, she read:

Dear Aurinda,

Yer father has turned for the worse. Please come home as soon as ye can.

Yer beloved aunt,
Primrose

She released the note and let it drop to the floor while she sat hard upon a wooden chair. "'Tis from Primrose. I need to return home." She stared up at Zadok. "Father is quite ill." Her lips quivered. "I never told him I forgive him. I must get home before 'tis too late."

Zadok pulled her up into his arms. "We shall find a way to get you back to Fairfield." He drew away from her and captured her gaze. "I cannot leave Mother and Mercy. Let me see what I can arrange." He kissed her forehead and helped her back to her chair. "I'll awaken Mother and have her fix you breakfast. Then I'll go find transport for you."

AFTER SPEAKING WITH HIS MOTHER, Zadok left for the post rider's home. Unfortunately, the man was out on another delivery and not expected home any time soon. Zadok stood in the middle of the road, unable to think clearly.

The parson approached him. "Zadok, how do ye fare? Ye look troubled."

"Aye." He rubbed his eyes then opened them wide. "Aurinda needs to return home. Her father has taken a turn, and she needs to speak with him before 'tis too late. I'd send her with the post rider who brought her here, but he is gone."

"Come with me. I have a plan." The parson motioned for Zadok to follow him.

For such an older man, the parson could move quickly when necessary. Zadok had to speed his steps to keep up with him.

"Where are we going?" It was difficult to get the parson's attention when he moved with such determination.

"The fort."

"The fort? Why?" Zadok's breathing quickened with his pace.

The parson's jaw set firmly, but he glanced at his companion before speaking. "Ye may not know this, Zadok, but for quite some time, Mercy has made it her mission to encourage the militia by bringing bread to the fort once a week. She wanted to thank them for their protection of New Haven." He coughed then cleared his throat.

"One of the men, a Private Levi Parlee, took quite a fancy to Mercy and was quite disturbed when she seemed smitten by her notorious attacker. When he heard Mercy had been abducted by the man, he took it quite hard. He was first to volunteer to try to find her and happened to be with the men who did. He carried her back to your home."

Zadok paused in their trek. Shaking his head, he narrowed his eyes. "I am all astonishment, Parson. Why did I not know of this?"

He placed his hand on Zadok's shoulder. "Ye were consumed with work and supporting your family, I imagine. 'Twould not be the first time a man was unaware of the goings on under his own roof." He winked at Zadok.

"But ... what does all this have to do with getting Aurinda home?"

"We can speak to Levi's superior officer and explain the situation. It might be a mission that would benefit both Levi and Aurinda."

Zadok frowned. "Are you sure this Levi fellow is trustworthy?"

"I'd stake my life on it."

34

After meeting with the officer commanding the fort, Zadok returned home. The meeting had gone well, with assurances Private Parlee would be there within the hour to accompany Aurinda to Fairfield. She and Mercy were in the bedroom when Zadok knocked on the door and announced the plan. Aurinda wrinkled her brow and pulled on a curl hanging down her shoulder.

"Zadok, are you certain the man is trustworthy?"

"I know Private Parlee." Mercy grabbed her hand. "He is a good man, and I know you can trust him. He helped rescue me." At the mention of the abduction, Mercy's lips quivered, and she turned her head and buried her face in her pillow.

"'Twill be all right, Mercy." Aurinda squeezed her shoulder. "You are safe now." She bit her lip and looked at Zadok.

He stood tall and placed his hands on his hips. "I'll look after her. So will Mother. But please, come back to us soon."

"I shall." Aurinda leaned over and kissed Mercy's hair. "I will come back, Mercy. I promise." She arose from sitting on the side of Mercy's bed and hurried out the door.

Z<small>ADOK WENT TO THE KITCHEN</small>, where Private Parlee drank coffee and spoke with Mother. They seemed to be old friends. He nodded at the soldier. "I wish to thank you personally for finding my sister. I shall forever be in your debt, sir."

Appearing youthful, Private Parlee bore the maturity of a seasoned soldier. He stood tall and saluted Zadok and visibly swallowed. "I only wish I could have found her sooner, sir."

Zadok tipped his head in agreement then turned toward Aurinda, who walked into the room carrying her travel bag. "This is my intended, Miss Aurinda Whitney of Fairfield. Her father was injured in the attack on that town and has taken an ill turn. She is required at her home forthwith."

"Understood, sir. Miss Whitney, 'tis my pleasure to see you safely to Fairfield."

"I am grateful to you, sir."

"I'll help you onto his horse." Zadok held onto her arm as he escorted her toward the mare.

His mother kissed Aurinda farewell and returned to Mercy's room.

After escorting Aurinda outdoors, Zadok held her close. "It seems I finally have you safe in my arms, and then I must let you go again." He struggled to smile.

"Aye. But I shall return to you. Of that, you can be certain."

He only intended to kiss her briefly, but her hungry lips drew him into a lingering embrace.

"I must go." She pulled away.

Private Parlee assisted her so she could sit behind him on the saddle. She glanced back at Zadok one more time, then faced the road to Fairfield.

He prayed God would give her the strength to face whatever lay ahead.

~

THE SPEED and stamina of Private Parlee's mount impressed Aurinda. The strength of the gelding that had carried her and Zadok to New Haven weeks ago paled in comparison. Because of the danger of enemy troops who might be on the main road, they still used the old trail from New Haven to Fairfield. The soldier seemed an expert in navigating its uneven path.

Several miles had sped by when he slowed the mare and dismounted. "Time for water for all of us. Have a seat on this boulder, miss, and I'll bring you a canteen."

His formal military training made even the simplest of tasks performed with expertise. After ensuring her thirst was satiated, he excused himself to find water for the mare. Aurinda observed his vigilant demeanor as he searched the woods for any sign of trouble. She put aside her concerns about her welfare. He was a professional soldier whom she could trust.

After returning from the stream with a hatful of water, he stroked the side of the mare's head and held the water-filled vessel in front of her. She guzzled down the liquid offering. He then returned to Aurinda's side and found another boulder to sit upon.

Her curiosity piqued. "Private Parlee, you are friends with Miss Wooding, I understand."

"I suppose we are friends." He tapped his hat with his fingers. "In truth, we've not spent more than a few words of conversation together. Mostly, 'Thank you for the bread. 'Twas most kind.'"

She thought his complexion grew redder. There seemed to be something he was not saying.

"Have … have you set your eyes upon Miss Wooding?" It was a bold question, under the circumstances.

"Miss Wooding preferred another, Miss Whitney." He turned

quite ruddy and cleared his throat. "She didna' care to speak with me."

"Yet, she told me I could trust you to see me safely to Fairfield."

He picked up a stick and chased a bug on the ground without speaking. Finally, he looked up. "I'll be forthright with ya, Miss Whitney. I wanted to see her and nearly asked her to a dance at the fort. Then I discovered she cared for that courier—that blaggart." His jaw contorted.

"I never did trust the man. She changed when she befriended him. Wasn't so kind. I knew I didna' have a chance with her." He sniffed. "And now ... Now she is so hurt. I saw her when he was through with her, and somethin' in me grew dark. I wanted to tear his heart out." He stood and wandered several feet from her.

The trembling of his shoulders made Aurinda ache. She gathered her gown, strode toward him, and touched his arm. "Mercy will need friends to help her through this terrible time. Friends who understand her and will not judge her for what has happened."

He swiped moisture from his chin. "Aye."

"You are a fine man, Private Parlee. A man any woman would be proud to call friend."

"Thank you, miss." He glanced up at the sunlight streaming through the trees. "We'd best be on our way."

"Aye."

When she settled on the saddle behind him, he turned toward her. "I am sorry about your father, Miss Wooding."

"Thank you, Private. I am sorry as well." *Sorry for so many things.*

He kicked the mare just enough to start her back on the trail toward Fairfield and the journey to her father's deathbed.

35

A hazy dusk with scorching temperatures stole the breath from both man and beast, extending a dubious welcome to Aurinda and Private Parlee when they arrived at the Whitney farm.

Aunt Primrose ran outside to greet them on this unseasonably hot September evening.

Aurinda slipped down from the horse and grabbed her aunt's forearms. "Am I too late?"

"Nay, but ye'd best come inside." Primrose turned toward the rider. "Bed ye mare down in the barn and come in for victuals."

He tipped his hat at her and led the horse toward the barn. The mare picked up her pace, likely anticipating rest and water.

Steeling herself to face her father, Aurinda clenched her gown when she saw his thinner, weaker form. Guilt filled her thoughts, regretting that she hadn't settled this unanswered question long ago. She knew forgiveness was not just an option in God's eyes, but a command. Why had she ignored that duty for too long, nearly allowing her father to enter eternity thinking she hated him?

"Father." She rushed to his bedside, and his delight at her

greeting increased her guilt. Had it been that hard to say she apologized for holding a grudge against him? To say she forgave him? Was it that hard even now? She inhaled a dose of courage. "Father, please forgive me for not loving you—for bearing ill toward you."

"Oh, daughter." His rheumy eyes reddened even more. "'Tis I who needs forgiveness. Please, can you forgive the terrible way I've treated you?"

She did not expect him to weep, but cry he did. It seemed there was a tear for every wicked insult he'd inflicted upon her through the years. The bed became soaked with his regret.

"Aye, Father. I do forgive you." Her tears now added to the pool of remorse that covered the quilts. The blankets were baptized with their mutual repentance. She lay her head on his chest but could hear the painful rasps of his breathing. Pulling her head upward, she sought Dr. Northrup.

He looked at her, then glanced downward without smiling. His expression informed her there was little hope Father would survive.

The door opened, and Private Parlee stepped inside. "Excuse me. I should have knocked first."

"Nay, nay, I told ye to come on in." Aunt Primrose stood. "Sit yerself down, Private ..."

"Parlee, ma'am. Private Levi Parlee, at your service." He nodded.

"Well, Private Parlee, ye are a welcome sight, bringing our lass home. Thank ye."

"My pleasure, ma'am." He looked around the room, and his eyes settled on the patient. "Oh, I am sorry, sir. I heard you were not well. Forgive my intrusion."

Her father's weak voice still carried enough strength to express his gratitude. "You have brought me my daughter, Private. I cannot thank you enough."

A raucous cough began, and Dr. Northrup went to his

friend's side to help him sit higher in the bed. "Let me get you more laudanum, Abijah."

"Nay, not yet, Isaac. Give me more time to visit with Aurinda. You know that wretched medicinal makes me sleepy."

"You do need rest." The doctor handed him a tankard with a drink inside.

"I'll have plenty of time to rest when I'm restin' in peace, Isaac."

Her father turned toward Aurinda. She took his hand and held it, amazed at how effortless and comfortable it seemed. A genuine smile curved her lips upward. She could not remember if she'd ever looked at him with tenderness before.

"You are so much like your mother. Your hair, your eyes, even that smile. And your heart—so full of love it seems to spread to everyone around you. That's how she was." His face glowed with joy.

Aurinda smiled through her tears. "I wish I'd known her."

"I miss her so much." Abijah's eyes darkened. "My comfort is I shall see her again soon." He looked up to the ceiling as though searching for her even now. "I know I shall see her because … I've asked God to forgive me for the wretched man I was. And I pray I'll ne'er be that man again."

"Father?"

"Aye?"

"I wish to tell you something." She leaned closer and whispered, "I'm to be married."

"I'm so happy for you, Aurinda. So happy." The painful coughing began again.

Dr. Northrup hurried over with a vial of laudanum and helped prop him up so he could drink. "Here, friend. Please take this."

Her father drank it down quickly, then winced at the taste. "Foul drink for the dyin'."

His breathing slowed, and he soon snored.

"He'll rest now. You should as well, Aurinda."

Glancing at Dr. Northrup, she looked back at the man whose time on this earth was nearing an end. "Nay, Dr. Northrup. I'll stay here."

She took her father's limp hand and held it to her lips, resting her cheek on his fingers. They were hands that never held her with affection all these many years. Yet in these last moments of his life, the warmth and connection with him could suffice for a lifetime. God's grace was sufficient for her.

When Aurinda woke the next morning, her father's eyes viewed heaven. She kissed his blue-tinged fingers. "I love you, Father."

Dr. Northrup stirred and, seeing Aurinda weeping quietly, hurried over and felt her father's pulse. "He's gone. But I guess you surmised that."

Numbness gripped her. She nodded and stood from the chair at Father's bedside. Wiping away the tears, she walked out to the barn, where Private Parlee lay asleep. The mare stomped her feet, ready for another day of travel.

Aurinda stroked the horse's flanks, admiring the shiny black coat. "You'll have to let your rider sleep a bit longer."

As she ambled toward the barn door, Aurinda watched the bits of hay and straw flutter through the air in the stream of sunlight. The dust from the fodder seemed to be everywhere, only visible in that ray of illumination. *Much like love—hidden until God's light reveals it.*

Oblivious to where she walked, she soon found herself at the edge of her lake. A mother duck swam by, surrounded by numerous other ducks nearly as large as herself. They all glided smoothly, confident of their journey and capable of foraging in the soil and water.

These were no longer frantic ducklings racing to follow their parent. They'd all outgrown the need for protection and direction. It was time for each of them to find their own mate and raise ducklings of their own.

An earnest desire to be with Zadok nearly overwhelmed her. She longed to feel the comfort of his arms, the tenderness of his kisses, the hint of the passion that promised even more on their wedding night.

"I love you, Zadok." She whispered the words into the breeze and prayed it would carry to his heart.

36

Private Parlee offered to wait for Aurinda until after her father's burial. That way he could accompany her back to New Haven.

"Nay, Private, but I am so grateful for your offer. With my father gone, I have unfinished business here I must attend to." She handed him a letter. "But if you would be so kind as to give this letter to Zadok, I would be most grateful."

Private Parlee stood at attention. "'Twould be my honor to deliver it, miss." He doffed his hat and mounted his horse.

"Private Parlee."

He held the reins fast.

"Please remember what I said about Mercy." She walked toward the mare. "She is in great need of friends."

"I shall remember." He nodded. "Fare thee well, Miss Wooding."

"Godspeed."

THE HOUSE SEEMED vacant with father gone. Yet new life now filled the corners of Aurinda's home with the presence of Aunt Primrose and the orphan, Hannah. And Dr. Northrup's visits did not lessen with Abijah Whitney's death. In fact, they seemed to increase.

"Aunt Primrose, you and Dr. Northrup have become good friends, have you not?" Aurinda worked with great difficulty to refrain from giggling, since she'd seen them behind the barn kissing the previous evening.

"Aye." Her aunt focused far too closely on her sewing as her cheeks bloomed red. "And yer meaning is what, Miss Aurinda? I told ye Isaac and I were close ... long ago."

"My meaning is this." She turned another page in her book. "You know I shall soon marry Zadok and be moving to New Haven. So, I would like to suggest a business proposal." She pretended to read.

"Business proposal?" Primrose stopped her sewing and wrinkled her nose at Aurinda. "What do ye mean?"

"Well, I cannot keep this farm going and live in New Haven. So, my proposal is this. You, Hannah ... and Dr. Northrup ... take over this farm and move in permanently."

Primrose gasped as her hand flew to her chest. "Miss Aurinda! Have ye lost yer senses, lass? The doctor and I ... living together? Such a scandal!"

"Well, 'twould not be a scandal if you were married to each other." Aurinda continued to feign reading her book while her aunt stared with her mouth agape.

"Well, Aurinda, you've managed to accomplish something I've ne'er been able to do. You made your Aunt Primrose unable to speak a word." Dr. Northrup had just arrived. His boyish grin beamed with mischief.

"Ye heard? I am so embarrassed." Primrose covered her mouth and turned red as a ripe apple. "Please do no' listen to my niece. She is full of fanciful thinking since she's fallen in love herself."

The doctor lowered his head, enjoying a laugh to himself. He walked over to Primrose and placed a hand on her shoulder. "Well, why should the young ones have all the fun? We could indeed get married. After all, Hannah needs a home. And I would not mind having someone warm to share my bed with in the winter."

Primrose dropped her sewing on the table and crossed her arms tightly over her breasts. Pushing away from the tableboard with her feet, she stood and raced outside. Dr. Northrup followed her.

As Aurinda and Hannah moved quickly to stand near the doorway and watch, they both tried to stifle their giggles, to no avail.

Kneeling in front of Aunt Primrose, Dr. Northrup took her hands. Primrose's hand went to her mouth, and she nodded vigorously. Then, the doctor stood and kissed her.

Aurinda grinned. Her plan had worked.

A WEEK LATER, the wedding took place in Aurinda's cabin that she gifted to the newly married couple. Aunt Primrose appeared ten years younger when she took her wedding vows and promised to love and cherish Dr. Northrup.

Hannah clung to Primrose's hand. The poor child must be so unsure what these new changes meant. At least she clung to the one person who'd been with her through all the difficulties. Aurinda prayed the orphan's life would be filled with love and stability from now on.

Aurinda offered to stay a few days after their wedding so the couple could have time together while she and Hannah slept in the barn. Dr. Northrup said he appreciated the offer.

Although anxious to return to Zadok in New Haven, she also knew her time in Fairfield would soon be relegated to occasional visits. It was bittersweet in some ways, yet sweeter at the thought of sharing her life with Zadok.

Dr. Northrup had promised to accompany Aurinda back to New Haven when she was ready.

Within a few days, her thoughts dwelt more on New Haven than Fairfield. As she washed the evening dishes, she wondered how Mercy fared. And Mrs. Wooding. And most of all, Zadok. Did he know how much she missed him?

Lord, I pray he will understand the depth of my love for him. And that I will be a wife who can make him happy and do him good all the days of my life.

When the lingering days ensued with few messages from her future husband, she worried all might not be well. Seven days after the wedding of Aunt Primrose and the doctor, she knew the time had come to return. If things were not going well in New Haven, Aurinda wanted to be there for Zadok.

37

The exhausting ride from Fairfield to New Haven never ended. At least it seemed that way.

The closer Aurinda and Dr. Northrup came to their destination, the more concerned she became. Her thoughts imagined every doomed scenario, including the most dreaded of possibilities—that Zadok no longer loved her. Fortunately, that fear quickly disappeared when he greeted her. His welcoming kiss and tight embrace reassured her his love remained steadfast and sure.

Dr. Northrup cleared his throat, reminding them they were not alone.

"Please forgive us, Dr. Northrup." Her cheeks burned with heat. She smoothed her gown and readjusted her sunbonnet, which had been knocked askew.

The grin of the newly married doctor provided sufficient pardon.

After tying the horse's reins to the metal post, Zadok led them both inside. Mrs. Wooding seemed paler than usual, if that were possible.

"Mrs. Wooding, how fare you? And Mercy?"

Instead of replying, she covered her trembling mouth and escaped to her room.

Aurinda's mouth dropped open. "Zadok, what has happened?"

His shoulders sagged. "Please, do sit, and I'll get you both refreshment."

Both Aurinda and the doctor drew chairs toward the tableboard and waited while Zadok filled two tankards with cider from the hogshead. As he placed them in front of the weary travelers, some of the cider splashed over the side of the tankards with the tremble of his hands. He grabbed a cloth from nearby and wiped the spilled cider before he sat next to Aurinda. He appeared at least two days unshaven.

With one of his hands resting on her arm, he held the other against his forehead. Finally, he spoke. "The worst has happened."

Aurinda gripped the side of the wooden table. "Your father?"

"Nay, that would indeed be the worst." He took a deep breath. "'Tis Mercy." He hesitated and seemed to search for words. Finally, he blurted out. "Perhaps ... perhaps Dr. Northrup might examine her."

The doctor gave a knowing nod then upended his tankard. Placing it empty on the table, he grew sober. "I must have your mother's permission, of course."

"Aye." Zadok went to her room and returned in a few moments.

A calmer Mrs. Wooding joined them in the kitchen with her gaze lowered. "I must apologize for my rudeness. 'Twas most inhospitable of me."

Aurinda stood and gathered the woman in her arms. "You have been a tower of strength after enduring so much, Mrs. Wooding. No one thinks ill of you when you need to be alone." She kissed the top of the woman's mobcap.

"Thank you, Aurinda." Her voice was strained. "Dr.

Northrup, I am relieved you have accompanied Aurinda here. May I speak with you in private before you examine Mercy?"

Dr. Northrup stretched before accompanying Mrs. Wooding outside.

"Zadok, what has happened?"

He shook his head.

"I have something of import I'd like to share with you." Aurinda placed her hand on his arm. "About Private Parlee."

"Private Parlee? He narrowed his eyebrows and shook his head. "Of what do you speak?"

"The private is someone who cares for her." She told him the story the soldier shared with her on their journey. "Perhaps he would befriend her if she'd give him a chance."

Zadok sat with a thud, placed his elbows on the table, and covered his eyes with both hands. He shook his head back and forth.

"Nay?" Aurinda's hopes dashed. "Why not?"

"Because Private Parlee would not wish to befriend her now." He swiped his face with one hand, and redness crept up his neck.

Swallowing became difficult, but she managed and lowered her voice to a whisper. "Why ever not?"

"Is it not obvious, Aurinda?" He took both of her hands in his. "My sister is with child. No one will want a tainted woman with a fatherless infant—especially when the baby is from the loins of a man hung for treason." He closed his eyes tightly. "Not even a lad so noble as Private Parlee."

Aurinda moved to stand behind Zadok and placed her arms around him. She kissed his hair and held him close.

Neither spoke. What could they say? She knew Zadok was right. In a situation already out of their hands, it had gone one step farther toward desperation. Only God held the answer, and Aurinda prayed He would show them the way.

~

DR. NORTHRUP WALKED with heavy steps back into the kitchen and sighed. He sat on a chair that Aurinda offered him.

"Well?" Zadok could not stand the silence.

The physician swallowed the ale he'd been offered, and he wiped his face with the other hand. "I think you know the answer. Aye, she is with child." He shook his head slowly. "The scoundrel. The blaggart. The …"

"We understand, Dr. Northrup." Zadok interrupted his oratory, lest the doctor's words grow more offensive. "And we agree."

"The question now is, what's to be done? You and your family must decide, since this is a burden you all must bear." The doctor's gaze captured Zadok's attention.

"What's to be done? What do you mean?" Zadok stared back.

"I mean, there are things that can be administered by certain midwives. Things that can change the situation."

Aurinda's jaw dropped open. "You mean to destroy the child? Dr. Northrup, what an appalling suggestion."

"You may deem this a horrific solution, yet I've seen infants conceived by force and then abandoned by their mothers. Is that any less appalling?"

"That will not happen, Dr. Northrup." Zadok resisted raising his voice. "We would never allow Mercy's baby to be left unwanted and uncared for."

"Despite the conduct of its father?" Dr. Northrup's voice rose in intensity.

"Did the child sin, Dr. Northrup?" Aurinda interrupted. "Must an innocent baby suffer for his parent's transgression? I cannot fathom such cruelty to a helpless child."

Zadok thought she would burst into tears.

A look of defeat crossed the doctor's countenance. "I only offer this information to let you know what you all face."

"You mean what I face." No one had heard Mercy slip into the kitchen from her room. "You all act as if this is your affliction. This child is my baby, not a burden. Despite how this little one began its existence, this wee one must be given a chance."

Aurinda hurried toward Zadok's sister and wrapped her arms around her. "Mercy, no one wishes to harm your child. And we are here to help if you need us. Please, let us know how we can."

"I've had much time to dwell on this." Mercy's eyes riveted upon her. "And I may give this child to someone who can love it, despite its father's sin." Mercy took her hand. "Aurinda, can you and Zadok raise it as your own?"

His bride-to-be tugged on one of the curls that had escaped her mobcap. "Zadok and me?"

Zadok searched Aurinda's face to discern her heart in the matter. He saw hope, but most of all, love. He knew immediately she would love the child as her own. But could he? Only God could help him look past the transgression of the father to see a child of Mercy's who needed love and care.

The whole room anticipated his verdict. He inhaled a deep and uncertain breath. "Aye, we can raise the child as our own."

"Thank you, my love." Aurinda ran to him and threw her arms around him.

Mercy joined the couple, and the threesome embraced.

Weariness prevented Zadok from dwelling on his fears for long. Too much work needed to be done to prepare for the child —and for their wedding. He hugged Aurinda and rejoiced at the thought of marrying her. That was the one commitment for which he carried no doubts.

38

Late September, 1779

The officer in charge of the militia offered the fort as the site for Aurinda and Zadok's wedding. With so many residents of New Haven gathering in one location, it seemed safer for the town if guards stood watch around the stockade. Word might have spread that the militia in New Haven had hung a traitor, and the Regulars would not be pleased about losing one of their spies.

Although Aurinda preferred the more intimate setting of the Wooding home, excitement filled her spirit at the prospect of music and dancing. It had been some time since revelry had been a part of their lives. What could be more reason to celebrate than the union of a man and woman? She shivered with anticipation.

Mrs. Wooding had offered to allow the bride to wear one of the gowns from her formal collection. "I no longer fit in it, Aurinda, and you shall be dazzling in this silk brocade."

"Thank you, Mrs. Wooding."

"If you like, since your mother is no longer alive, you may call me 'Mother'—unless that is asking too much."

Aurinda contemplated the suggestion. "How about Mother Wooding?"

"That sounds lovely." Her future mother-in-law grinned.

Mother Wooding and Mercy helped her dress for the wedding. They had been set up in the Army officer's bedchamber, which had been vacated for the bride and groom's wedding night. Aurinda nervously glanced at the officer's bed, which seemed entirely too small to accommodate two people.

The ladies brought out the voluminous wedding dress, and Aurinda gasped. She'd never worn such finery before. Mother Wooding and Mercy helped tighten her stays before assisting her in adjusting the layers of petticoat and gown then slipping on the matching shoes.

They were a bit tight, but Aurinda decided if her feet hurt too much, she would dance barefoot. Mercy helped style her hair, curling her ringlets and uplifting some of the strands to form a crown of tresses on top.

When the ladies brought out the looking glass from the closet in the officer's bedchamber, Mercy and Mother Wooding held it up for Aurinda to see. All she could do was stare. It did not seem possible it reflected her true image. The unfamiliar woman who stared back at her was far too refined and delicate to be herself.

Yet when she raised her hand to touch her hair, the image did the same. Tilting her head produced the duplicate action in the woman in the mirror. When she smiled, her heart warmed with the realization Zadok would see this woman on their wedding day, rather than the uncomely image she had carried in her mind for so many years.

There was a knock on the door, and Mercy answered it. Private Parlee. He looked at the floor and tugged at the cravat around his neck. He then lifted his eyes upward and seemed mesmerized by Zadok's sister.

"The parson is here and ready for the ceremony." He paused. "You look lovely, Miss Wooding."

Mercy glanced at her mother before replying, "Thank you, Private Parlee." She grew bolder and met the man's eyes with hers. "I never had an opportunity to thank you for rescuing me. I am most grateful."

"'Twas nothing, miss." The private fumbled with his buttons on his coat. His now-reddened face contrasted with his dark hair, which was pulled back neatly into a queue.

"'Twas everything to me, Private Parlee. Thank you."

He bowed awkwardly and left.

Mercy closed the door softly. Her eyes moistened, and she sniffed. Sucking in a deep breath, she said, "Well then, let us finish getting the bride ready."

Grasping Mercy's hand, Aurinda squeezed it. She took in several breaths, hoping they would give her courage to face her future husband in front of the large crowd. *Lord, calm me.*

While a violinist played a soft melody, Mother Wooding and Mercy entered the ceremony room first. Dr. Northrup met Aurinda outside the chamber doorway and gave her his arm. She searched for Zadok across the room, and when the crowd moved aside for her, there he stood.

Her heart thrilled at the sight of him, so handsome in a blue wool waistcoat, matching coat borrowed from Dr. Northrup, and leather breeches. His new linen shirt, accented with a white silk cravat at his neck, was a gift from his mother. Moisture crept onto her forehead. Soon the man in front of her would be her husband, and they would never have to part from one another again.

When she drew near him and he took her hand from the doctor's, the trembling in his fingers encouraged her to steady them with her own. His gaze captured her, and her breath caught in her throat as the parson spoke the words that would join them together to love one another 'til death would they part.

Death was the farthest thing from Aurinda's mind this day. This day celebrated life and the hope for a future of love and happiness. She wanted nothing more than to share that love with the man standing next to her.

She got lost in the words as their vows were spoken. When Zadok's soft lips caressed hers, she realized he'd been given permission to kiss the bride. She was now Mrs. Zadok Wooding.

The militia in attendance shouted "Huzzah!" and the crowd of friends repeated the sentiment while the fiddlers began a lively reel.

Zadok stared at her, and she blushed at the look in his eyes. "Would you care to dance with me?"

"Aye, Mr. Wooding, I would."

"Thank you, Mrs. Wooding."

Aurinda turned to look for his mother, then realized he called her by her married name. She covered her mouth and giggled before he swept her onto the dance floor. Surprised that a blacksmith could be so adept at twirling her to music, she grinned when he proved he had the dancing skills he'd learned in school.

A delightful dizziness overwhelmed her with joy. Too soon, the first song ceased, but then a slower tune took its place. She was so caught up in the enjoyment, she almost didn't realize her dance partner had abruptly changed.

"Congratulations, Mrs. Wooding. You have a husband to be proud of, and he, a wife to be enraptured by her beauty."

Her eyes widened, and she paused in her dancing. "Major Talmadge!"

"At your service, ma'am." He bowed before her in a gallant manner, then swept her back onto the dance floor.

"But ... why? How?"

"We have our sources." He winked. "General Washington wished me to express his congratulations to you on this joyful occasion. He was most grateful for the information you delivered to me some weeks ago."

"But ... the courier ... we were told he also worked for the enemy." She blinked several times and tilted her head.

"Aye, 'tis true. And 'twas the letter you delivered to us that verified that fact so that we could use that betrayal to our advantage." The major grinned.

Her stomach fluttered. "The missive I brought was that important?" She found it difficult to inhale deeply. Perhaps her stays were too tight.

"Aye. 'Twas quite important. We wanted to be sure you were paid for your efforts."

"Paid?" Her thoughts blurred. "Paid—for being a patriot?"

"Aye. Spying is dangerous business, and all our good ones are paid generously. If that is acceptable, of course."

"Well, I suppose you must ask my husband."

He leaned toward her ear. "I already have, and we gave him the coinage."

Aurinda nearly burst out in laughter. This was a most unexpected visitor with an equally unexpected gift. "I am most grateful, Major Talmadge."

"No need to thank me. You earned it." He whispered near her ear. "And if you ever wish to join in transporting messages in future, just send us word. You've already proven your skills."

Aurinda's eyes widened. She considered her new life as a wife and soon-to-be mother to Mercy's child. Not to mention the children she hoped to bear for Zadok. "I am quite flattered by your invitation, Major Talmadge. But at the moment, I have other responsibilities." She glanced at her husband briefly before her dance partner swirled her away from him.

Major Talmadge leaned close again. "Your husband is a fortunate man, Mrs. Wooding."

"'Tis I who am the fortunate one."

The reel finished, and Zadok came directly to her. "I believe this dance is mine, Major." The officer bowed from his waist and stepped back.

Once again, Aurinda was swept onto the dance floor by the man who held her heart. "Are you pleased with me, Zadok?"

His Adam's apple rolled when he swallowed. "I've ne'er been happier, Aurinda. I do not deserve you."

"I love you so much, Zadok." So much she could have kissed him at that very moment.

"I'm glad we need not travel far to our bedchamber tonight." His whisper near her ear elicited weakness in her knees. Her face burned with heat.

"You make me blush." She grinned and avoided looking him in the eye.

Wrapping both arms around her waist, he kissed her with a tenderness that sent tingles down to her toes. "That is just the first of many more this night."

"I cannot wait."

39

Two Months Later
November 1779

Sun streamed through their bedroom window as Aurinda heard her husband hammering outside in the smithy. Turning toward his empty pillow, she pulled its softness toward her and inhaled his scent. She would never tire of his presence.

Aurinda pushed up from the bed, wishing they could spend all day with each other. She knew that wouldn't be possible, no matter how much they desired it. She stretched out her arms and slipped a gown over her shift. Pulling her mass of curls into one bundle, she twisted it into submission and knotted it on top of her head with a wooden hairpin.

When she exited the bedroom, she found Mother Wooding standing by the hearth, stirring the gruel. Lines had furrowed more deeply into her mother-in-law's forehead of late.

"Forgive my sleeping in, Mother Wooding. Let me stir that for you."

"Thank you, Aurinda. 'Tis a pleasure to have your company during these dark days."

"In many ways, they are dark. Yet there will soon be new life in this home, however somber the circumstances. Your first grandchild. What pleasure you shall have holding the wee one, watching it grow, singing lullabies. After the babe is born, perhaps we can all put aside our hurt as we realize there is hope with a new life ... and so much love to be shared." Aurinda kissed her on the cheek.

"You are a blessing to this home, to be sure, Aurinda Wooding. You cast light into the shadows of despair. Not to mention the glint of light in your husband's eye." She winked at her.

Although Aurinda's cheeks burned with heat, she could not help but laugh.

The leaves on the maples had started turning to golds and reds more than a month ago, and the brilliance of the foliage on this November morning drew her to look outside. The image that filled every pane of the large window reminded her of the beauty of the Creator, Who designed the pallet of colors she beheld. It never grew old.

Mercy came down the hall toward the kitchen. "There's a chill in the air this morning."

"Aye. Come sit and have your gruel." Aurinda moved a cup that Zadok left on the table every morning.

Her sister-in-law winced and rubbed her lower back. "I ache this morning."

"Aye. 'Twill be a bigger problem as time goes on." Mother Wooding gave a knowing nod while wiping the tableboard clean. A knock sounded on the door. "Were we expecting anyone?"

Mercy and Aurinda shook their heads no.

Mother Wooding went to answer and opened the door just a few inches. "Praise be the good Lord!" She opened the door wider, revealing Private Levi Parlee holding a large buck across his shoulders.

"I thought you ladies could use some venison before the cold sets in." Private Parlee grinned like a schoolboy. "I know Zadok is likely too busy in the smithy to hunt."

The two young women squealed with delight.

"Let me run and get Zadok so you can get the beast into the barn." Aurinda threw on her shawl and ran out the door past her shy sister-in-law, who wrapped her arms across her enlarging waist.

"Zadok! We have venison."

He paused in his hammering. "What?

"Private Parlee brought us a buck he shot."

"A true blessin'." Zadok looked to heaven as if praying, then grinned at Aurinda. He wiped his hands on his apron, then he removed it before washing the soot off his fingers. "Let me help Levi."

Aurinda followed her husband to the barn, where Private Parlee sagged under the weight of the buck. She held the door wide open while the two men carried the eight-point catch, then hoisted it over a wooden rack separating stalls. She looked at the wooden enclosures and placed hands on her hips.

"Perhaps we might find a cow to live in one of these stalls. We could use some milk." She turned and went back to the house.

ZADOK STARED at the empty stall and sighed.

"Are ya expectin' a little one, you and your wife, Zadok?" The private grinned at the newly married man.

"What? Nay. Not so far as I know. Thank you for the venison. We must have you over for a feast after it's dressed and cooked." He started to leave the barn.

"Wait, Zadok. I ... I been meaning to speak with you. About Mercy." Private Parlee fidgeted with the buttons on his coat.

"Mercy."

"Aye. I know 'tis some time now since that terrible day." He glanced at the barn floor. "I've been biding my time, waiting for the right moment, but I'm not sure there is one." The young man tugged at his shirt collar. "I wondered if you think I could visit her. As a friend, of course."

"A friend." Zadok looked out the open door of the barn then back at Private Parlee. "My sister does need friends right now. But are you hopin' you will be more than friends someday?"

"Well, perhaps." Sweat beaded on his forehead, despite the chilled air. "I … I've long admired Mercy and always hoped she could find it in her heart to care about me." He shifted his weight from one foot to the other, then gripped his hands behind his back.

Zadok sighed. "Come, sit with me, Levi." He found an old milking stool that had been unused for years and directed the private to have a seat. Zadok pulled another rickety chair over and sat on it carefully. He held his hands together over his lips with his fingers pointed upward and mused about what he should say to this honorable man. "Levi, you are a good man. But there is something I must tell you before you set your eyes on my sister."

The private shifted on the milking stool. "Zadok, I'm well aware she has been defiled. And, I assume, she needs great tenderness and understanding in order to trust another man. But … I know I can be patient with her if she decides she cares for me. I can wait as long as it takes."

The man's love for his sister, who was broken and ruined by the actions of another, touched Zadok deeply. Did he dare share the truth? He knew he had to.

"Levi, there is something else I must tell you." This conversation dug trenches of pain in his heart. "My sister … Mercy … when that blaggart despoiled her …" Zadok had to take a deep breath, but he owed the private the truth. "Mercy is with child."

Motionless, Private Parlee stared at him. He did not speak for several moments. "With child?"

"Aye. Aurinda and I will raise the child as our own. But in the meantime, Mercy will be in confinement." Zadok drew a circle in the dust-covered floor of the barn with the tip of his finger.

Private Parlee clenched his hands into fists and placed them against his mouth. After what seemed an eternity, he uncovered his lips and spoke. "I've never shared this with any of my mates. Figured 'twas not their business. Besides, 'twas too painful to share." He cleared his throat. "My mother was accused of the crime of fornication. My father left our township when he knew my mother was expectin' me. I never knew the man.

"Lads at school made fun of me, calling me names that would make ladies blush. I learned to get tough, but it still hurt inside here." He pointed to his chest. "So, you see, I'm not too proud a man to care for your sister ... and marry her ... if she'll have me."

Without speaking a word, Zadok stood. Private Parlee rose to meet him. They shook hands with a tight grip.

"'Tis my sister's decision, but you have my blessing."

40

Private Parlee came by the Wooding home whenever he did not have military duty at the fort. At first, Aurinda thought Mercy did not enjoy the visits. But one day, the couple took a walk. Aurinda wasn't sure what they discussed, but when Mercy came home, her cheeks blushed pink, and a contented smile brightened her face.

November winds slipped through the cracks in the windows and doors, and Zadok set to work filling in the holes. When Aurinda saw Private Parlee chopping wood for their hearth, gratitude filled her heart. Zadok carried much of the workload these days, and she'd watched as weariness etched lines in his handsome face.

"Mercy, have you seen who is chopping our wood?"

Her sister-in-law pushed herself out of the chair and peeked out the window. "Levi." Her face brightened like a warm summer's sun. She grabbed a tankard, filled it with cider, and brought it outside to Private Parlee, no longer hiding her growing belly.

As Aurinda glanced out the window at the couple, she noted

the private glance downward at the protrusion and then smile at Mercy. She rejoiced at this unexpected and ever-changing relationship between her sister-in-law and Private Parlee. It was what she'd hoped for.

Yet an unsettling thought took root in Aurinda's mind, which would be the natural result if Mercy were to marry before the child's birth. *Will she decide to keep the child?*

Aurinda had not realized until now how much she wanted to raise this wee one. She'd loved this unseen infant from the time Zadok said they could raise him or her. Knitting small stockings, she stored them in a special drawer that held items just for the newest member of their family.

She'd been loved and raised by an aunt, so to love and raise her own niece or nephew seemed as natural as loving a child born from her womb. Anxiety that she may not have the opportunity plagued her.

What would she do if Mercy married Private Parlee and they, together, raised this little one? It was not as if Aurinda were yet with child. It had been months since she and Zadok had married, and still there was no sign of an impending pregnancy. What if they never had a child? Before anyone could see her struggling with tears, she sniffed and resumed her cleaning.

Thanksgiving preparations were underway, so Aurinda busied herself in the hearth, making pies and breads. Zadok had taken a day to go hunting and hoped to add wild turkey or pigeon to the offerings at table.

Consumed with her baking, she startled when Mercy and Private Parlee opened the door. They both smelled of the cold outdoors, a scent that reminded her of years past and the cold winters with her father. Although the aroma was pleasant, the memories were not.

She forced a smile. "Thank you for the chopped wood, Private Parlee."

"Please, call me Levi." The private had a most contented look on his face.

"Very well then, Levi." She resumed kneading the bread dough.

Mercy placed her hand on Aurinda's arm. "Levi and I have something to share with you."

"Very well, what is it?" She banged her fists against the lump of flour and yeast.

"Aurinda, can you sit for a moment?"

She knew what was coming and dreaded the revelation as she wiped her hands on her apron and sat.

Dimples pinched Mercy's cheeks when she smiled. "Levi and I are to be wed."

"I am so pleased for you both." Aurinda swallowed past the dry lump in her throat, stood and hugged her sister-in-law, then awkwardly hugged Levi. "You will make a very loving couple."

"Wait." She started to return to the bread dough, but Mercy held onto her arm. "There is something more."

Aurinda could not speak. She knew her hopes and dreams were about to crumble like the ashes in the hearth.

"Levi would like to raise my child as his own. As our own."

Unbidden tears erupted in Aurinda's eyes. Furious with her own selfishness, yet so grief-stricken she could not stop herself, she said, "Excuse me." Her pinched voice was so soft she didn't know if Mercy heard her. Grabbing her cloak, she ran toward the door, flung it open, and rushed toward the woods.

Although she didn't know her destination, she needed to escape. She longed for the lake in Fairfield, where she always cast her cares on the waters and pondered her circumstances. But there was no lake here. Just the Long Island Sound with its swishing waves and swirling pools of salty water that resembled the unrest in her heart. She turned and headed for the Sound, ignoring the increasing and very cold rain.

The longing for a child overwhelmed her. She hadn't

realized how much she wanted Mercy's baby until now. Although her arms hadn't even held the little one yet, Aurinda had dreamed of that moment when the newborn would be handed to her, and she would introduce herself as *Mama*.

But like the tumbling water wrenching away particles of sand at the beach, her image of that sweet moment of motherhood demolished in front of her eyes. Perhaps forever. She sat on the cold, damp granules and closed her eyes.

ZADOK RETURNED to the house after dark, satisfied with the success of the hunt. He laid the limp turkey on the tableboard and looked around, then blew warm breath onto his freezing fingers. No one was about.

"Aurinda?"

His mother hurried down the hallway. "Zadok, I'm so relieved you are here. Mercy and I are beside ourselves with concern. Aurinda has been gone for hours. Levi has gone looking for her."

"Gone?" His throat tightened, and his heart lurched. "What has occurred."

Mercy came into the room, weeping. "I fear 'tis my fault."

"What do you mean?" Zadok gripped the musket he took down from above the hearth.

"I told her that Levi and I were to marry."

"Why would that upset her?"

"We also told her Levi wants to raise the baby with me."

He gripped the musket tighter as his jaw clenched. "And you did not think to wait until I was present before you told her?"

"I'm so sorry." Mercy wept, and her mother wrapped her arms around her.

Trying to control his rage, he grabbed two blankets from their bedchamber and added them to the supplies in his haversack. "I'll not return 'til I find her." Flinging open the door, he slammed it shut behind him.

Dear God, please watch over her. He adjusted the collar on his coat to protect his neck from the cold. Throwing the haversack over his shoulder, he pushed against a wind that carried sleet against his face. He ignored the sting while he focused on the shadows that haunted the forest.

Stopping short, Zadok clenched his eyes shut. He had no idea where Aurinda had run. There was no lake haven for Aurinda here. He opened his eyes again. No lake. *But there is the Sound.*

He turned and raced toward the beach. Pushing against the unforgiving wind slowed his steps to what seemed like a crawl. With blood coursing through him at a faster pace than his muscles could accomplish, his legs seemed like heavy tree trunks hauled by a team of oxen—too slow and making little headway. He shouted his frustration into the wind.

When he finally made it to the beach, it looked deserted. He allowed his eyes to adjust to the dimming light on the edge of the horizon then wondered at the rock-like formation on the edge of the water. As he trudged across the sand, he paused. Aurinda lay huddled on the edge of the water, covered by her woolen cloak.

In desperation, he fought against the unrelenting blast of frigid air. The sand slowed his every step, but he finally reached her. He opened his haversack and grabbed a dry blanket to wrap around her.

"Aurinda, you must be freezing." The wind swallowed up his voice.

Reaching down for her, Zadok swept her up in his arms and started to carry her home.

"Nay, I do not wish to go to the house." She struggled against his grip.

He stood still for a moment before walking again. "You need a warm fire."

"Please, do not take me there." Her sobs wrenched his heart.

The cold sleet forced a rapid decision as they could both freeze in this weather.

Then he recalled the Lansford homestead nearby. It had belonged to a Tory who'd been run out of town, and no one had yet taken over the deserted buildings. Would they be accused of trespassing? At the moment, that seemed a minor concern when their lives were threatened by the cold.

It took every ounce of Zadok's strength to plow through the driving sleet. When they finally made it to the front entrance, he could barely grip the door handle, his hands were so benumbed by the cold. In desperation, he kicked against the portal until it flew open.

Booting the door closed, he waited for his eyes to adjust to the darkness inside. The disheveled condition of the main room, likely torn apart by angry patriots, shouldn't have surprised him. Scurrying movement in the corner revealed mice had likely taken over. *At least it wasn't a skunk.*

Most of the furniture had been taken—or plundered—but a few pillows offered a soft cushion on which she could rest.

Carefully, he undid the clasp at her neck and removed her sodden, woolen cloak as she shivered. After quickly removing his own soaked coat, he took a dry blanket out of his haversack and wrapped it around them both.

He stroked her cheek and drew Aurinda closer, holding her body next to his for warmth. He kissed her once, twice, then many times and paused to look at her. "I worried so. Please, never leave again." He kissed her slowly and deeply, then whispered near her ear. "Please."

"I never will. I love you, Zadok."

"I cannot imagine my life without you." His eyes grew moist. "When they said you were gone, I thought I'd go mad."

She touched his lips, and he kissed her fingers. "Love me now, Zadok."

Gently drawing her to the floor, his fears melted away in their passion.

41

Mercy and Levi were wed on Thanksgiving Day in the Wooding home. The only guests were Parson Stone and his wife. It was a simple ceremony, followed by a sumptuous meal of venison, turkey, breads and puddings, and numerous vegetables from the garden.

Everyone seemed satiated from the food offerings, but Aurinda only picked at the food in her trencher. Her usual appetite missing, she found Zadok staring at her often. An attempt at a reassuring smile felt forced.

With the meal consumed, the women cleared off the table. In a moment of privacy, Mercy reached toward her and grasped her arm. "Dear Aurinda, can you ever forgive me?"

Embarrassment flooded her whenever Mercy offered her repeated apologies. "'Tis I who must apologize, Mercy. I had no right to act the way I did. I am so ashamed of my actions."

"I should not have told you this news in the manner I did. Please forgive me."

She hugged her. "There is naught to forgive, dear sister."

LATE NOVEMBER SAW its first snow, but it was no ordinary storm. The ferocity of the blizzard vied with any other Zadok could remember. A foot of the white powder already covered the ground by December first, and he worried there would not be sufficient food or wood to survive the winter. But he also fretted over Aurinda. She'd not been the same since Mercy and Levi's announcement. She ate paltry amounts of food and often stayed in their bed late of a morning.

One day in early December, he threw on his coat and trudged through the knee-high snow to fetch the doctor. If something could be done to help his wife, he would do it at any expense. He wished Dr. Northrup lived close enough to come but, in this weather, it would put him in danger.

The doctor from New Haven, named Pritchard, was sufficiently qualified to help Aurinda and agreed to come see her. "And how is your sister, Mercy, doing these days?" The doctor placed medicinals in a sack.

"She is well. Getting larger by the day. 'Tis a wonder she and her husband can both fit in the same bed." Zadok grinned. Would he ever know that discomfort? He sighed.

"Well, now, let us be off." Dr. Pritchard placed his hat on his head over a wool scarf he tied at his neck.

Although just several rods from his home, the distance to the physician's office felt like many miles through the abundant snow. By the time the two men arrived at the Wooding home, their cheeks were ruddy, and their noses ran.

Looking paler than usual, Aurinda sat at the table. Zadok was relieved he'd brought the doctor.

"Aurinda, I've brought Dr. Pritchard. I'm worried about you and want him to examine you."

Her eyes blazed, and blotches of red colored her cheeks and neck. "Did you not think to ask me if the doctor could examine me?" She left the table and ran to their bedroom, thrusting the door shut.

"Well, now." Dr. Pritchard raised his eyebrows. "If she is not amenable to being examined, I can always come back later."

"I'm sorry, Doctor." Zadok rubbed the hair on his head. "I don't understand the change in her and am beside myself."

The physician looked directly into Zadok's face. "Did ye not consider having one of the midwives examine her? Just a thought." He plopped his hat back on his head and exited the house.

"Midwife?" He felt his mother's penetrating gaze and met her eyes.

"Men." She shook her head back and forth. After stirring the soup for a moment over the warm hearth, she set the spoon aside and retrieved her cloak hanging on a hook. "I shall return forthwith."

Zadok plopped on a chair, then stood. Inhaling a deep breath, he strode to their bedroom. Aurinda slept soundly on her side, and he pulled a quilt over her.

"I love you, Aurinda." He kissed her hair, then tiptoed back to the hearth, ladled warm cider into a tankard, and sat down.

Lord, give me wisdom.

It wasn't long before the midwife arrived. He took the cloak from the gray-haired woman. "My wife is asleep in our room."

"No matter." The cheery woman with the round face and reddened cheeks giggled. "Most of our young mothers rest quite frequently."

"No, but my wife ..."

Mrs. Wooding tilted her head toward the bedroom. "Let her examine Aurinda." She pressed her lips together to emphasize the instruction.

Raising his hands in surrender, he sat. Aurinda had already told him she was not with child. Why wouldn't they listen to him?

Mercy came into the room. "Who came to the door?"

"The midwife."

Mercy's face burst into a grin.

"Before you get any ideas, no." Zadok interrupted. "Aurinda is not with child."

"Oh." Mercy's demeanor changed from joy-filled to distressed. "Then why is she here?"

"Mother's idea." He rolled his eyes upward.

"Oh." Mercy sat next to him while they waited. "I've been concerned about Aurinda these last weeks. I fear a melancholy of sorts has set in." Mercy glanced downward and bit her lip.

Zadok watched the fire in the hearth. The flame burned brighter when a draft of air blew in from somewhere. His eyes grew heavy, and he started to nod off.

The door to the bedroom finally opened. "Mr. Wooding, can you come in?" The midwife stood with her hands on her ample hips.

Feeling for all the world like he was being sent to the gallows for the failure of being a good husband, he rose slowly and followed the midwife's instructions. He passed his mother when she exited their bedchamber. Was that a smile she tried to stifle?

"Zadok." Aurinda lay on the bed with eyes wide. She reached for his hand, and placed his palm on her belly. "'Tis a miracle. I am with child."

The midwife laughed so hard her girth quaked like a jar of jelly. "If 'tis a miracle, then 'tis the miracle of lovemaking." She continued to laugh while warmth crept up Zadok's neck.

"But, I thought ... Aurinda, you said ..."

"I know what I said. But I was wrong, and I am so sorry." He sat next to her on the side of their bed, and she gripped his hand. "Growing up with my father, I have been uninformed about what to look for. I've been with child nigh two months now."

"Two months?" His mouth opened wide.

"Aye." She nodded. "Are you pleased, Zadok?"

He was both shocked and pleased, and so many emotions

jarred through his head, he barely knew what to say. But he knew what he wanted to do. He leaned over and kissed her, and she responded with heartfelt enthusiasm.

"Well, it must be my time to leave now. I'll see you in seven months' time."

Unconcerned about seven months from now, Zadok barely heard the midwife leave. He embraced his wife and reveled in the love of the woman who'd captured his heart so long ago and now carried the fruit of that love within.

It was the passion that kindled in him even when his eyes could not see. But the eyes of his heart had understood her true beauty. And the elation of her returned devotion was his greatest joy and treasure—the steadfast love of the lass with the golden curls.

AUTHOR'S NOTE

I spent my growing up years in New England and, from two years of age to eight, I had the joy of living in Hartford, Connecticut. I treasure the memories of visiting Wethersfield Cove where an ancient warehouse still bore bullet holes in the thick wooden planks of the door.

My siblings and I imagined the scary building was an ocean-side prison. Its iron bars allowed tide to flow into the lower levels, making this a place where the worst offenders might drown in the salty water. Shiver! I suppose my author's imagination was being groomed even in those early years.

One summer, our family stayed in a cottage on the Long Island Sound and reveled in the warm, gritty sand. We listened to the seagulls and laughed amidst the waves that lured us into deeper waters. It was a peaceful time of joy, spent with my family, that I will always treasure. Never could I have imagined a war taking place on those very beaches.

Yet in July of 1779, that is exactly what happened. When I discovered archived documents recorded in 1879 about attacks that occurred during the American Revolution, I was spellbound. My treasured shores of Connecticut bore unseen scars from the Revolution.

When I asked many others if they knew about these attacks, they were as surprised as I was. The British attacking towns on the coast of Connecticut? It seemed impossible because none of us were taught this in our history books. Yet many of the "highlights" in United States

history miss such incidents that helped shape the details of the Dawn of America.

I hope you have enjoyed *Love's Kindling*, Book 1 in the Dawn of America series. Book 2 is entitled *Winter's Ravage*, and Book 3, *Courier's Return*. The story of Zadok and Aurinda continues!

ABOUT THE AUTHOR

Elaine Marie Cooper has been writing since she was a young girl. Her passion for history was nurtured by growing up near Boston, the seat of the American Revolution. Her vivid memories of exploring historical sites inspires her to tell the story of our country's roots. Although devastated as a child to discover her ancestry included a British redcoat, she has grown fond of the family connection, even using it as inspiration for some of her novels.

Before settling in to her author's role, she became a wife, mom of three, and is now a GiGi of 5. She continues to keep her

RN license current although retired from active nursing. Her interest in medicine is evident in the research of colonial "medicinals" that are included in many of her stories.

She is now an award-winning author of **Fields of the Fatherless** and **Bethany's Calendar**. Her 2016 release, **Saratoga Letters**, and **Love's Kindling** were both finalists in Historical Romance for the Selah Awards. She penned the three-book *Deer Run Saga* and has been published in numerous magazines and anthologies.

The first book in a new series entitled *Dawn of America*, is set in Colonial Connecticut. **Love's Kindling** will release this year, followed by two more novels.

Cooper is a member of American Christian Fiction Writers. She also contributes every month to Heroes, Heroines, and History blog (hhhistory.com). You can visit her own website/blog at www.elainemariecooper.com.

To contact Elaine for interviews or speaking engagements, please email her at: elainemariecooper@yahoo.com

ALSO BY ELAINE MARIE COOPER

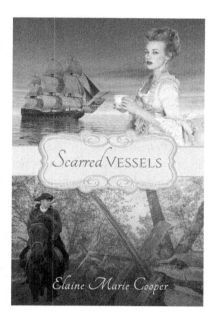

Scarred Vessels

by Elaine Marie Cooper

In a time when America battles for freedom, a man and woman seek to fight the injustice of slavery while discovering love in the midst of tragedy.

In 1778 Rhode Island, the American Revolution rallies the Patriots to fight for freedom. But the slavery of black men and women from Africa, bartered for rum, is a travesty that many in America cannot ignore. The seeds of abolition are planted even as the laws allowing slavery in the north still exist.

Lydia Saunders, the daughter of a slave ship owner, grew up with the horror of slavery. It became more of a nightmare when, at a young age, she is confronted with the truth about her father's occupation. Burdened with the guilt of her family's sin, she struggles to make a difference in whatever way she can. When she loses her husband in the battle for freedom from England, she makes a difficult decision that will change her life forever.

Sergeant Micah Hughes is too dedicated to serving the fledgling country of America to consider falling in love. When he carries the tragic news to Lydia Saunders about her husband's death, he is appalled by his attraction to the young widow. Micah wrestles with his feelings for Lydia while he tries to focus on helping the cause of freedom. He trains a group of former slaves to become capable soldiers on the battlefield.

Tensions both on the battlefield and on the home front bring hardship and turmoil that threaten to endanger them all. When Lydia and Micah are faced with saving the life of a black infant in danger, can they survive this turning point in their lives?

A groundbreaking book, honest and inspiring, showcasing black soldiers in the American Revolution. *Scarred Vessels* is peopled with flesh and blood characters and true events that not only inspire and entertain but educate. Well done!

~ Laura Frantz, Christy Award-winning author

of *An Uncommon Woman*

MORE HISTORICAL ROMANCE FROM SCRIVENINGS PRESS

Books Afloat

Columbia River Undercurrents

Book One

Blaming herself for her childhood role in the Oklahoma farm truck accident that cost her grandfather's life, Anne Mettles is determined to make her life count. She wants to do it all–captain her library boat and resist Japanese attacks to keep America safe. But failing her pilot's exam requires her to bring others onboard.

Will she go it alone? Or will she team with the unlikely but (mostly) lovable characters? One is a saboteur, one an unlikely hero, and one, she discovers, is the man of her dreams.

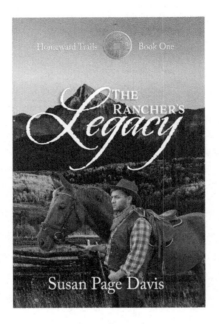

The Rancher's Legacy

Homeward Trails

Book One

Matthew Anderson and his father try to help neighbor Bill Maxwell when his ranch is attacked. On the day his daughter Rachel is to return from school back East, outlaws target the Maxwell ranch. After Rachel's world is shattered, she won't even consider the plan her father and Matt's cooked up—to see their two children marry and combine the ranches.

Meanwhile in Maine, sea captain's widow Edith Rose hires a private investigator to locate her three missing grandchildren. The children were abandoned by their father nearly twenty years ago. They've been adopted into very different families, and they're scattered across the country. Can investigator Ryland Atkins find them all while the elderly woman still lives? His first attempt is to find the boy now called

Matthew Anderson. Can Ryland survive his trip into the wild Colorado Territory and find Matt before the outlaws finish destroying a legacy?

~

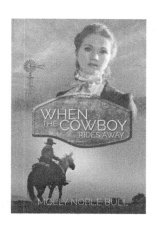

When the Cowboy Rides Away

Western Romance

Maggie Gallagher, twenty-one, runs the Gallagher Ranch in South Texas and has raised her little sister and orphaned nephew since her parents and older sister died. No wonder she can't find time for romance!

When the Cowboy Rides Away opens two years after Maggie loses her family members. Out for a ride with her sister, she discovers Alex Lancaster, a handsome cowboy, shot and seriously wounded, on her land. Kind-hearted and a Christian, Maggie nurses him back to health despite all her other chores.

How could she know that Alex has a secret that could break her heart?

~

Stay up-to-date on your favorite books and authors with our free e-newsletters.

ScriveningsPress.com

Made in the USA
Columbia, SC
01 May 2021